KT-172-781

Dame Ngaio Marsh was born in New Zealand in 1899 and died in February 1982.

She wrote over twenty-five detective novels and many of her stories have theatrical settings, for Ngaio Marsh's real passion was the theatre. She was both actress and producer and almost single-handedly revived the New Zealand public's interest in live theatre. It was for this work that she received what she called her 'damery' in 1966.

NGAIO MARSH

Grave Mistake

FONTANA/Collins

For Gerald Lascelles

First published by William Collins Sons & Co. Ltd 1978
First issued in Fontana Paperbacks 1979
Ninth impression June 1987

Copyright © Ngaio Marsh Limited 1978

Made and printed in Great Britain by
William Collins Sons & Co. Ltd, Glasgow

CONTENTS

CAST OF CHARACTERS

Verity Preston	of Keys House, Upper Quintern
The Hon. Mrs Foster (Sybil)	of Quintern Place, Upper Quintern
Claude Carter	her stepson
Prunella Foster	her daughter
Bruce Gardener	her gardener
Mrs Black	his sister
The Rev. Mr Walter Cloudesley	Vicar of St Crispin-in-Quintern
Nikolas Markos	of Mardling Manor, Upper Quintern
Gideon Markos	his son
Jim Jobbin	of Upper Quintern Village
Mrs Jim	his wife. Domestic helper
Dr Field-Innis, MB	of Upper Quintern
Mrs Field-Innis	his wife
Basil Schramm (né Smythe)	Medical incumbent, Greengages Hotel
Sister Jackson	his assistant
G. M. Johnson ⎫ Marleena Biggs ⎭	Housemaids, Greengages Hotel
The Manager	Greengages Hotel
Daft Artie	Upper Quintern Village
Young Mr Rattisbon	Solicitor
Chief Superintendent Roderick Alleyn	CID
Detective-Inspector Fox	CID
Detective-Sergeant Thompson	CID Photographic Expert
Sergeant Bailey	CID Fingerprint Expert
Sergeant McGuiness	Upper Quintern Police Force
PC Dance	Upper Quintern Police Force
A Coroner	
A Waiter	

Chapter One

UPPER QUINTERN

' "Bring me," ' sang the ladies of Upper Quintern, ' "my Bow of Burning Gold." '

' "Bring me," ' itemized the Hon. Mrs Foster, sailing up into a thready descant, ' "my Arrows of Desire." '

' "Bring me," ' stipulated the vicar's wife, adjusting her pince-nez and improvising into seconds, ' "my Chariot of Fire." '

Mrs Jim Jobbin sang with the rest. She had a high soprano and a sense of humour and it crossed her mind to wonder what Mrs Foster would do with Arrows of Desire or how nice Miss Preston of Keys House would manage a Spear, or how the vicar's wife would make out in a Chariot of Fire. Or for a matter of that how she herself, hard-working creature that she was, could ever be said to rest or stay her hand, much less build Jerusalem here in Upper Quintern or anywhere else in England's green and pleasant land.

Still, it was a good tune and the words were spirited if a little far-fetched.

Now they were reading the minutes of the last meeting and presently there would be a competition and a short talk from the vicar, who had visited Rome with an open mind.

Mrs Jim, as she was always called in the district, looked round the drawing-room with a practised eye. She herself had 'turned it out' that morning and Mrs Foster had done the flowers, picking white japonica with a more lavish hand than she would have dared to use had she known that McBride, her bad-tempered jobbing gardener, was on the watch.

Mrs Jim, pulling herself together as the chairwoman, using a special voice, said she knew they would all want to express their sympathy with Mrs Black in her recent sad loss. The ladies murmured and a little uncertain woman in a corner offered soundless acknowledgement.

Then followed the competition. You had to fill in the names of ladies present in answer to what were called cryptic clues. Mrs Jim was mildly amused but didn't score very highly. She guessed her own name, for which the clue was 'She doesn't work out'. 'Jobb-in'. Quite neat but inaccurate, she thought because her professional jobs were, after all, never 'in'. Twice a week she obliged Mrs Foster here at Quintern Place, where her niece, Beryl, was a regular. Twice a week she went to Mardling Manor to augment the indoor staff. And twice a week, including Saturdays, she helped Miss Preston at Keys House. From these activities she arrived home in time to get the children's tea and her voracious husband's supper. And when Miss Preston gave one of her rare parties, Mrs Jobbin helped out in the kitchen, partly because she could do with the extra money but mostly because she liked Miss Preston.

Mrs Foster she regarded as being a bit daft; always thinking she was ill and turning on the gushing act to show how nice she could be to the village.

Now the vicar, having taken a nervy look at the Vatican City, was well on his way to the Forum. Mrs Jobbin made a good-natured effort to keep him company.

Verity Preston stretched out her long corduroy legs, looked at her boots and wondered why she was there. She was fifty years old but carried about her an air of youth. This was not achieved by manipulation; rather it was as if, inside her middle-aged body, her spirit had neglected to grow old. Until five years ago she had worked in the theatre, on the production side. Then her father, an eminent heart-specialist, had died and left Keys House to her with just enough money to enable her to live in it and write plays, which she did from time to time with tolerable success.

She had been born at Keys, she supposed she would die there, and she had gradually fallen into a semi-detached acceptance of the rhythms of life at Upper Quintern which, in spite of war, bombs, crises and inflations, had not changed all that much since her childhood. The great difference was that, with the exception of Mr Nikolas Markos, a newcomer to the district, the gentry had very much less money nowadays and, again with the exception of Mr Markos, no resident domestic help. Just Mrs Jim, her niece Beryl, and some dozen lesser ladies who were precariously available and all in hot demand. Mrs Foster was cunning in securing their services and was thought to cheat by using bribery. She was known, privately, as the Pirate.

It was recognized on all hands that Mrs Jim was utterly impervious to bribery. Mrs Foster had tried it once and had invoked a reaction that made her go red in the face whenever she thought of it. It was only by pleading the onset of a genuine attack of lumbago that she had induced Mrs Jim to return.

Mrs Foster was a dedicated hypochondriac and nobody would have believed in the lumbago if McBride, the Upper Quintern jobbing gardener, had not confided that he had come across her on the gravelled drive, wearing her best tweeds, hat and gloves and crawling on all fours towards the house. She had been incontinently smitten on her way to the garage.

The vicar saw himself off at the Leonardo da Vinci airport, said his visit had given him much food for thought and ended on a note of ecumenical wistfulness.

Tea was announced and a mass move to the dining-room accomplished.

'Hullo, Syb,' said Verity Preston. 'Can I help?'

'Darling!' cried Mrs Foster. '*Would* you? Would you pour? I simply can't cope. *Such* arthritis! In the wrists.'

'Sickening for you.'

'Honestly. *Too* much. Not a wink all night and this party hanging over one, and Prue's off somewhere watching hang-gliding' (Prunella was Mrs Foster's daughter), 'so she's no use. And to put the final pot on it, ghastly McBride's given notice. Imagine!'

'*McBride* has? Why?'

'He *says* he feels ill. If you ask me it's bloody-mindedness.'

'Did you have words?' Verity suggested, rapidly filling up cups for ladies to carry off on trays.

'Sort of. Over my picking the japonica. This morning.'

'Is he still here? Now?'

'Don't ask me. Probably flounced off. Except that he hasn't been paid. I wouldn't put it past him to be sulking in the tool shed.'

'I must say I hope he won't extend his embargo to take me in.'

'Oh, dear me no!' said Mrs Foster, with a hint of acidity. 'You're his adored Miss Preston. You, my dear, can't do wrong in McBride's bleary eyes.'

'I wish I could believe you. Where will you go for honey, Syb? Advertise or what? Or eat humble pie?'

'Never that! Not on your life! Mrs *Black*!' cried Mrs Foster in a voice of mellifluous cordiality. '*How* good of you to come. *Where* are you sitting? Over there, are you? *Good*. Who's died?' she muttered as Mrs Black moved away. 'Why were we told to sympathize?'

'Her husband.'

'That's all right then. I wasn't overdoing it.'

'Her brother's arrived to live with her.'

'He wouldn't happen to be a gardener, I suppose.'

Verity put down the teapot and stared at her. 'You won't believe this,' she said, 'but I rather think I heard someone say he is. Mrs Jim, it was. Yes, I'm sure. A gardener.'

'My dear! I wonder if he's any good. My dear, *what* a smack in the eye that would be for McBride. Would it be all right to tackle Mrs Black now, do you think? Just to find out?'

'Well—'

'Darling, you know me. I'll be the soul of tact.'

'I bet you will,' said Verity.

She watched Mrs Foster insinuate herself plumply through the crowd. The din was too great for anything she said to be audible, but Verity could guess at the compliments sprinkled upon the vicar, who was a good-looking man, the playful badinage with the village. And all the time, while her pampered little hands dangled from her wrists, Mrs Foster's pink coiffure tacked this way and that, making towards Mrs Black, who sat in her bereavement upon a chair at the far end of the room.

Verity, greatly entertained, watched the encounter, the gradual response, the ineffable concern, the wide-open china-blue stare, the compassionate shakes of the head and, finally, the withdrawal of both ladies from the dining-room, no doubt into Syb's boudoir. Now, thought Verity, she'll put in the hard tackle.

Abruptly, she was aware of herself being under observation.

Mrs Jim Jobbin was looking at her and with such a lively expression on her face that Verity felt inclined to wink. It struck her that of all the company present – county, gentry, trade and village, operating within their age-old class structure – it was for Mrs Jim that she felt the most genuine respect.

Verity poured herself a cup of tea and began, because it was expected of her, to circulate. She was a shy woman but her work in the theatre had helped her to deal with this disadvantage. Moreover, she took a vivid interest in her fellow creatures.

'Miss Preston,' Mr Nikolas Markos had said, the only time they had met, 'I believe you look upon us all as raw material,' and his black eyes had snapped at her. Although this remark was a variant of the idiotic 'don't put me in it', it had not induced the usual irritation. Verity, in fact, had been wondering at that very moment if she could build a black comedy round

10

Upper Quintern ingredients.

She reached the french windows that opened on lawns, walks, rose-gardens and an enchanting view across the Weald of Kent.

A little removed from the nearest group, she sipped her tea and gazed with satisfaction at this prospect. She thought that the English landscape, more perhaps than any other, is dyed in the heraldic colours of its own history. It is *there*, she thought, and until it disintegrates, earth, rock, trees, grass, turf by turf, leaf by leaf and blade by blade, it will remain imperturbably itself. To it, she thought, the reed really *is* as the oak and she found the notion reassuring.

She redirected her gaze from the distant prospect to the foreground and became aware of a human rump, elevated above a box hedge in the rose-garden.

The trousers were unmistakable: pepper-and-salt, shapeless, earthy and bestowed upon Angus McBride or purchased by him at some long-forgotten jumble sale. He must be doubled up over a treasured seedling, thought Verity. Perhaps he had forgiven Sybil Foster or perhaps, with his lowland Scots rectitude, he was working out his time.

'Lovely view, isn't it?' said the vicar. He had come alongside Verity, unobserved.

'Isn't it? Although at the moment I was looking at the person behind the box hedge.'

'McBride,' said the vicar.

'I thought so, by the trousers.'

'I know so. They were once my own.'

'Does it,' Verity asked, after a longish pause, 'strike you that he is sustaining an exacting pose for a very long time?'

'Now you mention it.'

'He hasn't stirred.'

'Rapt, perhaps over the wonders of nature,' joked the vicar.

'Perhaps. But he must be doubled over at the waist like a two-foot rule.'

'One would say so, certainly.'

'He gave Sybil notice this morning on account of health.'

'Could he be feeling faint, poor fellow,' hazarded the vicar, 'and putting his head between his knees?' And after a moment, 'I think I'll go and see.'

'I'll come with you,' said Verity. 'I wanted to look at the rose-garden in any case.'

They went out by the french window and crossed the lawn.

11

The sun had come out and a charming little breeze touched their faces.

As they neared the box hedge the vicar, who was over six feet tall, said in a strange voice, 'It's very odd.'

'What is?' Verity asked. Her heart, unaccountably, had begun to knock at her ribs.

'His head's in the wheelbarrow. I fear,' said the vicar, 'he's fainted.'

But McBride had gone further than that. He was dead.

2

He had died, the doctor said, of a heart attack and his condition was such that it might have happened any time over the last year or so. He was thought to have raised the handles of the barrow, been smitten and tipped forward, head first, into the load of compost with which it was filled.

Verity Preston was really sorry. McBride was often maddening and sometimes rude but they shared a love of old-fashioned roses and respected each other. When she had influenza he brought her primroses in a jampot and climbed a ladder to put them on her window-sill. She was touched.

An immediate result of his death was a rush for the services of Mrs Black's newly arrived brother. Sybil Foster got in first, having already paved the way with his sister. On the very morning after McBride's death, with what Verity Preston considered indecent haste, she paid a follow-up visit to Mrs Black's cottage under cover of a visit of condolence. Ridiculously inept, Verity considered, as Mr Black had been dead for at least three weeks and there had been all those fulsomely redundant expressions of sympathy only the previous afternoon. She'd even had the nerve to take white japonica.

When she got home she telephoned Verity.

'My dear,' she raved, 'he's *perfect. So* sweet with that dreary little sister and *such* good manners with me. Called one Madam which is more than – well, never mind. He knew at once what would suit and said he could sense I had an understanding of the "bonny wee flooers". He's Scotch.'

'Clearly,' said Verity.

'But quite a different *kind* of Scotch from McBride. Highland I should think. Anyway – very superior.'

'What's he charge?'

'A little bit more,' said Sybil rapidly, 'but, my dear, the *difference*!'

'References?'

'Any number. They're in his luggage and haven't arrived yet. *Very* grand, I gather.'

'So you've taken him on?'

'Darling! What do you think? Mondays and Thursdays. All day. He'll tell me if it needs more. It well may. After all, it's been shamefully neglected – I know you won't agree, of course.'

'I suppose I'd better do something about him.'

'You'd better hurry. Everybody will be grabbing. I hear Mr Markos is a man short up at Mardling. Not that I think my Gardener would take an under-gardener's job.'

'What's he called?'

'Who?'

'Your gardener.'

'You've just said it. Gardener.'

'You're joking.'

Sybil made an exasperated noise into the receiver.

'So he's gardener-Gardener,' said Verity. 'Does he hyphenate it?'

'Very funny.'

'Oh, come *on*, Syb!'

'All right, my dear, you may scoff. Wait till you see him.'

Verity saw him three evenings later. Mrs Black's cottage was a short distance along the lane from Keys House and she walked to it at 6.30, by which time Mrs Black had given her brother his tea. She was a mimbling little woman, meekly supporting the prestige of recent widowhood. Perhaps with the object of entrenching herself in this state, she spoke in a whimper.

Verity could hear television blaring in the back parlour and said she was sorry to interrupt. Mrs Black, alluding to her brother as Mr Gardener, said without conviction that she supposed it didn't matter and she'd tell him he was wanted.

She left the room. Verity stood at the window and saw that the flower-beds had been recently dug over and wondered if it was Mr Gardener's doing.

He came in. A huge sandy man with a trim golden beard, wide mouth and blue eyes, set far apart and slightly, not unattractively, strabismic. Altogether a personable figure. He contemplated Verity quizzically from aloft, his head thrown back and slightly to one side and his eyes half-closed.

'I didna just catch the name,' he said, 'ma-am.'

Verity told him her name and he said, ou aye, and would she no' tak' a seat.

She said she wouldn't keep him a moment and asked if he could give her one day's gardening a week.

'That'll be the residence a wee piece up the lane, I'm thinking. It's a bonny garden you have there, ma-am. What I call perrrsonality. Would it be all of an acre that you have there, now, and an orchard, forby?'

'Yes. But most of it's grass and that's looked after by a contractor,' explained Verity, and felt angrily that she was adopting an apologetic, almost a cringing attitude.

'Ou aye,' said Mr Gardener again. He beamed down upon her. 'And I can see fine that it's highly prized by its leddy-mistress.'

Verity mumbled self-consciously.

They got down to brass tacks. Gardener's baggage had arrived. He produced glowing references from, as Sybil had said, grand employers, and photographs of their quellingly superior grounds. He was accustomed, he said, to having at the verra least a young laddie working under him but realized that in coming to keep his sister company in her ber-r-rievement, pure lassie, he would be obliged to dra' in his horns a wee. Ou, aye.

They arrived at wages. No wonder, thought Verity, that Sybil had hurried over the topic: Mr Gardener required almost twice the pay of Angus McBride. Verity told herself she ought to say she would let him know in the morning and was just about to do so when he mentioned that Friday was the only day he had left and in a panic she suddenly closed with him.

He said he would be glad to work for her. He said he sensed they would get along fine. The general impression was that he preferred to work at a derisive wage for somebody he fancied rather than for a pride of uncongenial millionaires and/or noblemen, however open-handed.

On that note they parted.

Verity walked up the lane through the scents and sounds of a spring evening. She told herself that she could afford Gardener, that clearly he was a highly experienced man and that she would have kicked herself all round her lovely garden if she'd funked employing him and fallen back on the grossly incompetent services of the only other jobbing gardener now available in the district.

But when she had gone in at her gate and walked between burgeoning lime trees up to her house, Verity, being an honest-minded creature, admitted to herself that she had taken a scunner on Mr Gardener.

As soon as she opened her front door she heard the telephone ringing. It was Sybil, avid to know if Verity had secured his services. When she learnt that the deed had been done she adopted an irritatingly complacent air as if she herself had scored some kind of triumph.

Verity often wondered how it had come about that she and Sybil seemed to be such close friends. They had known each other all their lives, of course, and when they were small had shared the same governess. But later on, when Verity was in London and Sybil, already a young widow, had married her well-heeled, short-lived stockbroker, they seldom met. It was after Sybil was again widowed, being left with Prunella and a highly unsatisfactory stepson from her first marriage, that they picked up the threads of their friendship. Really they had little in common.

Their friendship in fact was a sort of hardy perennial, re-appearing when it was least expected to do so.

The horticultural analogy occurred to Verity while Sybil gushed away about Gardener. He had started with her that very day, it transpired, and, my dear, the *difference*! And the *imagination*! And the *work*, the sheer *hard work*. She raved on. She really is a bit of an ass, is poor old Syb, Verity thought.

'And don't you find his Scots *rather* beguiling?' Sybil was asking.

'Why doesn't his sister do it?'

'Do what, dear?'

'Talk Scots?'

'Good Heavens, Verity, how should I know? Because she came south and married a man of Kent, I dare say. Black spoke broad Kentish.'

'So he did,' agreed Verity pacifically.

'I've got news for you.'

'Have you?'

'You'll never guess. An invitation. From *Mardling Manor*, no less,' said Sybil in a put-on drawing-room-comedy voice.

'Really?'

'For dinner. Next Wednesday. He rang up this morning. Rather unconventional if one's to stickle, I suppose, but that sort of tommy-rot's as dead as the dodo in my book. And we

15

have met. When he lent Mardling for that hospital fund-raising garden-party. Nobody went inside, of course. I'm told lashings of lolly have been poured out – redecorated, darling, from attic to cellar. You were there, weren't you? At the garden-party?'

'Yes.'

'Yes. I was sure you were. Rather intriguing, I thought, didn't you?'

'I hardly spoke to him,' said Verity inaccurately.

'I hoped you'd been asked,' said Sybil much more inaccurately.

'Not I. I expect you'll have gorgeous grub.'

'I don't know that it's a *party*.'

'Just you?'

'My dear. Surely not! But no. Prue's come home. She's met the son somewhere and so she's been asked – to balance him, I suppose. Well,' said Sybil on a dashing note, 'we shall see what we shall see.'

'Have a lovely time. How's the arthritis?'

'Oh, *you* know. Pretty ghastly, but I'm learning to live with it. Nothing else to be done, is there? If it's not that it's my migraine.'

'I thought Dr Field-Innis had given you something for the migraine.'

'Hopeless, my dear. If you ask me Field-Innis is getting beyond it. *And* he's become very offhand, I don't mind telling you.'

Verity half-listened to the so-familiar plaints. Over the years Sybil had consulted a procession of general practitioners and in each instance enthusiasm had dwindled into discontent. It was only because there were none handy, Verity sometimes thought, that Syb had escaped falling into the hands of some plausible quack.

'– and I had considered,' she was saying, 'taking myself off to Greengages for a fortnight. It does quite buck me up, that place.'

'Yes, why don't you?'

'I think I'd like to just be *here*, though, while Mr Gardener gets the place into shape.'

'One calls him "Mr Gardener", then?'

'Verity, he *is* very superior. Anyway I hate those old snobby distinctions. You don't, evidently.'

'I'll call him the Duke of Plaza-Toro if he'll get rid of my weeds.'

'I really must go,' Sybil suddenly decided, as if Verity had been preventing her from doing so. 'I can't make up my mind about Greengages.'

Greengages was an astronomically expensive establishment; a hotel with a resident doctor and a sort of valetudinarian sideline where weight was reduced by the exaction of a deadly diet while appetites were stimulated by compulsory walks over a rather dreary countryside. If Sybil decided to go there, Verity would be expected to drive through twenty miles of dense traffic to take a luncheon of inflationary soup and a concoction of liver and tomatoes garnished with mushrooms to which she was uproariously allergic.

She had no sooner hung up her receiver when the telephone rang again.

'Damn,' said Verity, who hankered after her cold duck and salad and the telly.

A vibrant male voice asked if she were herself and on learning that she was, said it was Nikolas Markos speaking.

'Is this a bad time to ring you up?' Mr Markos asked. 'Are you telly-watching or thinking about your dinner, for instance?'

'Not quite yet.'

'But almost, I suspect. I'll be quick. Would you like to dine here next Wednesday? I've been trying to get you all day. Say you will, like a kind creature. Will you?'

He spoke as if they were old friends and Verity, accustomed to this sort of approach in the theatre, responded.

'Yes,' she said. 'I will. I'd like to. Thank you. What time?'

3

Nobody in Upper Quintern knew much about Nikolas Markos. He was reputed to be fabulously rich, widowed and a financier. Oil was mentioned as the almost inescapable background. When Mardling Manor came on the market Mr Markos had bought it, and when Verity went to dine with him, had been in residence, off and on, for about four months.

Mardling was an ugly house. It had been built in mid-Victorian times on the site of a Jacobean mansion. It was large, pepper-potted and highly inconvenient; not a patch on Sybil Foster's Quintern Place, which was exquisite. The best that could be said of Mardling was that, however hideous, it looked clumsily important both inside and out.

As Verity drove up she saw Sybil's Mercedes parked along-side a number of other cars. The front door opened before she got to it and revealed that obsolete phenomenon, a manservant.

While she was being relieved of her coat she saw that even the ugliest of halls can be made beautiful by beautiful posses-sions. Mr Markos had covered the greater part of the stupidly carved walls with smoky tapestries. These melted upwards into an almost invisible gallery and relinquished the dominant posi-tion above an enormous fireplace to a picture. Such a picture! An imperious quattrocento man, life-size, ablaze in a scarlet cloak on a round-rumped charger. The rider pointed his sword at an immaculate little Tuscan town.

Verity was so struck with the picture that she was scarcely conscious that behind her a door had opened and closed.

'Ah!' said Nikolas Markos, 'you like my arrogant equestrian? Or are you merely surprised by him?'

'Both,' said Verity.

His handshake was quick and perfunctory. He wore a green velvet coat. His hair was dark, short and curly at the back. His complexion was sallow and his eyes black. His mouth, under a slight moustache, seemed to contradict the almost too plushy ensemble. It was slim-lipped, and, Verity thought, ex-tremely firm.

'Is it a Uccello?' she asked, turning back to the picture.

'I like to think so, but it's a borderline case. "School of" is all the pundits will allow me.'

'It's extraordinarily exciting.'

'Isn't it, just? I'm glad you like it. And delighted, by the way, that you've come.'

Verity was overtaken by one of her moments of middle-aged shyness. 'Oh. Good,' she mumbled.

'We're nine for dinner: my son, Gideon, a Dr Basil Schramm who's yet to arrive, and you know all the rest, Mrs Foster and her daughter, the vicar (*she's* indisposed) and Dr and Mrs Field-Innis. Come and join them.'

Verity's recollection of the drawing-room at Mardling was of a great ungainly apartment, over-furnished and nearly al-ways chilly. She found herself in a bird's-egg blue and white room, sparkling with firelight and a welcoming elegance.

There, expansively on a sofa, was Sybil at her most feminine, and that was saying a great deal. Hair, face, pampered little hands, jewels, dress and, if you got close enough, scent – they all came together like the ingredients of some exotic pudding. She fluttered a minute handkerchief at Verity and pulled an arch grimace.

'This is Gideon,' said Mr Markos.

He was even darker than his father and startlingly handsome. 'My dear, an Adonis,' Sybil was to say of him, and later was to add that there was 'something' wrong and that she was never deceived, she sensed it at once, let Verity mark her words. When asked to explain herself she said it didn't matter but she always *knew*. Verity thought that she knew, too. Sybil was hell-bent on her daughter Prunella encouraging the advances of a hereditary peer with the unlikely name of Swingletree and took an instant dislike to any attractive young man who hove into view.

Gideon looked about twenty, was poised and had nice manners. His black hair was not very long and was well kept. Like his father, he wore a velvet coat. The only note of extravagance was in the frilled shirt and flowing tie. These lent a final touch to what might have been an unendurably romantic appearance, but Gideon had enough natural manner to get away with them.

He had been talking to Prunella Foster, who was like her mother at the same age; ravishingly pretty and a great talker. Verity never knew what Prunella talked about as she always spoke in a whisper. She nodded a lot and gave mysterious little smiles and, because it was the fashion of the moment, seemed to be dressed in expensive rags partly composed of a patchwork quilt. Under this supposedly evening attire she wore a little pair of bucket boots.

Dr Field-Innis was an old Upper Quintern hand. The younger son of a brigadier, he had taken to medicine instead of arms and had married a lady who sometimes won point-to-points and more often fell off.

The vicar we have already met. He was called Walter Cloudesley, and ministered, a little sadly, to twenty parishioners in a very beautiful old church that had once housed three hundred.

Altogether, Verity thought, this was a predictable Upper Quintern dinner-party with an unpredictable host in a highly exceptional setting.

They drank champagne cocktails.

Sybil, sparkling, told Mr Markos how clever he was and went into an ecstasy over the house. She had a talent that never failed to tickle Verity's fancy, for making the most unexceptionable remark to a gentleman sound as if it carried some frisky innuendo. She sketched an invitation for him to join her on the sofa but he seemed not to notice it. He stood over her and replied in kind. Later on, Verity thought, she will tell me he's a man of the world.

He moved to his hearthrug and surveyed his guests with an air of satisfaction. 'This is great fun,' he said. 'My first Quintern venture. Really, it's a kind of christening party for the house, isn't it? What a good thing you could come, Vicar.'

'I certainly give it my blessing,' the vicar hardily countered. He was enjoying a second champagne cocktail.

'And, by the way, the party won't be undiluted Quintern. There's somebody still to come. I do hope he's not going to be late. He's a man I ran across in New York, a Basil Schramm. I found him—' Mr Markos paused and an odd little smile touched his mouth – 'quite interesting. He rang up out of a clear sky this morning, saying he was going to take up a practice somewhere in our part of the world and was driving there this evening. We discovered that his route would bring him through Upper Quintern and on the spur of the moment I asked him to dine. He'll unbalance the table a bit but I hope nobody's going to blench at that.'

'An American?' asked Mrs Field-Innis. She had a hoarse voice.

'He's Swiss by birth, I fancy.'

'Is he taking a locum,' asked Dr Field-Innis, 'or a permanent practice?'

'The latter, I supposed. At some hotel or nursing home or convalescent place or something of the sort. Green - something.'

'*Not* "gages",' cried Sybil, softly clapping her hands.

'I knew it made me think of indigestion. Greengages it is,' said Mr Markos.

'Oh,' said Dr Field-Innis. 'That place.'

Much was made of this coincidence, if it could be so called. The conversation drifted to gardeners. Sybil excitedly introduced her find. Mr Markos became *grand signorial* and when Gideon asked if they hadn't taken on a new man, said they had but he didn't know what he was called. Verity, who, a-political at heart, drifted guiltily from left to right and back again, felt her redder hackles rising. She found that Mr Markos was looking at her in a manner that gave her the sense of having been rumbled.

Presently he drew a chair up to hers.

'I very much enjoyed your play,' he said. 'Your best, up to date, I thought.'

'Did you? Good.'

'It's very clever of you to be civilized as well as penetrating. I want to ask you, though—'

He talked intelligently about her play. It suddenly dawned on Verity that there was nobody in Upper Quintern with whom she ever discussed her work and she felt as if she spoke the right lines in the wrong theatre. She heard herself eagerly discussing her play and fetched up abruptly.

'I'm talking shop,' she said. 'Sorry.'

'Why? What's wrong with shop? Particularly when your shop's one of the arts.'

'Is yours?'

'Oh,' he said, 'mine's as dull as ditchwater.' He looked at his watch. 'Schramm *is* late,' he said. 'Lost in the Weald of Kent, I dare say. We shall not wait for him. Tell me—'

He started off again. The butler came in. Verity expected him to announce dinner but he said, 'Dr Schramm, sir.'

When Dr Schramm walked into the room it seemed to shift a little. Her mouth dried. She waited through an unreckoned interval for Nikolas Markos to arrive at her as he performed the introductions.

'But we have already met,' said Dr Schramm. 'Some time ago.'

4

Twenty-five years to be exact, Verity thought. It was ludicrous – grotesque almost – after twenty-five years, to be put out by his reappearance.

'Somebody should say "What a small world",' said Dr Schramm.

He had always made remarks like that. And laughed like that and touched his moustache.

He didn't know me at first, she thought. That'll learn me.

He had moved on towards the fire with Mr Markos and been given, in quick succession, two cocktails. Verity heard him explain how he'd missed the turn-off to Upper Quintern.

But why 'Schramm'? she wondered. He could have hyphenated himself if 'Smythe' wasn't good enough. And 'Doctor'? So he qualified after all.

'Very difficult country,' Mrs Field-Innis said. She had been speaking for some time.

'Very,' Verity agreed fervently and was stared at.

Dinner was announced.

She was afraid they might find themselves together at the table but after, or so she fancied, a moment's hesitation, Mr Markos put Schramm between Sybil and Dr Field-Innis who was on Verity's right, with the vicar on her left. Mr Markos himself was on Sybil's right. It was a round table.

She managed quite well at dinner. The vicar was at all times prolific in discourse and, being of necessity as well as by choice, of an abstemious habit, he was a little flown with unaccustomed wine. Dr Field-Innis was also in talkative form. He coruscated with anecdotes concerning high jinks in his student days.

On his far side, Dr Schramm, whose glass had been twice replenished, was much engaged with Sybil Foster, which meant that he was turned away from Dr Field-Innis and Verity. He bent towards Sybil, laughed a great deal at everything she said and established an atmosphere of flirtatious understanding. This stabbed Verity with the remembrance of long-healed injuries. It had been his technique when he wished to show her how much another woman pleased him. He had used it at the theatre in the second row of the stalls, prolonging his laughter beyond the rest of the audience so that she, as well as the actress concerned, might become aware of him. She realized that even now, idiotically after twenty-five years, he aimed his performance at her.

Sybil, she knew, although she had not looked at them, was bringing out her armoury of delighted giggles and upward glances.

'And then,' said the vicar, who had returned to Rome, 'there was the Villa Giulia. I can't describe to you—'

In turning to him, Verity found herself under observation from her host. Perhaps because the vicar had now arrived at the Etruscans, it occurred to Verity that there was something knowing about Mr Markos's smile. You wouldn't diddle that one in a hurry, she thought.

Evidently he had asked Mrs Field-Innis to act as hostess.

When the port had gone round once she surveyed the ladies and barked out orders to retire.

Back in the drawing-room it became evident that Dr Schramm had made an impression. Sybil lost no time in tackling Verity. Why, she asked, had she never been told about him? Had Verity known him well? Was he married?

'I've no idea. It was a thousand years ago,' Verity said. 'He was one of my father's students, I think. I ran up against him at some training-hospital party as far as I can remember.'

Remember? He had watched her for half the evening and then, when an 'Excuse me' dance came along, had relieved her of an unwieldy first-year student and monopolized her for the rest of the evening.

She turned to the young Prunella, whose godmother she was, and asked what she was up to these days, and made what she could of a reply that for all she heard of it might have been in mime.

'Did you catch any of that?' asked Prunella's mother wearily.

Prunella giggled.

'I think I may be getting deaf,' Verity said.

Prunella shook her head vigorously and became audible. 'Not you, Godmama V,' she said. 'Tell us about your super friend. What a dish!'

'*Prue,*' expostulated Sybil, punctual as clockwork.

'Well, Mum, he is,' said her daughter, relapsing into her whisper. 'And you can't talk, darling,' she added. 'You gobbled him up like a turkey.'

Mrs Field-Innis said, 'Really!' and spoilt the effect by bursting into a gruff laugh.

To Verity's relief this passage had the effect of putting a stop to further enquiries about Dr Schramm. The ladies discussed local topics until they were joined by the gentlemen.

Verity had wondered whether anybody – their host or the vicar or Dr Field-Innis – had questioned Schramm as she had been questioned about their former acquaintanceship, and if so, how he had answered and whether he would think it advisable to come and speak to her. After all, it would look strange if he did not.

He did come. Nikolas Markos, keeping up the deployment of his guests, so arranged it. Schramm sat beside her and the first thought that crossed her mind was that there was something unbecoming about not seeming, at first glance, to have grown old. If he had appeared to her, as she undoubtedly did to him, as a greatly changed person, she would have been able to get their confrontation into perspective. As it was he sat there like a hangover. His face at first glance was scarcely changed, although when he turned it into a stronger light, a system of lines seemed to flicker under the skin. His eyes were more protuberant, now, and slightly bloodshot. A man, she thought, of whom people would say he could hold his liquor. He used the stuff she remembered, on hair that was only vestigially thinner at the temples.

As always he was, as people used to say twenty-five years ago, extremely well turned out. He carried himself like a soldier.

'How are you, Verity?' he said. 'You look blooming.'

'I'm very well, thank you.'

'Writing plays, I hear.'

'That's it.'

'Absolutely splendid. I must go and see one. There is one, isn't there? In London?'

'At the Dolphin.'

'Good houses?'

'Full,' said Verity.

'Really! So they wouldn't let me in. Unless you told them to. Would you tell them to? Please?'

He bent his head towards her in the old way. Why on earth, she thought, does he bother?

'I'm afraid they wouldn't pay much attention,' she said.

'Were you surprised to see me?'

'I was, rather.'

'Why?'

'Well—'

'Well?'

'The name for one thing.'

'Oh, that!' he said, waving his hand. 'That's an old story. It's my mother's maiden name. Swiss. She always wanted me to use it. Put it in her Will, if you'll believe it. She suggested that I made myself "Smythe-Schramm" but that turned out to be such a wet mouthful I decided to get rid of Smythe.'

'I see.'

'So I qualified after all, Verity.'

'Yes.'

'From Lausanne, actually. My mother had settled there and I joined her. I got quite involved with that side of the family and decided to finish my course in Switzerland.'

'I see.'

'I practised there for some time – until she died to be exact.

Since then I've wandered about the world. One can always find something to do as a medico.' He talked away, fluently. It seemed to Verity that he spoke in phrases that followed each other with the ease of frequent usage. He went on for some time, making, she thought, little sorties against her self-possession. She was surprised to find how ineffectual they proved to be. Come, she thought, I'm over the initial hurdle at least, and began to wonder what all the fuss was about.

'And now you're settling in Kent,' she said politely.

'Looks like it. A sort of hotel-cum-convalescent home. I've made rather a thing of dietetics – specialized actually – and this place offers the right sort of scene. Greengages, it's called. Do you know it at all?'

'Sybil – Mrs Foster – goes there quite often.'

'Yes,' he said. 'So she tells me.'

He looked at Sybil who sat, discontentedly, beside the vicar. Verity had realized that Sybil was observant of them. She now flashed a meaning smile at Schramm as if she and he shared some exquisite joke.

Gideon Markos said, 'Pop, may I show Prue your latest extravagance?'

'Do,' said his father. 'By all means.'

When they had gone he said, 'Schramm, I can't have you monopolizing Miss Preston like this. You've had a lovely session and must restrain your remembrance of things past. I'm going to move you on.'

He moved him on to Mrs Field-Innis and took his place by Verity.

'Gideon tells me,' he said, 'that when I have company to dine I'm bossy, old hat and a stuffed shirt or whatever the "in" phrase is. But what should I do? Invite my guests to wriggle and jerk to one of his deafening records?'

'It might be fun to see the vicar and Florence Field-Innis having a go.'

'Yes,' he said, with a sidelong glance at her, 'it might indeed. Would you like to hear about my "latest extravagance"? You would? It's a picture. A Troy.'

'From her show at the Arlington?'

'That's right.'

'How lovely for you. Which one? Not by any chance "Several Pleasures"?'

'But you're brilliant! '

'It *is*?'

'Come and look.'

He took her into the library where there was no sign of the young people: a large library it was, and still under renovation. Open cases of books stood about the floors. The walls, including the backs of shelves, had been redone in a lacquer-red Chinese paper. The Troy painting stood on the chimney-piece – a glowing flourish of exuberance, all swings and roundabouts.

'You *do* collect lovely pictures,' she said.

'Oh, I'm a dedicated magpie. I even collect stamps.'

'Seriously?'

'Passionately,' he said. He half-closed his eyes and contemplated his picture.

Verity said. 'You're going to hang it where it is, are you?'

'I think so. But whatever I do with it in this silly house is bound to be a compromise,' he said.

'Does that matter very much?'

'Yes, it does. I lust,' said Mr Markos, 'after Quintern Place.'

He said this with such passion that Verity stared at him. 'Do you?' she said. 'It's a lovely house, of course. But just seeing it from the outside—'

'Ah, but I've seen it from inside too.'

Verity thought what a slyboots old Syb was not to have divulged this visit but he went on to say that on a house-hunting drive through Kent he saw Quintern Place from afar and had been so struck that he had himself driven up to it there and then.

'Mrs Foster,' he said, 'was away but a domestic was persuaded to let me catch a glimpse of the ground floor. It was enough. I visited the nearest land agency only to be told that Quintern was not on their or anybody else's books and that former enquiries had led to the flattest of refusals. Mine suffered a like fate; there was no intention to sell. So, you may say that in a fit of pique, I bought this monster where I can sit down before my citadel in a state of fruitless siege.'

'Does Sybil know about all this?'

'Not she. The approach has been discreet. Be a dear,' said Mr Markos, 'and don't tell her.'

'All right.'

'How nice you are.'

'But I'm afraid you haven't a hope.'

'One can but try,' he said and Verity thought if ever she saw fixity of purpose in a human face, she saw it now, in Mr Markos's.

As she drove home, Verity tried to sort out the events of the evening but had not got far with them when, at the bottom of the drive, her headlamps picked up a familiar trudging figure. She pulled up alongside.

'Hullo, Mrs Jim,' she said. 'Nip in and I'll take you home.'

'It's out of your way, Miss Preston.'

'Doesn't matter. Come on.'

'Very kind, I'm sure. I won't say no,' said Mrs Jim.

She got in neatly and quickly but settled in her seat with a kind of relinquishment of her body that suggested fatigue. Verity asked her if she'd had a long day and she said she had, a bit.

'But the money's good,' said Mrs Jim, 'and with Jim on half-time you can't say no. There's always something,' she added and Verity understood that she referred to the cost of living.

'Do they keep a big staff up there?' she asked.

'Five if you count the housekeeper. Like the old days,' Mrs Jim said, 'when I was in regular service. You don't see much of them ways now, do you? Like I said to Jim, they're selling the big houses when they can, for institutions and that. Not trying all out to buy them, like Mr Markos.'

'Is Mr Markos doing that?'

'He'd like to have Quintern,' said Mrs Jim. 'He come to ask if it was for sale when Mrs Foster was at Greengages a year ago last April. He was that taken with it, you could see. I was helping springclean at the time.'

'Did Mrs Foster know?'

'He never left 'is name. I told her a gentleman had called to enquire, of course. It give me quite a turn when I first see him after he come to the Manor.'

'Did you tell Mrs Foster it was he who'd called?'

'I wasn't going out to Quintern Place at the time,' said Mrs Jim shortly, and Verity remembered that there had been a rift.

'It come up this evening in conversation. Mr Alfredo, that's the butler,' Mrs Jim continued, 'reckons Mr Markos is still dead set on Quintern. He says he's never known him not to get his way once he's made up his mind to it. You're suited with a gardener, then?'

Mrs Jim had a habit of skipping, without notice, from one topic to another. Verity thought she detected a derogatory note but could not be sure. 'He's beginning on Friday,' she said. 'Have you met him, Mrs Jim?'

'Couldn't miss 'im, could I?' she said, rubbing her arthritic knee. 'Annie Black's been taking him up and down the village like he was Exhibit A in the horse show.'

'He'll be company for her.'

'He's all of that,' she said cryptically.

Verity turned into the narrow lane where the Jobbins had their cottage. When they arrived no light shone in any of the windows. Jim and the kids all fast asleep, no doubt. Mrs Jim was slower leaving the car than she had been in entering it and Verity sensed her weariness. 'Have you got an early start?' she asked.

'Quintern at eight. It was very kind of you to bring me home, Miss Preston. Ta, anyway. I'll say good night.'

That's two of us going home to a dark house, Verity thought as she turned the car.

But being used to living alone, she didn't mind letting herself into Keys House and feeling for the light switch.

When she was in bed she turned over the events of the evening and a wave of exhaustion came upon her together with a nervous condition she thought of as 'restless legs'. She realized that the encounter with Basil Schramm (as she supposed she should call him) had been more of an ordeal than she had acknowledged at the time. The past rushed upon her, almost with the impact of her initial humiliation. She made herself relax, physically, muscle by muscle, and then tried to think of nothing.

She did not think of nothing but she thought of thinking of nothing and almost, but not quite, lost the feeling of some kind of threat waiting offstage like the return of a baddie in one of the old moralities. And at last after sundry heart-stopping jerks she fell asleep.

Chapter Two

GREENGAGES (1)

There were no two ways about it, Gardener was a good gardener. He paid much more attention to his employers' quirks and fancies than McBride had ever done and he was a conscientious worker.

When he found his surname caused Verity some embarrassment, he laughed and said it wad be a' the same to him if she calt him by his first name which was Brrruce. Verity herself was no Scot but she couldn't help thinking his dialect was laid on with a trowel. However, she availed herself of the offer and Bruce he became to all his employers. Praise of him rose high in Upper Quintern. The wee laddie he had found in the village was nearly six feet tall and not quite all there. One by one as weeks and then months went by, Bruce's employers yielded to the addition of the laddie, with the exception of Mr Markos's head gardener who was adamant against him.

Sybil Foster continued to rave about Bruce. Together they pored over nurserymen's catalogues. At the end of his day's work at Quintern he was given a pint of beer and Sybil often joined him in the staff sitting-room to talk over plans. When odd jobs were needed indoors he proved to be handy and willing.

'He's such a comfort,' she said to Verity. 'And, my dear, the energy of the man! He's made up his mind I'm to have home-grown asparagus and has dug two enormous deep, deep graves, beyond the tennis court of all places, and is going to fill them up with all sorts of stuff – seaweed, if you can believe me. The maids have fallen for him in a big way, thank God.'

She alluded to her 'outside help', a girl from the village, and Beryl, Mrs Jim's niece. Both, according to Sybil, doted on Bruce and she hinted that Beryl actually had designs. Mrs Jim remained cryptic on the subject. Verity gathered that she thought Bruce 'hated himself', which meant that he was conceited.

Dr Basil Schramm had vanished from Upper Quintern as if he had never appeared there and Verity, after a time, was almost, but not quite, able to get rid of him.

The decorators had at last finished their work at Mardling

and Mr Markos was believed to have gone abroad. Gideon, however, came down from London most weekends, often bringing a house-party with him. Mrs Jim reported that Prunella Foster was a regular attendant at these parties. Under this heading Sybil displayed a curiously ambivalent attitude. She seemed on the one hand to preen herself on what appeared, in her daughter's highly individual argot, to be a 'grab'. On the other hand she continued to drop dark, incomprehensible hints about Gideon, all based, as far as Verity could make out, on an infallible instinct. Verity wondered if, after all, Sybil merely entertained some form of maternal jealousy. It was OK for Prue to be all set about with ardent young men, but it was less gratifying if she took a fancy to one of them. Or was it simply that Sybil had set her sights on the undynamic Lord Swingletree for Prue?

'Of course, darling,' she had confided on the telephone one day in July, 'there's lots of lovely lolly but you know me, that's not everything, and one doesn't know, does one, anything *at all* about the background. Crimpy hair and black eyes and large noses. Terribly good-looking, I grant you, like profiles on old pots, but what is one to think?' And sensing Verity's reaction to this observation she added hurriedly, 'I don't mean what you mean, as you very well know.'

Verity said, 'Is Prue serious, do you suppose?'

'Don't ask me,' said Sybil irritably. 'She whispers away about him. Just when I was so pleased about John Swingletree. *Devoted*, my dear. All I can say is, it's playing havoc with my health. Not a wink last night and I dread my back. She sees a lot of him in London. I prefer not to know what goes on there. I really can't take much more, Verry. I'm going to Greengages.'

'When?' asked Verity, conscious of a jolt under her ribs.

'My dear, on Monday. I'm hoping your chum can do something for me.'

'I hope so, too.'

'What did you say? Your voice sounded funny.'

'I hope it'll do the trick.'

'I wrote to him personally, and he answered at once. A charming letter, so understanding and informal.'

'Good.'

When Sybil prevaricated she always spoke rapidly and pitched her voice above its natural register. She did so now and Verity would have taken long odds that she fingered her hair at the back of her head.

'Darling,' she gabbled, 'you couldn't give me a boiled egg, could you? For lunch? Tomorrow?'

'Of course I could,' said Verity.

She was surprised, when Sybil arrived, to find that she really did look unwell. She was a bad colour and clearly had lost weight. But apart from that there was a look of – how to define it? – a kind of blankness, of a mask almost. It was a momentary impression and Verity wondered if she had only imagined she saw it. She asked Sybil if she'd seen a doctor and was given a fretful account of a visit to the clinic in Great Quintern, the nearest town. An unknown practitioner, she said, had 'rushed over her' with his stethoscope, 'pumped up her arm' and turned her on to a dim nurse for other indignities. Her impression had been one of complete professional detachment. 'One might have been drafted, darling, into some yard, for all he cared. The deadliest of little men with a signet ring on the wrong finger. All right, I'm a snob,' said Sybil crossly and jabbed at her cutlet.

Presently she reverted to her gardener. Bruce as usual had been 'perfect', it emerged. He had noticed that Sybil looked done up and had brought her some early turnips as a present. 'Mark my words,' she said. 'There's something *in* that man. You may look sceptical, but there is.'

'If I look sceptical it's only because I don't understand. What sort of thing is there in Bruce?'

'You know *very* well what I mean. To be perfectly frank and straightforward – breeding. Remember,' said Sybil surprisingly, 'Ramsay MacDonald.'

'Do you think Bruce is a blue-blooded bastard? Is that it?'

'Stranger things have happened,' said Sybil darkly. She eyed Verity for a moment or two and then said airily, 'He's not very comfortable with the dreary little Black sister – tiny dark room and nowhere to put his things.'

'Oh?'

'Yes. I've been considering,' said Sybil rapidly, 'the possibility of housing him in the stable block – you know, the old coachman's quarters. They'd have to be done up, of course. It'd be a good idea to have somebody on the premises when we're away.'

'You'd better watch it, old girl,' Verity said, 'or you'll find yourself doing a Queen Victoria to Bruce's Brown.'

'Don't be ridiculous,' said Sybil.

She tried without success to get Verity to fix a day when she would come to a weight-reducing luncheon at Greengages.

'I do think it's the least you can do,' she said piteously. 'I'll be segregated among a tribe of bores and dying for gossip. And besides you can bring me news of Prue.'

'But I don't see Prue in the normal course of events.'

'Ask her to lunch, darling. Do—'

'Syb, she'd be bored to sobs.'

'She'd adore it. You *know* she thinks you're marvellous. It's odds on she'll confide in you. After all, you're her godmother.'

'It doesn't follow as the night the day. And if she should confide I wouldn't hear what she said.'

'There *is* that difficulty, I know,' Sybil conceded. 'You must tell her to scream. After all, her friends seem to hear her. Gideon Markos does, presumably. And that's not all.'

'Not all what?'

'All my woe. Guess who's turned up?'

'I can't imagine. *Not*,' Verity exclaimed on a note of real dismay, '*not* Charmless Claude? Don't tell me!'

'I do tell you. He left Australia weeks ago and is working his way home on a ship called *Poseidon*. As a steward. I've had a letter.'

The young man Sybil referred to was Claude Carter, her stepson – a left-over from her first marriage in whose favour not even Verity could find much to say.

'Oh Syb,' she said, 'I *am* sorry.'

'He wants me to forward a hundred pounds to Tenerife.'

'Is he coming to Quintern?'

'My dear, he doesn't say so but of course he will. Probably with the police in hot pursuit.'

'Does Prue know?'

'I've told her. Horrified, of course. She's going to make a bolt to London when the time comes. This is why, on top of everything else, I'm hell-bent for Greengages.'

'Will he want to stay?'

'I expect so. He usually does. I can't stop that.'

'Of course not. After all—'

'Verry, he gets the very generous allowance his father left him and blues the lot. I'm always having to yank him out of trouble. And what's more – absolutely for your ears alone – when I pop off he gets everything his father left me for my life-time. God knows what he'll do with it. He's been in jail and I dare say he dopes. I'll go on paying up, I suppose.'

'So he'll arrive and find – who?'

'Either Beryl, who's caretaking, or Mrs Jim who's relieving her and springcleaning, or Bruce, if it's one of his days. They're all under strict instructions to say I'm away ill and not seeing anybody. If he insists on being put up nobody can stop him. Of course he might—' There followed a long pause. Verity's mind misgave her.

'Might what?' she said.

'Darling, I wouldn't know but he *might* call on you. Just to enquire.'

'What,' said Verity, 'do you want me to do?'

'Just not tell him where I am. And then let me know and come to Greengages. Don't just ring or write, Verry. Come. Verry, as my oldest friend I ask you.'

'I don't promise.'

'No, but you will. You'll come to awful lunch with me at Greengages and tell me what Prue says and whether Charmless Claude has called. Think! You'll meet your gorgeous boy-friend again.'

'I don't want to.'

As soon as she had made this disclaimer, Verity realized it was a mistake. She visualized the glint of insatiable curiosity in Sybil's large blue eyes and knew she had aroused the passion that, second only to her absorption in gentlemen, consumed her friend – a devouring interest in other people's affairs.

'*Why* not?' Sybil said quickly. 'I knew there was something. That night at Nikolas Markos's dinner-party. I sensed it. What was it?'

Verity pulled herself together. 'Now, then,' she said. 'None of that. Don't you go making up nonsenses about me.'

'There *was* something,' Sybil repeated. 'I'm never wrong. I sensed there was something. I know!' she sang out. 'I'll ask Basil Schramm – Dr Schramm I mean – himself. He'll tell me.'

'You'll do nothing of the sort,' Verity said, and tried not to sound panicstricken. She added too late, 'He wouldn't know what on earth you were driving at. Syb – please don't go making a fool of me. And of yourself.'

'*Tum-te-tiddily. Tum-te-tee,*' sang Sybil idiotically. 'See what a tizzy we've got into.'

Verity kept her temper.

Wild horses, she decided, would not drag her to luncheon at Greengages. She saw Sybil off with the deepest misgivings.

Gideon Markos and Prunella Foster lay on a magnificent hammock under a striped canopy beside the brand-new swimming pool at Mardling Manor. They were brown, wet and almost nude. Her white-gold hair fanned across his chest. He held her lightly as if some photographer had posed them for a glossy advertisement.

'Because,' Prunella whispered, 'I don't want to.'

'I don't believe you. You do. Clearly, you want me. Why pretend?'

'All right, then. I do. But I'm not going to. I don't choose to.'

'But why, for God's sake? Oh,' said Gideon with a change of voice, 'I suppose I know. I suppose, in a way, I understand. It's the "Too rash, too ill-advised, too sudden" bit. Is that it? What?' he asked, bending his head to hers. 'What did you say? Speak up.'

'I like you too much.'

'Darling Prue, it's extremely nice of you to like me too much but it doesn't get us anywhere, now does it?'

'It's not meant to.'

Gideon put his foot to the ground and swung the hammock violently. Prunella's hair blew across his mouth.

'Don't,' she said and giggled. 'We'll capsize. Stop.'

'No.'

'I'll fall off. I'll be sick.'

'Say you'll reconsider the matter.'

'Gideon, *please*.'

'Say it.'

'I'll reconsider the matter, damn you.'

He checked the hammock but did not release her.

'But I'll come to the same conclusion,' said Prunella. 'No, darling. Not again! *Don't*. Honestly, I'll be sick. I promise you I'll be sick.'

'You do the most dreadful things to me,' Gideon muttered after an interval. 'You beastly girl.'

'I'm going in again before the sun's off the pool.'

'Prunella, are you really fond of me? Do you think about me when we're not together?'

'Quite often.'

'Very well, then, would you like – would you care to entertain the idea – I mean, couldn't we try it out? To see if we suit?'

'How do you mean?'

'Well – in my flat? Together. You like my flat, don't you? Give it, say, a month and then consider?'

She shook her head.

'I could beat you like a gong,' said Gideon. 'Oh, come *on*, Prunella, for Christ's sake. Give me a straight answer to a straight question. Are you fond of me?'

'I think you're fantastic. You know I do. Like I said, I'm too fond of you for a jolly affair. Too fond to face it all turning out to be a dead failure and us going back to square one and wishing we hadn't tried. We've seen it happen among our friends, haven't we? Everything super to begin with. And then the not-so-hot situation develops.'

'Fair enough. One finds out and no bones broken, which is a damn sight better than having to plough through the divorce court. Well, isn't it?'

'It's logical and civilized and liberated but it's just not on for me. No way. I must be a throwback or simply plain chicken. I'm sorry. Darling Gideon,' said Prunella, suddenly kissing him. 'Like the song said, "I do, I do, I do, I do".'

'What?'

'Love you,' she mumbled in a hurry. 'There. I've said it.'

'*God!*' said Gideon with some violence. 'It's not fair. Look here, Prue. Let's be engaged. Just nicely and chastely and frustratingly engaged to be married and you can break it off whenever you want to. And I'll swear, if you like, not to pester you with my ungentlemanly attentions. No. Don't answer. Think it over and in the meantime, like Donne says, "for God's sake hold your tongue and let me love".'

'He didn't say it to the lady. He said it to some irritating acquaintance.'

'Come here.'

The sun-baked landscape moved into late afternoon. Over at Quintern Place Bruce, having dug a further and deeper asparagus bed, caused the wee lad, whose name was Daft Artie, to fill it up with compost, fertilizer and soil while he himself set to work again with his long-handled shovel. Comprehensive drainage and nutrition was needed if his and his employer's plans were to be realized.

Twenty miles away at Greengages in the Weald of Kent, Dr Basil Schramm completed yet another examination of Sybil Foster. She had introduced into her room a sort of overflow of her own surplus femininity – beribboned pillows, cushions, a negligée and a bedcover both rose-coloured. Photographs. Slippers trimmed with marabou, a large box of *petits-fours au massepain* from the 'Marquise de Sévigné' in Paris, which she had made but a feeble attempt to hide from the dietetic notice of her doctor. Above all, there was the pervasive scent of oil enclosed in a thin glass container that fitted over the light bulb of her table-lamp. Altogether the room, like Sybil herself, went much too far but, again like Sybil, contrived to get away with it.

'Splendid,' said Dr Schramm, withdrawing his stethoscope. He turned away and gazed out of the window with professional tact while she rearranged herself.

'There!' she said presently.

He returned and gazed down at her with the bossy, possessive air that she found so satisfactory.

'I begin to be pleased with you,' he said.

'Truly?'

'Truly. You've quite a long way to go, of course, but your general condition is improved. You're responding.'

'I feel better.'

'Because you're not allowed to take it out of yourself. You're a highly strung instrument, you know, and mustn't be at the beck and call of people who impose upon you.'

Sybil gave a deep sigh of concealed satisfaction.

'You do so understand,' she said.

'Of course I do. It's what I'm here for. Isn't it?'

'Yes,' said Sybil, luxuriating in it. 'Yes, indeed.'

He slid her bracelet up her arm and then laid his fingers on her pulse. She felt sure it was going like a train. When, after a final pressure, he released her she said as airily as she could manage, 'I've just written a card to an old friend of yours.'

'Really?'

'To ask her to lunch on Saturday. Verity Preston.'

'Oh yes?'

'It must have been fun for you, meeting again after so long.'

'Well, yes. It was,' said Dr Schramm, '*very* long ago. We used to run up against each other sometimes in my student days.' He looked at his watch. 'Time for your rest,' he said.

'You must come and talk to her on Saturday.'

'That would have been very pleasant.'

But it turned out that he was obliged to go up to London on Saturday to see a fellow medico who had arrived unexpectedly from New York.

Verity, too, was genuinely unable to come to Greengages, having been engaged for luncheon elsewhere. She rang Sybil up and said she hadn't seen Prue but Mrs Jim reported she was staying with friends in London.

'Does that mean Gideon Markos?'

'I've no idea.'

'I'll bet it does. What about ghastly C.C.?'

'Not a sign of him as far as I know. I see by the shipping news that *Poseidon* came into Southampton the day before yesterday.'

'Keep your fingers crossed. Perhaps we'll escape after all.'

'I think not,' said Verity.

She was looking through her open window. An unmistakable figure shambled towards her up the avenue of limes.

'Your stepson,' she said, 'has arrived.'

3

Claude Carter was one of those beings whose appearance accurately reflects their character. He looked, and in fact was, damp. He seemed unable to face anything or anybody. He was well into his thirties but maintained a rich crop of post-adolescent pimples. He had very little chin, furtive eyes behind heavy spectacles, a vestigial beard and mouse-coloured hair which hung damply, of course, half way down his neck.

Because he was physically so hopeless, Verity entertained a kind of horrified pity for him. This arose from a feeling that he couldn't be as awful as he looked and that anyway he had been treated unfairly – by his Maker in the first instance and probably in the second by his masters (he had been sacked from three schools), his peers (he had been bullied at all of them) and life in general. His mother had died in childbirth and he was still a baby when Sybil married his father, who was killed in the blitz six months later and of whom Verity knew little beyond the fact that he collected stamps. Claude was brought up by his grandparents who didn't care for him. These circumstances, when she thought of them, induced in Verity a muddled sense of guilt for which she could advance no justification and which was certainly not shared by Claude's stepmother.

When he became aware of Verity at her window he pretended, ineffectually, that he hadn't seen her and approached the front door with his head down. She went out to him. He did not speak but seemed to offer himself feebly for her inspection.

'Claude,' said Verity.

'That's right.'

She asked him in and he sat in her sunny drawing-room as if, she thought, he had been left till called for. He wore a T-shirt that had been made out of a self-raising-flour bag and bore the picture of a lady who thrust out a vast bosom garnished with the legend 'Sure to Rise'. His jeans so far exceeded in fashionable shrinkage as to cause him obvious discomfort.

He said he'd been up to Quintern Place where he'd found Mrs Jim Jobbin who told him Mrs Foster was away and she couldn't say when she would return.

'Not much of a welcome,' he said. 'She made out she didn't know Prue's address, either. I asked who forwarded their letters.' He blew three times down his nose, which was his manner of laughing, and gave Verity a knowing glance. 'That made Mrs Jim look pretty silly,' he said.

'Sybil's taking a cure,' Verity explained. 'She's not seeing anybody.'

'What, again! What is it this time?'

'She was run down and needs a complete rest.'

'I thought you'd tell me where she was. That's why I came.'

'I'm afraid not, Claude.'

'That's awkward,' he said fretfully. 'I was counting on it.'

'Where are you staying?'

'Oh, up there for the time being. At Quintern.'

'Did you come by train?'

'I hitched.'

Verity felt obliged to ask him if he'd had any lunch and he said, not really. He followed her into the kitchen where she gave him cold meat, chutney, bread, butter, cheese and beer. He ate a great deal and had a cigarette with his coffee. She asked him about Australia and he said it was no good, really, not unless you had capital. It was all right if you had capital.

He trailed back after her to the drawing-room and she began to feel desperate.

'As a matter of fact,' he said, 'I was depending on Syb. I happen to be in a bit of a patch. Nothing to worry about really, but, you know.'

'What sort of patch?' she asked against her will.

'I'm short.'

'Of money?'

'What else is there to be short of?' he asked and gave his

three inverted sniffs.

'How about the hundred pounds she sent to Tenerife?'

He didn't hesitate or look any more hang-dog than he was already.

'Did she *send* it!' he said. 'Typical of the bloody Classic Line, that is. Typical inefficiency.'

'Didn't it reach you?'

'Would I be cleaned out if it had?'

'Are you sure you haven't spent it?'

'I resent that, Miss Preston,' he said, feebly bridling.

'I'm sorry if it was unfair. I can let you have twenty pounds. That should tide you over. And I'll let Sybil know about you.'

'It's a bit off not telling where she is. But thanks, anyway, for helping out. I'll pay it back of course, don't worry.'

She went to her study to fetch it and again he trailed after her. Horrid to feel that it was not a good idea for him to see where she kept her housekeeping money.

In the hall she said, 'I've a telephone call to make. I'll join you in the garden. And then I'm afraid we'll have to part. I've got work on hand.'

'I quite understand,' he said with an attempt at dignity.

When she rejoined him he was hanging about outside the front door. She gave him the money. 'It's twenty-three pounds,' she said. 'Apart from loose change, it's all I've got in the house at the moment.'

'I quite understand,' he repeated grandly, and after giving her one of his furtive glances said, 'Of course, if I had my own I wouldn't have to do this. Do you know that?'

'I don't think I understand.'

'If I had the Stamp.'

'The Stamp?'

'The one my father left me. The famous one.'

'I'd forgotten about it.'

'You wouldn't have if you were in my boots. The Black Alexander.'

Then Verity remembered. The story had always sounded like something out of a boy's annual. Claude's father had inherited the stamp which was one of a set that had been withdrawn on the day of issue because of an ominous fault: a black spot in the centre of the Czar Alexander's brow. It was reputed to be the only specimen known to be extant and worth a fabulous amount. Maurice Carter had been killed in the blitz while on leave. When his stamp collection was uplifted from his bank the Black Alexander was missing. It was never recovered.

'It was a strange business, that,' Verity said.

'From what they've told me it was a very strange business indeed,' he said, with his laugh.

She didn't answer. He shuffled his feet in the gravel and said he supposed he'd better take himself off.

'Goodbye then,' said Verity.

He gave her a damp and boneless handshake and had turned away when a thought seemed to strike him.

'By the way,' he said. 'If anyone asks for me I'd be grateful if you didn't know anything. Where I am and that. I don't suppose they will but, you know, if they do.'

'Who would they be?'

'Oh – boring people. You wouldn't know them.' He smiled and for a moment looked fully at her. 'You're so good at not knowing where Syb is,' he said, 'the exercise ought to come easy to you, Miss Preston.'

She knew her face was red. He had made her feel shabby.

'Look here. Are you in trouble?' she asked.

'Me? Trouble?'

'With the police?'

'Well, I must say! Thank you very much! What on earth could have given you that idea!' She didn't answer. He said, 'Oh well, thanks for the loan anyway,' and walked off. When he had got half way to the gate he began, feebly, to whistle.

Verity went indoors meaning to settle down to work. She tried to concentrate for an hour, failed, started to write to Sybil, thought better of it, thought of taking a walk in the garden and was called back by the telephone.

It was Mrs Jim, speaking from Quintern Place. She sounded unlike herself and said she was sure she begged pardon for giving the trouble but said she was that worried. After a certain amount of preliminary explanation it emerged that it was about 'that Mr Claude Carter'.

Sybil had told the staff it was remotely possible that he might appear and that if he did and wanted to stay they were to allow it. And then earlier this afternoon someone had rung up asking if he was there and Mrs Jim had replied truthfully that he wasn't and wasn't expected and that she didn't know where he could be found. About half an hour later he arrived and said he wanted to stay.

'So I put him in the green bedroom, according,' said Mrs Jim, 'and I told him about the person who'd rang and he says he don't want to take calls and I'm to say he's not there and I don't know nothing about him. Well, Miss Preston, I don't like it. I won't take the responsibility. There's something funny going on and I won't be mixed up. And I was wondering if you'd be kind enough to give me a word of advice.'

'Poor Mrs Jim,' Verity said. 'What a bore for you. But Mrs Foster said you were to put him up and, difficult as that may be, that's what you've done.'

'I didn't know then what I know now, Miss Preston.'

'What do you know now?'

'I didn't like to mention it before. It's not a nice thing to have to bring up. It's about the person who rang earlier. It was – somehow I knew it was, before he said – it was the police.'

'Oh lor', Mrs Jim.'

'Yes, miss. And there's more. Bruce Gardener come in for his beer when he finished at five and he says he'd run into a gentleman in the garden, only he never realized it was Mr Claude. On his way back from you, it must of been, and Mr Claude told him he was a relation of Mrs Foster's and they got talking and—'.

'Bruce doesn't know – ? Does he know? – Mrs Jim, Bruce didn't tell him where Mrs Foster can be found?'

'That's what I was coming to. She won't half be annoyed, won't she? Yes, Miss Preston, that's just what he did.'

'Oh *damn*,' said Verity after a pause. 'Well, it's not your fault, Mrs Jim. Nor Bruce's if it comes to that. Don't worry about it.'

'But what'll I say if the police rings again?'

Verity thought hard but any solution that occurred to her seemed to be unendurably shabby. At last she said, 'Honestly, Mrs Jim, I don't know. Speak the truth, I suppose I ought to say, and tell Mr Claude about the call. Beastly though it sounds, at least it would probably get rid of him.'

There was no answer. 'Are you there, Mrs Jim?' Verity asked. 'Are you still there?'

Mrs Jim had begun to whisper, 'Excuse me, I'd better hang up.' And in loud, artificial tones added, 'That will be all, then, for today, thank you.' And did hang up. Charmless Claude, thought Verity, was in the offing.

Verity was now deeply perturbed and at the same time couldn't help feeling rather cross. She was engaged in making extremely tricky alterations to the last act of a play which, after a promising try-out in the provinces, had attracted nibbles from a London management. To be interrupted at this stage was to become distraught.

She tried hard to readjust and settle to her job but it was no good. Sybil Foster and her ailments and problems, real or synthetic, weighed in against it. Should she, for instance, let Sybil know about the latest and really most disturbing news of her awful stepson. Had she any right to keep Sybil in the dark? She knew that Sybil would be only too pleased to be kept there but that equally some disaster might well develop for which she, Verity, would be held responsible. She would be told she had been secretive and had bottled up key information. It wouldn't be the first time that Sybil had shovelled responsibility all over her and then raised a martyred howl when the outcome was not to her liking.

It came to Verity that Prunella might reasonably be expected to take some kind of share in the proceedings but where, at the moment, was Prunella and would she become audible if rung up and asked to call?

Verity read the same bit of dialogue three times without reading it at all, cast away her pen, swore and went for a walk in her garden. She loved her garden. There was no doubt that Bruce had done all the right things. There was no greenfly on the roses. Hollyhocks and delphiniums flourished against the lovely brick wall round her elderly orchard. He had not attempted to foist calceolarias upon her or indeed any objectionable annuals, only night-scented stocks. She had nothing but praise for him and wished he didn't irritate her so often.

She began to feel less badgered, picked a leaf of verbena, crushed and smelt it and turned back towards the house.

I'll put the whole thing aside, she thought, until tomorrow. I'll sleep on it.

But when she came through the lime trees she met Prunella Foster streaking hot-foot up the drive.

4

Prunella was breathless, a condition that did nothing to improve her audibility. She gazed at her godmother and flapped her hands in a manner that reminded Verity of her mother.

'Godma,' she whispered, 'are you alone?'

'Utterly,' said Verity.

'Could I talk to you?'

'If you can contrive to make yourself heard, darling, of course you may?'

'I'm sorry,' said Prunella, who was accustomed to this admonishment. 'I will try.'

'Have you walked here?'

'Gideon dropped me. He's in the lane. Waiting.'

'Come indoors. I wanted to see you.'

Prunella opened her eyes very wide and they went indoors where without more ado she flung her arms round her godmother's neck, almost shouted the information that she was engaged to be married, and burst into excitable tears.

'My dear child!' said Verity. 'What an odd way to announce it. Aren't you pleased to be engaged?'

A confused statement followed during which it emerged Prunella was very much in love with Gideon but was afraid he might not continue to be as much in love with her as now appeared because one saw that sort of thing happening all over the place, didn't one, and she knew if it happened to her she wouldn't be able to keep her cool and put it into perspective and she had only consented to an engagement because Gideon promised that for him it was for keeps but how could one be sure he knew what he was talking about?

She then blew her nose and said that she was fantastically happy.

Verity was fond of her god-daughter and pleased that she wanted to confide in her. She sensed that there was more to come.

And so there was.

'It's about Mummy,' Prunella said. 'She's going to be livid.'

'But why?'

'Well, first of all she's a roaring snob and wants me to marry John Swingletree because he's a peer. Imagine!'

'I don't know John Swingletree.'

'The more lucky, you. The bottom. And then, you see, she's got one of her things about Gideon and his papa. She thinks they've sprung from a mid-European ghetto.'

'None the worse for that,' said Verity.

'Exactly. But you know what she is. It's partly because Mr Markos didn't exactly make a big play for her at that dinner-party when they first came to Mardling. You know,' Prunella repeated, 'what she is. Well, don't you, Godma?'

There being no way out of it, Verity said she supposed she did.

'Not,' Prunella said, 'that she's all that hooked on him. Not now. She's all for the doctor at Greengages – you remember? Wasn't he an ex-buddy of yours, or something?'

'Not really.'

'Well, anyway, she's in at the deep end, boots and all. Potty about him. I do so wish,' Prunella said as her large eyes refilled with tears, 'I didn't have to have a mum like that. Not that I don't love her.'

'Never mind.'

'And now I've got to tell her. About Gideon and me.'

'How do you think of managing that? Going to Greengages? Or writing?'

'Whatever I do she'll go ill at me and say I'll be sorry when she's gone. Gideon's offered to come too. He's all for taking bulls by the horns. But I don't want him to see what she can be like if she cuts up rough. You know, don't you? If anything upsets her applecart when she's nervy it can be a case of screaming hysterics. Can't it?'

'Well—'

'You know it can. I'd hate him to see her like that. Darling, darling Godma V, I was wondering—'

Verity thought, She can't help being a bit like her mother, and was not surprised when Prunella said she had *just* wondered if Verity was going to visit her mother and if she did whether she'd kind of prepare the way.

'I hadn't thought of going. I really am busy, Prue.'

'Oh,' said Prunella, falling back on her whisper and looking desolate. 'Yes. I see.'

'In any case, shouldn't you and Gideon go together and Gideon – well—'

'Ask for my hand in marriage like Jack Worthing and Lady Bracknell?'

'Yes.'

'That's what *he* says. Darling Godma V,' said Prunella, once more hanging herself round Verity's neck, 'if we took you with us and you just sort of – you know – first. Couldn't you? We've come all the way from London just this minute almost, to ask. She pays more attention to you than anybody. Please.'

'Oh, Prue.'

'You *will*? I can see you're going to. And you can't possibly refuse when I tell you my other hideous news. Not that Gideon-and-me is hideous but just you wait.'

'Charmless Claude?'

'You *knew*! I rang up Quintern from Mardling and Mrs Jim told me. Isn't it *abysmal*? When we all thought he was safely stowed in Aussie.'

'Are you staying tonight?'

'There! With Claudie-boy? Not on your Nelly. I'm going to Mardling. Mr Markos is back and we'll tell him about us. He'll be super about it. I ought to go.'

'May I come to the car and meet your young man?'

'Oh, you mustn't trouble to do that. He'll come,' Prunella said. She put a thumb and finger between her teeth, leant out of the window and emitted a piercing whistle. A powerful engine started up in the lane, a rakish sports model shot through the drive in reverse and pulled up at the front door. Gideon Markos leapt out.

He really was an extremely good-looking boy, thought Verity, but she could see, without for a moment accepting the disparagement, what Sybil had meant by her central European remark. He was an exotic. He looked like a Latin member of the jet set dressed by an English tailor. But his manner was unaffected as well as assured and his face alive with a readiness to be amused.

'Miss Preston,' he said, 'I gather you're not only a godmother but expected to be a fairy one. Are you going to wave your wand and give us your blessing?'

He put his arm round Prunella and talked away cheerfully about how he'd bullied her into accepting him. Verity thought he was exalted by his conquest and that he would be quite able to manage not only his wife but if need be his mother-in-law as well.

'I expect Prue's confided her misgivings,' he said, 'about her mama being liable to cut up rough over us. I don't quite see why she should take against me in such a big way, but perhaps that's insufferable. Anyway, I hope *you* don't feel I'm not a good idea?' He looked quickly at her and added, 'But then, of course, you don't know me so that was a pretty gormless remark, wasn't it?'

'The early impression,' said Verity, 'is not unfavourable.'

'Well, thank the Lord for that,' said Gideon.

'Darling,' breathed Prunella, 'she's coming to Greengages with us. You are, Godma, you know you are. To temper the wind. Sort of.'

'That's very kind of her,' he said and bowed to Verity.

Verity knew she had been out-manoeuvred, but on the whole did not resent it. She saw them shoot off down the drive. It had been settled that they would visit Greengages on the coming Saturday but not, as Prunella put it, for a cabbage-water soup and minced grass luncheon. Gideon knew of a super restaurant en route.

Verity was left with a feeling of having spent a day during which unsought events converged upon her and brought with them a sense of mounting unease, of threats, even. She suspected that the major ingredient of this discomfort was an extreme reluctance to suffer another confrontation with Basil Schramm.

The following two days were uneventful but Thursday brought Mrs Jim to Keys for her weekly attack upon floors and furniture. She reported that Claude Carter kept very much to his room up at Quintern, helped himself to the food left out for him and, she thought, didn't answer the telephone. Beryl, who was engaged to sleep in while Sybil Foster was away, had said she didn't fancy doing so with that Mr Claude in residence. In the upshot the difficulty had been solved by Bruce who offered to sleep in, using a coachman's room over the garage formerly occupied by a chauffeur-handyman.

'I knew Mrs Foster wouldn't have any objections to *that*,' said Mrs Jim, with a stony glance out of the window.

'Perhaps, though, she ought just to be asked, don't you think?'

'He's done it,' said Mrs Jim sparsely. 'Bruce. He rung her up.'

'At Greengages?'

'That's right, miss. He's been over there to see her,' she added. 'Once a week. To take flowers and get orders. By bus. Of a Saturday. She pays.'

Verity knew that she would be expected by her friends to snub Mrs Jim for speaking in this cavalier manner of an employer but she preferred not to notice.

'Oh, well,' she generalized, 'you've done everything you can, Mrs Jim.' She hesitated for a moment and then said, 'I'm going over there on Saturday.'

After a fractional pause Mrs Jim said, 'Are you, miss? That's very kind of you, I'm sure,' and switched on the vacuum-cleaner. 'You'll be able to see for yourself,' she shouted above the din.

Verity nodded and returned to the study. But what? she wondered. *What* shall I be able to see?

Gideon's super restaurant turned out to be within six miles of Greengages. It seemed to be some sort of club of which he was a member and was of an exalted character with every kind of discreet attention and very good food. Verity seldom lunched at this level and she enjoyed herself. For the first time she wondered what Gideon's occupation in life might be. She also remembered that Prunella was something of a *partie*.

At half past two they arrived at Greengages. It was a converted Edwardian mansion approached by an avenue, sheltered by a stand of conifers and surrounded by ample lawns in which flower-beds had been cut like graves.

There were a number of residents strolling about with visitors or sitting under brilliant umbrellas on exterior furnishers' contraptions.

'She does know we're coming, doesn't she?' Verity asked. She had begun to feel apprehensive.

'You and me, she knows,' said Prunella. 'I didn't mention Gideon. Actually.'

'Oh, Prue!'

'I thought you might sort of ease him in,' Prue whispered.

'I really don't think—'

'Nor do I,' said Gideon. 'Darling, why can't we just—'

'There she is!' cried Verity. 'Over there beyond the calceolarias and lobelia under an orange brolly. She's waving. She's seen us.'

'Godma V, *please*. Gideon and I'll sit in the car and when you wave we'll come. Please.'

Verity thought, I've eaten their astronomical luncheon and drunk their champagne so now I turn plug-ugly and refuse? 'All right,' she said, 'but don't blame me if it goes haywire.'

She set off across the lawn.

Nobody has invented a really satisfactory technique for the gradual approach of people who have already exchanged greetings from afar. Continue to grin while a grin dwindles into a grimace? Assume a sudden absorption in the surroundings? Make as if sunk in meditation? Break into a joyous canter? Shout? Whistle? Burst, even, into song?

Verity tried none of these methods. She walked fast and when she got within hailing distance cried, 'There you are!'

Sybil had the advantage in so far as she wore enormous dark

sunglasses. She waved and smiled and pointed, as if in mock astonishment or admiration at Verity and when she arrived extended her arms for an embrace.

'Darling Verry!' she cried. 'You've come after all.' She waved Verity into a canvas chair, seemed to gaze at her fixedly for an uneasy moment or two and then said with a change of voice, 'Whose car's that? Don't tell me. It's Gideon Markos's. He's driven you both over. You needn't say anything. They're engaged!'

This, in a way, was a relief. Verity, for once, was pleased by Sybil's prescience. 'Well, yes,' she said, 'they are. And honestly, Syb, there doesn't seem to me to be anything against it.'

'In that case,' said Sybil, all cordiality spent, 'why are they going on like this? Skulking in the car and sending you to soften me up. If you call that the behaviour of a civilized young man! Prue would never be like that on her own initiative. He's persuaded her.'

'The boot's on the other foot. He was all for tackling you himself.'

'Cheek! Thick-skinned push. One knows where he got that from.'

'Where?'

'God knows.'

'You've just said you do.'

'Don't quibble, darling,' said Sybil.

'I can't make out what, apart from instinctive promptings, sets you against Gideon. He's intelligent, eminently presentable, obviously rich—'

'Yes, and where does it come from?'

'—and, which is the only basically important bit, he seems to be a young man of good character and in love with Prue.'

'John Swingletree's devoted to her. Utterly devoted. And she was—' Sybil boggled for a moment and then said loudly – 'she was getting to be very fond of him.'

'The Lord Swingletree, would that be?'

'Yes, it would, and you needn't say it like that.'

'I'm not saying it like anything. Syb, they're over there waiting to come to you. Do be kind. You won't get anywhere by being anything else.'

Sybil was silent for a moment and then said, 'Do you know what I think? I think it's a put-up job between him and his father. They want to get their hands on Quintern.'

'Oh, my *dear* old Syb!'

'All right. You wait. Just you wait.'

This was said with all her old vigour and obstinacy and yet with a very slight drag, a kind of flatness in her utterance. Was it because of this that Verity had the impression that Sybil did not really mind all that much about her daughter's engagement? There was an extraordinary suggestion of hesitancy and yet of suppressed excitement – almost of jubilation.

The pampered little hand she raised to her sunglasses quivered. It removed the glasses and for Verity the afternoon turned cold.

Sybil's face was blankly smooth as if it had been ironed. It had no expression. Her great china-blue eyes really might have been those of a doll.

'All right,' she said. 'On your own head be it. Let them come. I won't make scenes. But I warn you I'll never come round. Never.'

A sudden wave of compassion visited Verity.

'Would you rather wait a bit?' she asked. 'How are you, Syb? You haven't told me. Are you better?'

'Much, much better. Basil Schramm is fantastic. I've never had a doctor like him. Truly. He so *understands*. I expect,' Sybil's voice luxuriated, 'he'll be livid when he hears about this visit. He won't let me be upset. I told him about Charmless Claude and he said I must on no account see him. He's given orders. Verry, he's quite fantastic,' said Sybil. The warmth of these eulogies found no complementary expression in her face or voice. She wandered on, gossiping about Schramm and her treatment and his nurse, Sister Jackson, who, she said complacently, resented his taking so much trouble over her. 'My dear,' said Sybil, 'jealous! Don't you worry, I've got that one buttoned up.'

'Well,' Verity said, swallowing her disquietude, 'perhaps you'd better let me tell these two that you'll see Prue by herself for a moment. How would that be?'

'I'll see them both,' said Sybil. 'Now.'

'Shall I fetch them, then?'

'Can't you just wave?' she asked fretfully.

As there seemed to be nothing else for it, Verity walked into the sunlight and waved. Prunella's hand answered from the car. She got out, followed by Gideon, and they came quickly across the lawn. Verity knew Sybil would be on the watch for any signs of a conference however brief and waited instead of going to meet them. When they came up with her she said under her breath, 'It's tricky. Don't upset her.'

Prunella broke into a run. She knelt by her mother and looked into her face. There was a moment's hesitation and then she kissed her.

'Darling Mummy,' she said.

Verity returned to the car.

There she sat and watched the group of three under the orange canopy. They might have been placed there for a painter like Troy Alleyn. The afternoon light, broken and diffused, made nebulous figures of them so that they seemed to shimmer and swim a little. Sybil had put her sunglasses on again so perhaps, thought Verity, Prue won't notice anything.

Now Gideon had moved. He stood by Sybil's chair and raised her hand to his lips. She ought to like that, Verity thought. That ought to mean she's yielding but I don't think it does.

She found it intolerable to sit in the car and decided to stroll back towards the gates. She would be in full view. If she was wanted Gideon could come and get her.

A bus had drawn up outside the main gates. A number of people got out and began to walk up the drive. Among them were two men, one of whom carried a great basket of lilies. He wore a countrified tweed suit and hat and looked rather distinguished. It came as quite a shock to recognize him as Bruce Gardener in his best clothes. Sybil would have said he was 'perfectly presentable'.

And a greater and much more disquieting shock to realize that his shambling, ramshackle companion was Claude Carter.

6

When Verity was a girl there had been a brief craze for what were known as rhymes of impending disaster – facetious couplets usually on the lines of 'Auntie Maude's mislaid her glasses and thinks the burglar's making passes', accompanied by a childish drawing of a simpering lady being man-handled by a masked thug.

Why was she now reminded of this puerile squib? Why did she see her old friend in immediate jeopardy, threatened by something undefined but infinitely more disquieting than any nuisance Claude Carter could inflict upon her? Why should Verity feel as if the afternoon, now turned sultry, was closing about Sybil? Had she only imagined that there was an odd immobility in Sybil's face?

And what ought she to do about Bruce and Claude?

Bruce was delighted to see her. He raised his tweed hat high in the air, beamed across the lilies and greeted her in his richest and most suspect Scots. He was, he said, paying his usual wee Saturday visit to his pure leddy and how had Miss Preston found her the noo? Would there be an improvement in her condeetion, then?

Verity said she didn't think Mrs Foster seemed very well and that at the moment she had visitors to which Bruce predictably replied that he would bide a wee. And if she didna fancy any further visitors he'd leave the lilies at the desk to be put in her room. 'She likes to know how her garden prospers,' he said. Claude had listened to this exchange with a half-smile and a shifting eye.

'You found your way here, after all?' Verity said to him, since she could scarcely say nothing.

'Oh yes,' he said. 'Thanks to Bruce. He's sure she'll be glad to see me.'

Bruce looked, Verity thought, as if he would like to disown this remark and indeed began to say he'd no' put it that way when Claude said, 'That's her, over there, isn't it? Is that Prue with her?'

'Yes,' said Verity shortly.

'Who's the jet-set type?'

'A friend.'

'I think I'll just investigate,' he said with a pallid show of effrontery and made as if to set out.

'Claude, please wait,' Verity said, and in her dismay turned to Bruce. He said at once, 'Ou, now, Mr Carter, would you no' consider it more advisable to bide a while?'

'No,' said Claude, over his shoulder, 'thank you, I wouldn't,' and continued on his way.

Verity thought, I can't run after him and hang on his arm and make a scene. Prue and Gideon will have to cope.

Prue certainly did. The distance was too great for words to be distinguished and the scene came over like a mime. Sybil reached out a hand and clutched her daughter's arm. Prue turned, saw Claude and rose. Gideon made a gesture of enquiry. Then Prue marched down upon Claude.

They faced each other, standing close together, Prue very upright, rather a dignified little figure, Claude with his back to Verity, his head lowered. And in the distance Sybil being helped to her feet by Gideon and walked towards the house.

'She'll be better indoors,' said Bruce in a worried voice, 'she will that.'

Verity had almost forgotten him but there he stood gazing anxiously over the riot of lilies he carried. At that moment Verity actually liked him.

Prue evidently said something final to Claude. She walked quickly towards the house, joined her mother and Gideon on the steps, took Sybil's arm and led her indoors. Claude stared after them, turned towards Verity, changed his mind and sloped off in the direction of the trees.

'It wasna on any invitation of mine he came,' said Bruce hotly. 'He worrumed the information oot of me.'

'I can well believe it,' said Verity.

Gideon came to them.

'It's all right,' he said to Verity. 'Prue's taking Mrs Foster up to her room.' And to Bruce, 'Perhaps you could wait in the entrance hall until Miss Prunella comes down.'

'I'll do that, sir, thank you,' Bruce said and went indoors.

Gideon smiled down at Verity. He had, she thought, an engaging smile. 'What a very bumpy sort of a visit,' he said.

'How was it shaping up? Before Charmless Claude intervened?'

'Might have been worse, I suppose. Not much worse, though. The reverse of open arms and cries of rapturous welcome. You must have done some wonderful softening-up, Miss Preston, for her to receive me at all. We couldn't be more grateful.' He hesitated for a moment. 'I hope you don't mind my asking but is there – is she – Prue's mother – I don't know how to say it. Is there something – ?' He touched his face.

'I know what you mean. Yes. There is.'

'I only wondered.'

'It's new.'

'I think Prue's seen it. Prue upset. She managed awfully well but she *is* upset.'

'Prue's explained Charmless Claude, has she?'

'Yes. Pretty ghastly specimen. She coped marvellously,' said Gideon proudly.

'Here she comes.'

When Prunella joined them she was white-faced but perfectly composed. 'We can go now,' she said and got into the car.

'Where's your bag?' asked Gideon.

'What? Oh, *damn*,' said Prunella, 'I've left it up there. Oh, *what* a fool! Now I'll have to go back.'

'Shall I?'

'It's in her room. And she's been pretty beastly to you.'

'Perhaps I could better myself by a blithe change of manner.'

'*What* a good idea,' cried Prunella. 'Yes, do let's try it. Say she looks like Mrs Onassis.'

'She doesn't. Not remotely. Nobody less.'

'She thinks she does.'

'One can but try,' Gideon said. 'There's nothing to lose.'

'No more there is.'

He was gone for longer than they expected. When he returned with Prunella's bag he looked dubious. He started up the car and drove off.

'Any good?' Prunella ventured.

'She didn't actually throw anything at me.'

'Oh,' said Prunella. 'Like that, was it?'

She was very quiet on the homeward drive. Verity, in the back seat, saw her put her hand on Gideon's knee. He laid his own hand briefly over it and looked down at her. He knows exactly how to handle her, Verity thought. There's going to be no doubt about who's the boss.

When they arrived at Keys she asked them to come in for a drink but Gideon said his father would be expecting them.

'I'll see Godma V in,' said Prue as Gideon prepared to do so.

She followed Verity indoors and kissed and thanked her very prettily. Then she said, 'About Mummy. Has she had a stroke?'

'My dear child, why?'

'You noticed. I could see you did.'

'I don't think it looked like that. In any case they – the doctor – would have let you know if anything serious was wrong.'

'P'raps he didn't know. He may not be a good doctor. Sorry, I forgot he was a friend.'

'He's not. Not to matter.'

'I think I'll ring him up. I think there's something wrong. Honestly, don't you?'

'I did wonder.'

'And yet—'

'What?'

'In a funny sort of way she seemed – well – excited, pleased.'

'I thought so, too.'

'It's very odd,' said Prunella. 'Everything was odd. Out of focus, kind of. Anyway, I will ring up that doctor. I'll ring him tomorrow. Do you think that's a good idea?'

Verity said, 'Yes, darling. I do. It should put your mind at rest.'

But it was going to be a long time before Prunella's mind would be in that enviable condition.

7

At five minutes past nine that evening, Sister Jackson, the resident nurse at Greengages, paused at Sybil Foster's door. She could hear the television. She tapped, opened and after a long pause approached the bed. Five minutes later she left the room and walked rather quickly down the passage.

At eleven o'clock Dr Schramm telephoned Prunella to tell her that her mother was dead.

Chapter Three

ALLEYN

Basil looked distinguished, Verity had to admit, exactly as he ought to look under the circumstances, and he behaved as one would wish him to behave, with dignity and propriety, with deference and with precisely the right shade of controlled emotion.

'I had no reason whatever to suspect that, beyond symptoms of nervous exhaustion which had markedly improved, there was anything the matter,' he said. 'I feel I must add that I am astonished that she should have taken this step. She was in the best of spirits when I last saw her.'

'When was that, Dr Schramm?' asked the Coroner.

'On that same morning. About eight o'clock. I was going up to London and looked in on some of my patients before I left. I did not get back to Greengages until a few minutes after ten in the evening.'

'To find?'

'To find that she had died.'

'Can you describe the circumstances?'

'Yes. She had asked me to get a book for her in London – the autobiography of a Princess somebody – I forget the name. I went to her room to deliver it. Our bedrooms are large and comfortable and are often used as sitting-rooms. I have been told that she went up to hers late that afternoon. Long before her actual bedtime. She had dinner there, watching television. I knocked and there was no reply but I could hear the television and presumed that because of it she had not heard me. I went in. She was in bed and lying on her back. Her bedside table-lamp was on and I saw at once that a bottle of tablets was overturned and several – five, in fact – were scattered over the surface of the table. Her drinking glass was empty but had been used and was lying on the floor. Subsequently, a faint trace of alcohol – whisky – was found in the glass. A small whisky bottle, empty, was on the table. She sometimes used to take a modest nightcap. Her jug of water was almost empty. I examined her and found that she was dead. It was then twenty minutes past ten.'

'Can you give a time for when death occurred?'

'Not exactly, no. Not less than an hour before I found her.'

'What steps did you take?'

'I made absolutely certain there was no possibility of recovery. I then called up our resident nurse. We employed a stomach pump. The results were subsequently analysed and a quantity of barbiturates was found.' He hesitated and then said, 'I would like, sir, if this in an appropriate moment, to add a word about Greengages and its general character and management.'

'By all means, Dr Schramm.'

'Thank you. Greengages is not a hospital. It is a hotel with a resident medical practitioner. Many, indeed most, of our guests are not ill. Some are tired and in need of a change and rest. Some come to us simply for a quiet holiday. Some for a weight-reducing course. Some are convalescents preparing to return to normal life. A number of them are elderly people who are reassured by the presence of a qualified practitioner and a registered nurse. Mrs Foster had been in the habit of coming from time to time. She was a nervy subject and a chronic worrier. I must say at once that I had not prescribed the barbiturate tablets she had taken and have no idea how she had obtained them. When she first came I did, on request, prescribe phenobarbiturates at night to help her sleep but after her first week they were discontinued as she had no further need of them. I apologize for the digression but I felt it was perhaps indicated.'

'Quite. Quite. Quite,' chattered the complacent Coroner.

'Well then, to continue. When we had done what had to be done, I got in touch with another doctor. The local practitioners were all engaged or out but finally I reached Dr Field-Innis of Upper Quintern. He very kindly drove over and together we made a further examination.'

'Finding?'

'Finding that she had died of an overdose. There was no doubt of it at all. We found three half-dissolved tablets at the back of the mouth and one on the tongue. She must have taken the tablets, four or five at a time and lost consciousness before she could swallow the last ones.'

'Dr Field-Innis is present, is he not?'

'He is,' Basil said, with a little bow in the right direction. Dr Field-Innis bobbed up and down in his seat.

'Thank you very much, Dr Schramm,' said the Coroner with evident respect.

Dr Field-Innis was called.

Verity watched him push his glasses up his nose and tip back his head to adjust his vision just as he always did after he had listened to one's chest. He was nice. Not in the least dynamic or lordly, but nice. And conscientious. And, Verity thought, at the moment very clearly ill-at-ease.

He confirmed everything that Basil Schramm had deposed as to the state of the room and the body and the conclusion they had drawn and added that he himself had been surprised and shocked by the tragedy.

'Was the deceased a patient of yours, Dr Field-Innis?'

'She consulted me about four months ago.'

'On what score?'

'She felt unwell and was nervy. She complained of sleeplessness and general anxiety. I prescribed a mild barbiturate. *Not* the proprietary tranquillizer she was found to have taken that evening, by the way.' He hesitated for a moment. 'I suggested that she should have a general overhaul,' he said.

'Had you any reason to suspect there was something serious the matter?'

There was a longer pause. Dr Field-Innis looked for a moment at Prunella. She sat between Gideon and Verity who thought, irrelevantly, that like all blondes, especially when they were as pretty as Prunella, mourning greatly became her.

'That,' said Dr Field-Innis, 'is not an easy question to answer. There were, I thought, certain possible indications, very slight indeed, that should be followed up.'

'What were they?'

'A gross tremor in the hands. That does not necessarily imply a conspicuous tremor. And – this is difficult to define – a certain appearance in the face. I must emphasize that this was slight and possibly of no moment but I had seen something of the sort before and felt it should not be disregarded.'

'What might these symptoms indicate, Dr Field-Innis? A stroke?' hazarded the Coroner.

'Not necessarily.'

'Anything else?'

'I say this with every possible reservation. But yes. Just possibly – Parkinson's disease.'

Prunella gave a strange little sound, half cry, half sigh. Gideon took her hand.

The Coroner asked, 'And did the deceased, in fact, follow your advice?'

'No. She said she would think it over. She did not consult me again.'

'Had she any idea you suspected—?'

'Certainly not,' Dr Field-Innis said loudly. 'I gave no indication whatever. It would have been most improper to do so.'

'Have you discussed the matter with Dr Schramm?'

'It has been mentioned, yes.'

'Had Dr Schramm remarked these symptoms?' The Coroner turned politely to Basil Schramm. 'Perhaps,' he said, 'we may ask?'

He stood up. 'I had noticed the tremor,' he said. 'On her case-history and on what she had told me I attributed this to the general nervous condition.'

'Quite,' said the Coroner. 'So, gentlemen, we may take it, may we not, that fear of this tragic disease cannot have been a motive for suicide? We may rule that out?'

'Certainly,' they said together and together they sat down. Tweedledum and Tweedledee, Verity thought.

The resident nurse was now called, Sister Jackson, an opulent lady of good looks, a highish colour and an air of latent sexiness, damped down, Verity thought, to suit the occasion. She confirmed the doctors' evidence and said rather snootily that of course if Greengages had been a hospital there would have been no question of Mrs Foster having a private supply of any medicaments.

And now Prunella was called. It was a clear day outside and a ray of sunlight slanted through a window in the parish hall. As if on cue from some zealous stage-director it found Prunella's white-gold head and made a saint of her.

'How lovely she is,' Gideon said quite audibly. Verity thought he might have been sizing up one of his father's distinguished possessions. 'And how obliging of the sun,' he added and gave her a friendly smile. This young man, she thought, takes a bit of learning.

The Coroner was considerate with Prunella. She was asked about the afternoon visit to Greengages. Had there been anything unusual in her mother's behaviour? The Coroner was sorry to trouble her but would she mind raising her voice, the acoustics of the hall no doubt were at fault. Verity heard Gideon chuckle.

Prunella gulped and made a determined attempt to become fully vocal. 'Not really,' she said. 'Not unusual. My mother was rather easily fussed and – well – you know. As Dr Schramm said, she worried.'

'About anything in particular, Miss Foster?'

'Well – about me, actually.'

'I beg your pardon?'

'About *me*,' Prunella shrilled and flinched at the sound of her own voice. 'Sorry,' she said.

'About you?'

'Yes. I'd just got engaged and she fussed about that, sort of. But it was all right. Routine, really.'

'And you saw nothing particularly unusual?'

'Yes. I mean,' said Prunella, frowning distressfully and looking across at Dr Field-Innis, 'I did think I saw something – different – about her.'

'In what way?'

'Well, she was – her hands – like Dr Field-Innis said – were trembly. And her speech – I thought – you know – kind of dragged. And there was – or I thought there was – something about her face. As if it had kind of, you know, blanked out or sort of smoothed over, sort of – well – slowed up. I can't describe it. I wasn't even quite sure it was there.'

'But it troubled you?'

'Yes. Sort of,' whispered Prunella.

She described how she and Gideon took her mother back to the house and how she went up with her to her room.

'She said she thought she'd have a rest and go to bed early and have dinner brought up to her. There was something she wanted to see on television. I helped her undress. She asked me not to wait. So I turned the box on and left her. She truly seemed all right, apart from being tired and upset about – about me and my engagement.' Prunella's voice wavered into inaudibility, and her eyes filled with tears.

'Miss Foster,' said the Coroner, 'just one more question. Was there a bottle of tablets on her bedside table?'

'Yes, there was.' Prunella said quickly. 'She asked me to take it out of her beauty box, you know, a kind of face box. It was on the table. She said they were sleeping-pills she'd got from a chemist ages ago and she thought if she couldn't go to sleep after her dinner she'd take one. I found them for her and put them out. And there was a lamp on the table, a book and an enormous box of *petits-fours au massepain*. She gets – she used to get them from that shop the "Marquise de Sévigné" – in

Paris. I ate some before I left.'

Prunella knuckled her eyes like a small girl and then hunted for her handkerchief. The Coroner said they would not trouble her any more and she returned to Gideon and Verity.

Verity heard herself called and found she was nervous. She was taken over the earlier ground and confirmed all that Prunella had said. Nothing she was asked led to any mention of Bruce Gardener's and Claude Carter's arrival at Greengages and as both of them had been fended off from meeting Sybil she did not think it incumbent on her to say anything about them. She saw that Bruce was in the hall, looking stiff and solemn as if the inquest was a funeral. He wore his Harris tweed suit and a black tie. Poor Syb would have liked that. She would have probably said there was 'good blood there' and you could tell by the way he wore his clothes. Meaning blue blood. And suddenly and irrelevantly there came over Verity the realization that she could never believe ridiculous old Syb had killed herself.

She had found Dr Field-Innis's remarks about Sybil's appearance deeply disturbing, not because she thought they bore the remotest relation to her death but because she herself had for so long paid so little attention to Sybil's ailments. Suppose, all the time, there had been ominous signs? Suppose she had felt as ill as she said she did? Was it a case of 'wolf, wolf'? Verity was miserable.

She did not pay much attention when Gideon was called and said that he had returned briefly to Mrs Foster's room to collect Prunella's bag and that she had seemed to be quite herself.

The proceedings now came to a close. The Coroner made a short speech saying in effect that the jury might perhaps consider it was most unfortunate that nothing had emerged to show why the deceased had been moved to take this tragic and apparently motiveless step, so out of character according to all that her nearest and dearest felt about her. Nevertheless, in face of what they had heard they might well feel that the circumstances all pointed in one direction. However – at this point Verity's attention was distracted by the sight of Claude Carter, whom she had not noticed before. He was sitting at the end of a bench against the wall, wearing a superfluous raincoat with the collar turned up and feasting quietly upon his fingernails.

'–and so,' the Coroner was saying, 'you may think that in view of the apparent absence of motive and notwithstanding the entirely appropriate steps taken by Dr Schramm, an autopsy should be carried out. If you so decide I shall, of course, adjourn the inquest *sine die*.'

The jury, after a short withdrawal, brought in a verdict along these lines and the inquest was accordingly adjourned until after the autopsy.

The small assembly emptied out into the summery quiet of the little village.

As she left the hall Verity found herself face to face with Young Mr Rattisbon. Young Mr Rattisbon was about sixty-five years of age and was the son of Old Mr Rattisbon who was ninety-two. They were London solicitors of eminent respectability and they had acted for Verity's family and for Sybil's unto the third and fourth generation. His father and Verity's were old friends. As the years passed, the son grew more and more like the father, even to adopting his eccentricities. They both behaved as if they were character-actors playing themselves in some dated comedy. Both had an extraordinary mannerism – when about to pronounce upon some choice point of law they exposed the tips of their tongues and vibrated them as if they had taken sips of scalding tea. They prefaced many of their remarks with a slight whinny.

When Mr Rattisbon saw Verity he raised his out-of-date city hat very high and said, 'Good morning' three times and added, 'Very sad, yes,' as if she had enquired whether it was or was not so. She asked him if he was returning to London but he said no, he would find himself something to eat in the village and then go up to Quintern Place if Prunella Foster found it convenient to see him.

Verity rapidly surveyed her larder and then said, 'You can't lunch in the village. There's only the Passcoigne Arms and it's awful. Come and have an omelette and cheese and a glass of reasonable hock with me.'

He gave quite a performance of deprecating whinnies but was clearly delighted. He wanted, he said, to have a word with the Coroner and would drive up to Keys when it was over.

Verity, given this start, was able to make her unpretentious preparations. She laid her table, took some cold sorrel soup with cream from the refrigerator, fetched herbs from the orchard, broke eggs into a basin and put butter in her omelette pan. Then she paid a visit to her cellar and chose one of the few remaining bottles of her father's sherry and one of the more than respectable hock.

When Mr Rattisbon arrived she settled him in the drawing-room, joined him in a glass of sherry and left him with the bottle at his elbow while she went off to make the omelette.

They lunched successfully, finishing off with ripe Stilton and biscuits. Mr Rattisbon had two and a half glasses of hock to Verity's one. His face, normally the colour of one of his own parchments, became quite pink.

They withdrew into the garden and sat in weather-worn deckchairs under the lime trees.

'How very pleasant, my dear Verity,' said Mr Rattisbon. 'Upon my word, how quite delightful! I suppose, alas, I must keep my eyes upon the time. And, if I may, I shall telephone Miss Prunella. I mustn't overstay my welcome.'

'Oh, fiddle, Ratsy!' said Verity, who had called him by this Kenneth Grahamish nickname for some forty years. 'What did you think about the inquest?'

The professional change came over him. He joined his finger-tips, rattled his tongue and made his noise.

'M'nah,' he said. 'My dear Verity. While you were preparing our delicious luncheon I thought a great deal about the inquest and I may say that the more I thought the less I liked it. I will not disguise from you, I am uneasy.'

'So am I. What exactly is *your* worry? Don't go all professionally rectitudinal like a diagram. Confide. Do, Ratsy, I'm the soul of discretion. My lips shall be sealed with red-tape, I promise.'

'My dear girl, I don't doubt it. I had, in any case, decided to ask you. You were, were you not, a close friend of Mrs Foster?'

'A very *old* friend. I think perhaps the closeness was more on her side than mine, if that makes sense.'

'She confided in you?'

'She'd confide in the Town Crier if she felt the need, but yes, she did quite a lot.'

'Do you know if she has recently made a Will?'

'Oh,' said Verity, 'is that your trouble?'

'Part of it, at least. I must tell you that she did in fact execute a Will four years ago. I have reason to believe that she may have made a later one but have no positive knowledge of such being the case. She – yah – she wrote to me three weeks ago advising me of the terms of a new Will she wished me to prepare. I was – frankly appalled. I replied, as I hoped, temperately, asking her to take thought. *She* replied at once that I need concern myself no further in the matter with additions of a – of an intemperate – I would go so far as to say a hostile, character. So much so that I concluded that I had been given the – not to put too fine a point upon it – sack.'

'Preposterous!' cried Verity. 'She couldn't!'

'As it turned out she didn't. On my writing a formal letter asking if she wished the return of the Passcoigne documents which we hold, and, I may add, have held since the Barony was created, she merely replied by telegram.'

'What did it say?'

'It said "Don't be silly".'

'How like Syb!'

'Upon which,' said Mr Rattisbon, throwing himself back in his chair, 'I concluded that there was to be no severance of the connection. That is the last communication I had from her. I know not if she made a new Will. But the fact that I – yah – jibbed, might have led her to act on her own initiative. Provide herself,' said Mr Rattisbon, lowering his voice as one who speaks of blasphemy, 'with a Form. From some stationer. Alas.'

'Since she was in cool storage at Greengages, she'd have had to ask somebody to get the form for her. She didn't ask me.'

'I think I hear your telephone, my dear,' Mr Rattisbon said.

It was Prunella. 'Godma V,' she said with unusual clarity, 'I saw you talking to that fantastic old Mr Rattisbon. Do you happen to know where he was going?'

'He's here. He's thinking of visiting you.'

'Oh, good. Because I suppose he ought to know. Because, actually, I've found something he ought to see.'

'What have you found, darling?'

'I'm afraid,' Prunella's voice escalated to a plaintive squeak, 'it's a Will.'

When Mr Rattisbon had taken his perturbed leave and departed, bolt upright, at the wheel of his car, Prunella rang again to say she felt that before he arrived she must tell her godmother more about her find.

'I can't get hold of Gideon,' she said, 'so I thought I'd tell you. Sorry, darling, but you know what I mean.'

'Of course I do.'

'Sweet of you. Well. It was in Mummy's desk in the boudoir, top-drawer. In a stuck-up envelope with "Will" on it. It was signed and witnessed ten days ago. At Greengages, of course, and it's on a printed form thing.'

'How did it get to Quintern?'

'Mrs Jim says Mummy asked Bruce Gardener to take it and put it in the desk. He gave it to Mrs Jim and she put it in the desk. Godma V, it's a stinker.'

'Oh dear.'

'It's – you'll never believe this – I can't myself. It starts off by saying she leaves half her estate to me. You do know, don't you, that darling Mummy was a Rich Bitch. Sorry, that's a fun-phrase. But true.'

'I did suppose she was.'

'I mean *really* rich. Rolling.'

'Yes.'

'Partly on account of Grandpapa Passcoigne and partly because Daddy was a wizard with the lolly. Where was I?'

'Half the estate to you,' Verity prompted.

'Yes. That's over and above what Daddy entailed on me if that's what it's called. And Quintern's entailed on me, too, of course.'

'Nothing the matter with *that*, is there?'

'Wait for it. You'll never, never believe this – half to me *only* if I marry awful Swingles – John Swingletree. I wouldn't have thought it possible. Not even with Mummy, I wouldn't. It doesn't *matter*, of course, I mean, I've got more than is good for me with the entailment. Of course it's a lot less on account of inflation and all that but I've been thinking, actually, that I ought to give it away when I marry. Gideon doesn't agree.'

'You astonish me.'

'But he wouldn't stop me. Anyway, he's rather more than OK for lolly.' Prunella's voice trembled. 'But Godma V,' she said, 'how she *could*! How she could think it'd make me do it! Marry Swingles and cut Gideon just for the cash. It's repulsive.'

'I wouldn't have believed it of her. Does Swingletree *want* you to marry him, by the way?'

'Oh yes,' said Prunella impatiently. 'Never stops asking, the poor sap.'

'It must have been when she was in a temper,' said Verity. 'She'd have torn it up when she came round.'

'But she didn't, did she? And she'd had plenty of time to come round. And you haven't heard anything yet. Who do you suppose she's left the rest to? – well, all but £25,000? She's left £25,000 to Bruce Gardener, as well as a super little house in the village that is part of the estate and provision for him to be kept on as long as he likes at Quintern. But the rest – including the half if I don't marry Swingles – to whom do you suppose?'

A wave of nausea came over Verity. She sat down by her

telephone and saw with detachment that the receiver shook in her hand.

'Are you there?' Prunella was saying. 'Hullo! Godma V?'

'I'm here.'

'I give you three guesses. You'll never get it. Do you give up?'

'Yes.'

'Your heart-throb, darling. Dr Basil Schramm.'

A long pause followed. Verity tried to speak but her mouth was dry.

'Godma, are you there? Is something the matter with your telephone? Did you hear me?'

'Yes, I heard. I – I simply don't know what to say.'

'Isn't it awful?'

'It's appalling.'

'I told you she was crackers about him, didn't I?'

'Yes, yes, you did and I saw it for myself. But to do this –!'

'I know. When I don't marry that ass Swingles, Schramm'll get the lot.'

'Good God!' said Verity.

'Well, won't he? *I* don't know. Don't ask me. Perhaps it'll turn out to be not proper. The Will, I mean.'

'Ratsy will pounce on that – Mr Rattisbon – if it is so. Is it witnessed?'

'It seems to be. By G. M. Johnson and Marleena Biggs. Housemaids at Greengages I should think, wouldn't you?'

'I dare say.'

'Well, I thought I'd just tell you.'

'Yes. Thank you.'

'I'll let you know what Mr Rats thinks.'

'Thanks.'

'Goodbye then, Godma darling.'

'Goodbye, darling. I'm sorry. Especially,' Verity managed, 'about the Swingletree bit.'

'I know. Bruce is chicken feed, compared,' said Prunella. 'And what a name!' she added. 'Lady Swingletree! I ask you!' and hung up.

It was exactly a week after this conversation and on just such another halcyon afternoon that Verity answered her front doorbell to find a very tall man standing in the porch.

He took off his hat. 'Miss Preston?' he said. 'I'm sorry to bother you. I'm a police officer. My name is Alleyn.'

Afterwards, when he had gone away, Verity thought it strange that her first reaction had not been one of alarm. At the moment of encounter she had simply been struck by Alleyn himself, by his voice, his thin face and – there was only one word she could find – his distinction. There was a brief feeling of incredulity and then the thought that he might be on the track of Charmless Claude. He sat there in her drawing-room with his knees crossed, his thin hands clasped together and his eyes, which were bright, directed upon her. It came as a shock when he said, 'It's about the late Mrs Foster that I hoped to have a word with you.'

Verity heard herself say, 'Is there something wrong?'

'It's more a matter of making sure there isn't,' he said. 'This is a routine visit and I know that's what we're always supposed to say.'

'Is it because something's turned up at the – examination – the – I can't remember the proper word.'

'Autopsy?'

'Yes. Stupid of me.'

'You might say it's arisen out of that, yes. Things have turned out a bit more complicated than was expected.'

After a pause, Verity said, 'I'm sure one's not meant to ask questions, is one?'

'Well,' he said, and smiled at her, 'I can always evade answering but the form is supposed to be for me to ask.'

'I'm sorry.'

'Not a bit. You shall ask me anything you like as the need arises. In the meantime, shall I go ahead?'

'Please.'

'My first one is about Mrs Foster's room.'

'At Greengages?'

'Yes.'

'I was never in it.'

'Do you know if she habitually used a sort of glass sleeve contraption filled with scented oil that fitted over a lamp bulb?'

' "Oasis"? Yes, she used it in the drawing-room at Quintern and sometimes, I think, in her bedroom. She adored what she called a really groovy smell.'

' "Oasis", if that's what it was, is all of that. They tell me the memory lingers on in the window curtains. Did she usually have a nightcap, do you know? Whisky?'

'I think she did, occasionally, but she wasn't much of a drinker. Far from it.'

'Miss Preston, I've seen the notes of your evidence at the inquest but if you don't mind I'd like to go back to the talk you had with Mrs Foster on the lawn that afternoon. It's simply to find out if by any chance, and on consideration, hindsight if you like, something was said that now seems to suggest she contemplated suicide.'

'Nothing. I've thought and thought. Nothing.' And as she said this Verity realized that with all her heart she wished there had been something and at the same time told herself how appalling it was that she could desire it. I shall never get myself sorted out over this, she thought and realized that Alleyn was speaking to her.

'If you could just run over the things you talked about. Never mind if they seem irrelevant or trivial.'

'Well, she gossiped about the hotel. She talked a lot about – the doctor – and the wonders of his cure and about the nurse – Sister something – who she said resented her being a favourite. But most of all we talked about Prunella – her daughter's – engagement.'

'Didn't she fancy the young man?'

'Well – she *was* upset,' Verity said. 'But – well, she was often upset. I suppose it would be fair to say she was inclined to get into tizzies at the drop of a hat.'

'A fuss-pot?'

'Yes.'

'Spoilt, would you say?' he asked, surprisingly.

'Rather indulged, perhaps.'

'Keen on the chaps?'

He put this to her so quaintly that Verity was startled into saying, 'You *are* sharp!'

'A happy guess, I promise you,' said Alleyn.

'You must have heard about the Will,' she exclaimed.

'Who's being sharp now?'

'I don't know,' Verity said crossly, 'why I'm laughing.'

'When, really, you're very worried, aren't you? Why?'

'I don't *know*. Not really. It's all so muddling,' she broke out. 'And I *hate* being muddled.'

She stared helplessly at Alleyn. He nodded and gave a small affirmative sound.

'You see,' Verity began again, 'when you asked if she said anything that suggested suicide I said "nothing" didn't I? And if you'd known Syb as well as I did, there *was* nothing. But when you ask if she's ever suggested anything of the sort – well, yes. If you count her being in a bit of a stink over some dust-up and throwing a temperament and saying life wasn't worth living and she might as well end it all. But that was just histrionics. I often thought Syb's true métier was the theatre.'

'Well,' said Alleyn, 'you ought to know.'

'Have you seen Prunella? Her daughter?' Verity asked.

'Not yet. I've read her evidence. I'm on my way there. Is she at home, do you know?'

'She has been, lately. She goes up to London quite a lot.'

'Who'll be there if she's out?'

'Mrs Jim Jobbin. General factotum. It's her morning at Quintern.'

'Anyone else?'

Damn! thought Verity, here we go. She said, 'I haven't been in touch. Oh, it's the gardener's day up there.'

'Ah yes. The gardener.'

'Then you *do* know about the Will?'

'Mr Rattisbon told me about it. He's an old acquaintance of mine. May we go back to the afternoon in question? Did you discuss Miss Foster's engagement with her mother?'

'Yes. I tried to reconcile her to the idea.'

'Any success?'

'Not much. But she did agree to see them. Is it all right to ask – did they find – did the pathologist find – any signs of disease?'

'He thinks on Dr Field-Innis's report that she might have had Parkinson's disease.'

'If she had known that,' Verity said, 'it might have made a difference. If she was told – but Dr Field-Innis didn't tell her.'

'And Dr Schramm, apparently, didn't spot it.'

Sooner or later it had to come. They'd arrived at his name.

'Have you met Dr Schramm?' Alleyn asked casually.

'Yes.'

'Know him well?'

'No. I used to know him many years ago but we had entirely lost touch.'

'Have you seen him lately?'

'I've only met him once at a dinner-party some months ago. At Mardling – Mardling Manor, belonging to Mr Nikolas

Markos. It's his son who's engaged to Prunella.'

'The millionaire Markos would that be?'

'Not that I know. He certainly seems to be extremely affluent.'

'The millionaire who buys pictures,' said Alleyn, 'if that's any guide.'

'This one does that. He'd bought a Troy.'

'That's the man,' said Alleyn. 'She called it "Several Pleasures".'

'But – how did you – ? Oh, I see,' said Verity, 'you've been to Mardling.'

'No. The painter is my wife.'

'Curiouser,' said Verity, after a long pause, 'and curiouser.'

'Do you find it so? I don't quite see why.'

'I should have said how lovely. To be married to Troy.'

'Well, we like it,' said Troy's husband. 'Could I get back to the matter in hand, do you think?'

'Of course. Please,' said Verity, with a jolt of vertigo under her diaphragm.

'Where were we?'

'You asked me if I'd met Basil Smythe.'

'Smythe?'

'I should have said Schramm,' Verity amended quickly. 'I believe Schramm was his mother's maiden name. I think she wanted him to take it. He said something to that effect.'

'When would that have happened, would you suppose?'

'Some time after I knew him, which was in 1951, I think,' Verity added and hoped it sounded casual.

'How long had Mrs Foster known him, do you imagine?'

'Not – very long. She met him first at that same dinner-party. But,' said Verity quickly, 'she'd been in the habit of going to Greengages for several years.'

'Whereas he only took over the practice last April,' he said casually. 'Do you like him? Nice sort of chap?'

'As I said, I've only met him that once.'

'But you knew him before?'

'It was – so very long ago.'

'I don't think you liked him very much,' he murmured as if to himself. 'Or perhaps – but it doesn't matter.'

'Mr Alleyn,' Verity said loudly and, to her chagrin, in an unsteady voice. 'I know what was in the Will.'

'Yes, I thought you must.'

'And perhaps I'd better just say it: the Will might have hap-

pened at any time in the past if Sybil had been thoroughly
upset. On the rebound from a row, she could have left anything
to anyone who was in favour at the time.'

'But did she to your knowledge ever do this in the past?'

'Perhaps she never had the same provocation in the past.'

'Or was not sufficiently attracted?'

'Oh,' said Verity, 'she took fancies. Look at this whacking
great legacy to Bruce.'

'Bruce? Oh yes. The gardener. She thought a lot of him, I
suppose? A faithful and tried old retainer? Was that it?'

'He'd been with her about six months and he's middle-aged
and rather like a resurrection from the more dubious pages of
J. M. Barrie, but Syb thought him the answer to her prayers.'

'As far as the garden was concerned?'

'Yes. He does my garden too.'

'It's enchanting. Do you dote on him as well?'

'No. But I must say I like him better than I did. He took
trouble over Syb. He visited her once a week with flowers and
I don't think he was sucking up. I just think he puts on a bit of
an act like a guide doing his sob-stuff over Mary Queen of Scots
in Edinburgh Castle.'

'I've never heard of a guide doing sob-stuff in Edinburgh
Castle.'

'They drool. When they're not having a go at William and
Mary, they get closer and closer to you and the tears seem to
come into their eyes and they drool about Mary Queen of
Scots. I may have been unlucky of course. Bruce is positively
taciturn in comparison. He overdoes the nature-lover bit but
only perhaps because his employers encourage it. He *is*, in fact,
a dedicated gardener.'

'And he visited Mrs Foster at Greengages?'

'He was there that afternoon.'

'While you were there?'

Verity explained how Bruce and she had encountered in the
grounds and how she'd told him Sybil wouldn't be able to see
him then and how Prunella had suggested later on that he left
his lilies at the desk.

'So he did just that?'

'I think so. I suppose they both went back by the next bus.'

'Both?'

'I'd forgotten Charmless Claude.'

'What?'

'He's Syb's ghastly stepson.'

Verity explained Claude but avoided any reference to his more dubious activities, merely presenting him as a spineless drifter. She kept telling herself she ought to be on her guard with this atypical policeman in whose company she felt so inappropriately conversational. At the drop of a hat, she thought, she'd find herself actually talking about that episode of the past that she had never confided to anyone and which still persisted so rawly in her memory.

She pulled herself together. He had asked her if Claude was the son of Sybil's second husband.

'No, of her first husband, Maurice Carter. She married him when she was seventeen. He was a very young widower. His first wife died in childbirth – leaving Claude who was brought up by his grandparents. They didn't like him very much, I'm afraid. Perhaps he might have turned out better if they had, but there it is. And then Maurice married Syb who was in the WRNS. She was on duty somewhere in Scotland when he got an unexpected leave. He came down here to Quintern – Quintern Place is *her* house, you know – and tried to ring her up but couldn't get through so he wrote a note. While he was doing this he was recalled urgently to London. The troop-train he caught was bombed and he was killed. She found the note afterwards. That's a sad story, isn't it?'

'Yes. Was this stepson, Claude, provided for?'

'Very well provided for, really. His father wasn't an enormously rich man but he left a trust fund that paid for Claude's upbringing. It still would be a reasonable standby if he didn't contrive to lose it as fast as it comes in. Of course,' Verity said, more to herself than to Alleyn, 'it'd have been different if the stamp had turned up.'

'Did you say "stamp"?'

'The Black Alexander. Maurice Carter inherited it. It was a pre-revolution Russian stamp that was withdrawn on the day it was issued because of a rather horrid little black flaw that looked like a bullet-hole in the Czar's forehead. Apparently no other specimen was known to be in existence and so this one was worth some absolutely fabulous amount of money. Maurice's own collection was medium-valuable and it went to Claude, who sold it, but the Black Alexander couldn't be found. He was known to have taken it out of his bank the day before he died. They searched and searched but with no luck and it's generally thought he must have had it on him when he was killed. It was a direct hit. It was bad luck for Claude about the stamp.'

'Where is Claude now?'

Verity said uncomfortably that he had been staying at Quintern but she didn't know if he was still there.

'I see. Tell me, when did Mrs Foster re-marry?'

'In – when was it? In 1958. A large expensive stockbroker who adored her. He had a heart condition and died of it in 1964. You know,' Verity said suddenly, 'when one tells the whole story, bit by bit, it turns almost into a classic tragedy, and yet, somehow one can't see poor old Syb as a tragic figure. Except when one remembers the *look*.'

'The look that was spoken of at the inquest?'

'Yes. It would have been quite frightful if she, of all people, had suffered that disease.'

After a longish pause, Verity said, 'When will the inquest be reopened?'

'Quite soon. Probably early next week. I don't think you will be called again. You've been very helpful.'

'In what way? No, don't tell me,' said Verity. 'I – I don't think I want to know. I don't think I want to be helpful.'

'Nobody loves a policeman,' he said cheerfully and stood up. So did Verity. She was a tall woman but he towered over her.

He said, 'I think this business has upset you more than you realize. Will you mind if I give you what must sound like a professionally motivated word of advice? If it turns out that you're acquainted with some episode or some piece of behaviour, perhaps quite a long way back in time, that might throw a little light on – say, on the character of one or other of the people we have discussed – don't withhold it. You never know. By doing so you might be doing a disservice to a friend.'

'We're back to the Will again. Aren't we?'

'Oh, that? Yes. In a sense we are.'

'You think she may have been influenced? Or that in some way it might be a cheat? Is that it?'

'The possibility must be looked at when the terms of a Will are extravagant and totally unexpected and the Will itself is made so short a time before the death of the testator.'

'But that's not all? Is it? You're not here just because Syb made a silly Will. You're here because she died. You think it wasn't suicide. Don't you?'

He waited so long and looked so kindly at her that she was

answered before he spoke.

'I'm afraid that's it,' he said at last. 'I'm sorry.'

Again he waited, expecting, perhaps, that she might ask more questions or break down but she contrived, as she put it to herself, to keep up appearances. She supposed she must have gone white because she found he had put her back in her chair. He went away and returned with a glass of water.

'I found your kitchen,' he said. 'Would you like brandy with this?'

'No – why? There's nothing the matter with me,' said Verity and tried to steady her hand. She took a hurried gulp of water.

'Dizzy spell,' she improvised. ' "Age with his stealing steps" and all that.'

'I don't think he can be said to have "clawed you in his clutch".'

'Thank you.'

'Anyway, I shan't bother you any longer. Unless there's something I can do?'

'I'm perfectly all right. Thank you very much, though.'

'Sure? I'll be off then. Goodbye.'

Through the drawing-room window she watched him go striding down the drive and heard a car start up in the lane.

Time, of course, does heal as people say in letters of condolence, she thought. But they don't mention the scars and twinges that crop up when the old wound gets an unexpected jolt. And this is a bad jolt, thought Verity. This is a snorter.

And Alleyn, being driven by Inspector Fox to Quintern Place, said, 'That's a nice intelligent creature, Br'er Fox. She's got character and guts but she couldn't help herself going white when I talked about Schramm. She was much concerned to establish that they hadn't met for many years and then only once. Why? An old affair? On the whole, I can't wait to meet Dr Schramm.'

3

But first they must visit Quintern Place. It came into view, unmistakably as soon as they had passed through the village – a Georgian house half way up a hill, set in front of a stand of oaks and overlooking a rose-garden, lawns, a ha-ha and a sloping field and woodlands. Facing this restrained and lovely house, and separated from it by a shallow declivity, was a monstrous Victorian pile, a plethora of towers and pepper-pots approached by a long avenue which opened, by way of grandiloquent gates, off the lane leading to Quintern. 'That's Mardling Manor, that is,' said Alleyn, 'the residence of Mr Nikolas Markos who had the good sense and taste to buy Troy's "Several Pleasures".'

'I wouldn't have thought the house was quite his style,' said Mr Fox.

'And you'd have been dead right. I can't imagine what possessed him to buy such a monumental piece of complacency unless it was to tease himself with an uninterrupted view of a perfect house,' said Alleyn and little knew how close to the mark he had gone.

'Did you pay a call on the local Super?' he asked.

'Yes. He's looking forward to meeting you. I got a bit of info out of him,' said Mr Fox, 'which came in handy, seeing I've only just been brought in on the case. It seems they're interested in the deceased lady's stepson, a Mr Carter. He's a bit of a ne'er-do-well. Worked his way home from Australia in the *Poseidon* as a ship's steward. He's done porridge for attempted blackmail and he's sussy for bringing the hard stuff ashore but they haven't got enough for a catch. He's staying up at Quintern Place.'

'So Miss Preston thought. And here we go.'

The approach was through a grove of rhododendrons from which they came out rather unexpectedly on a platform in front of the house.

Looking up at the façade, Alleyn caught a fractional impression of someone withdrawing from a window at the far end of the first floor. Otherwise there was no sign of life.

The door was opened by a compact little person in an apron. She looked quickly at the car and its driver and then, doubtfully, at Alleyn who took off his hat.

'You must be Mrs Jim Jobbin,' he said.

Mrs Jim looked hard at him. 'That's correct,' she said.

'Do you think Miss Foster could give me a moment if she's in?'

'She's not.'

'Oh.'

Mrs Jim gave a quick look across the little valley to where Mardling Manor shamelessly exhibited itself. 'She's out,' she said.

'I'm sorry about that. Would you mind if I came in and had

a word with you? I'm a police officer but there's no need to let that bother you. It's only to tidy up some details about the inquest on Mrs Foster.'

He had the impression that Mrs Jim listened for something to happen inside the house and, not hearing it, waited for him to speak and not hearing that either, was relieved. She gave him another pretty hard look and then stood away from the door.

'I'll just ask my colleague to wait if I may?' Alleyn said and returned to the car.

'A certain amount of caginess appears,' he murmured. 'If anything emerges and looks like melting away ask it if it's Mr Carter and keep it here. Same goes for the gardener.' Aloud he said, 'I won't be long,' and returned to the house.

Mrs Jim stood aside for him and he went into a large and beautifully proportioned hall. It was panelled in parchment-coloured linenfold oak with a painted ceiling and elegant stairway. 'What a lovely house,' Alleyn said. 'Do you look after it?'

'I help out,' said Mrs Jim guardedly.

'Miss Preston told me about you. Mrs Foster's death must have been a shock after knowing her for so long.'

'It seemed a pity,' Mrs Jim conceded economically.

'Did you expect anything of the kind?'

'I didn't expect anything. I never thought she'd make away with herself if that's what's meant. She wasn't the sort.'

'Everybody seems to think that,' Alleyn agreed.

The hall went right through the house and at the far end looked across rose-gardens to the misty Weald of Kent. He moved to the windows and was in time to see a head and shoulders bob up and down behind a box hedge. The owner seemed to be crouched and running.

'You've got somebody behaving rather oddly in your garden,' said Alleyn. 'Come and look.'

She moved behind him.

'He's doubled up,' Alleyn said, 'behind that tallish hedge. Could he be chasing some animal?'

'I don't know, I'm sure.'

'Who could it be?'

'The gardener's working here today.'

'Has he got long fair hair?'

'No,' she said quickly, and passed her working hand across her mouth.

'Would the gentleman in the garden, by any chance, be Mr Claude Carter?'

'It might.'

'Perhaps he's chasing butterflies.'

'He might be doing anything,' said Mrs Jim woodenly.

Alleyn, standing back from the window and still watching the hedge, said: 'There's only one point I need bother you with, Mrs Jobbin. It's about the envelope that I believe you put in Mrs Foster's desk after her death.'

'She give it to the gardener about a week before she died and said he was to put it there. He give it to me and asked me to. Which I did.'

'And you told Miss Foster it was there?'

'Correct. I remembered it after the inquest.'

'Do you know what was in it?'

'It was none of my business, was it, sir?' said Mrs Jim, settling for the courtesy title. 'It had "Will" written on the outside and Miss Prue said it was a stinker. She give it to the lawyer.'

'Was it sealed, do you remember?'

'It was gummed up. Sort of.'

'Sort of, Mrs Jim?'

'Not what you'd call a proper job. More of a careless lick. She was like that with her letters. She'd think of something she'd meant to say and open them up and then stick them down with what was left of the gum. She was great on afterthoughts.'

'Would you mind letting me see the desk?'

Mrs Jim's face reddened and she stuck out her lower lip.

'Mrs Jobbin,' Alleyn said, 'don't think we're here for any other purpose than to try and sort matters out in order that there shall be no injustice done to anybody, including Miss Prunella Foster, or if it comes to that, to the memory of her mother. I'm not setting traps at the moment, which is not to say a copper never does. As I expect you very well know. But not here and not now. I would simply like to see the desk, if you'll show me where it is.'

She looked fixedly at him for an appreciable interval, then broke out, 'It's no business of mine, this isn't. I don't know anything that goes on up here, sir, and if you'll excuse my speaking out, I don't want to. Miss Prue's all right. She's a nice young lady, for all you can't hear half she says and anyone can see she's been upset. But she's got her young man and he's sharp enough for six and he'll look after her. So'll his old – his

76

father,' amended Mrs Jim. 'He's that pleased, anyway, with the match seeing he's getting what he'd set his heart on.'

'Really? What was that?' Alleyn asked, still keeping an eye on the box hedge.

'This property. He wanted to buy it and they say he would have paid anything to get it. Well, in a sort of way he'll get his wish now, won't he? It's settled he's to have his own rooms – self-contained, like. I'll show you the desk, then, if you'll come this way.'

It was in a smallish room known in her lifetime as Sybil's boudoir, which lay between the great drawing-room and the dining-room where, on the day of the old gardener's death, the Upper Quintern ladies had held their meeting. The desk, a nice piece of Chippendale, stood in the window. Mrs Jim indicated the centre drawer and Alleyn opened it. Letter paper, stamps and a diary were revealed.

'The drawer wasn't locked?' he asked.

'Not before, it wasn't. I left the envelope on top of some papers and then I thought it best to turn the key in the lock and keep it. I handed the key to Miss Prue. She doesn't seem to have locked it.'

'And was the envelope sealed?'

'Like I said.' She waited for a moment and then, for the second time, broke out: 'If you want to know any more about it you can ask Bruce. He fetched it. Mrs Foster give it to him.'

'Do you think he knows what was in it? The details, I mean?'

'Ask him. I don't know. *I* don't discuss the business of the house and I don't ask questions, no more than I expect them to ask me.'

'Mrs Jobbin, I'm sure you don't and I won't bother you much further.'

He was about to shut the drawer when he noticed a worn leather case. He opened it and it disclosed a photograph, in faded sepia, of a group from a Scottish regiment. Among the officers was a second lieutenant, so emphatically handsome as to stand out from among his fellows.

'That's her first,' said Mrs Jim, at Alleyn's back. 'Third from the left. Front row. Name of Carter.'

'He must have been a striking chap to look at.'

'Like a Greek god,' Mrs Jim startled him by announcing, still in her wooden voice. 'That's what they used to say, them in the village that remembered him.'

Wondering which of the Upper Quintern worthies had employed this classy simile, Alleyn pushed the drawer shut and looked at the objects on the top of the desk. Prominent among them was a photograph of pretty Prunella Foster, one of the ultra-conservative kind, destined for glossy magazines and thought of, by Alleyn, as 'Cabinet Pudding'. Further off, and equally conventional, was a middle-aged man of full habit and slightly prominent eyes who had signed himself 'John'. That would be Foster, the second husband and Prunella's father. Alleyn looked down into the pink-shaded lamp on Sybil Foster's desk. The bulb was covered by a double-glass slipper. A faint odour of sweet almonds still hung about it.

'Was there anything else you was wanting?' asked Mrs Jim.

'Not from you, thank you, Mrs Jobbin. I'd like a word with the gardener. I'll find him somewhere out there, I expect.' He waited for a moment and then said cheerfully, 'I gather you're not madly keen on him.'

'Him,' said Mrs Jim. 'I wouldn't rave and that's a fact. Too much of the Great I Am.'

'The—?'

'Letting on what a treat he is to all and sundry.'

'Including Mrs Foster?'

'Including everybody. It's childish. One of these days he'll burst into poetry and stifle himself,' said Mrs Jim and then seemed to think better of it. 'No harm in 'im, mind,' she amended. 'Just asking for attention. Like a child, pathetic, reely. And good at his work, he is. You've got to hand it to him. He's all right at bottom even if it is a long way down.'

'Mrs Jobbin,' said Alleyn, 'you are a very unexpected and observant lady. I will leave my card for Miss Foster and I wish you a grateful good morning.'

He held out his hand. Mrs Jobbin, surprised into a blush, put her corroded little paw into it and then into her apron pocket.

'Bid you good day, then,' she said. 'Sir. You'll likely find him near the old stables. First right from the front door and right again. Growing mushrooms, for Gawd's sake.'

Bruce was not near the old stables but in them. As Alleyn approached he heard the drag and slam of a door and when he 'turned right again' found his man.

Bruce had evidently taken possession of what had originally been some kind of open-fronted lean-to abutting on the stables.

He had removed part of the flooring and dug up the ground beneath. Bags of humus and a heap of compost awaited his attention.

In response to Alleyn's greeting he straightened up, squared his shoulders and came forward. 'Guid day, sir,' he said. 'Were you looking for somebody?'

'For you,' Alleyn said, 'if your name's Gardener?'

'It is that. Gardener's the name and gardener's the occupation,' he said, evidently cracking a vintage quip. 'What can I do for you, then?'

Alleyn made the usual announcement.

'Police?' said Bruce loudly and stared at him. 'Is that a fact? Ou, aye, who'd have thowt it?'

'Would you like me to flash a card at you?' Alleyn asked lightly. Bruce put his head on one side, gazed at him, waited for a moment and then became expansive.

'Och, na, na, na, na,' he said. 'Not at a', not at a'. There's no call for anything o' the sort. You didna strike me at first sight as a constabulary figure, just. What can I do for you?'

Members of the police force develop a sixth sense about the undeclared presence of offstage characters. Alleyn had taken the impression that Bruce was aware, but not anxiously, of a third person somewhere in the offing.

'I wanted to have a word with you, if I might,' he said, 'about the late Mrs Foster. I expect you know about the adjourned inquest?'

Bruce looked fixedly at him. He's re-focusing, thought Alleyn. He was expecting something else.

'I do that,' Bruce said. 'Aye. I do that.'

'You'll realize, of course, that the reason for the adjournment was to settle, beyond doubt, the question of suicide.'

Bruce said slowly, 'I wad never have believed it of her. Never. She was aye fu' of enthusiasm. She liked fine to look ahead to the pleasures of her garden. Making plans! What for would we be planning for mushrooms last time I spoke with her if she was of a mind to make awa' wi' herself?'

'When was that?'

He pushed his gardener's fingers through his sandy hair and said it would have been when he visited her a week before it happened and that she had been in great good humour and they had drawn plans on the back of an envelope for a lily-pond and had discussed making a mushroom bed here in the old stables. He had promised to go into matters of plumbing and mulching and here he was, carrying on as if she'd be coming home to see it. Something, he said, must have happened during that last week to put sic' awfu' thoughts into her head.

'Was it on that visit,' Alleyn asked, 'that she gave you her Will to put in her desk here at Quintern?'

Bruce said aye, it was that, and intimated that he hadn't fancied the commission but that her manner had been so light-hearted he had not entertained any real misgivings.

Alleyn said, 'Did Mrs Foster give you any idea of the terms of this Will?'

For the first time he seemed to be discomfited. He bent his blue unaligned gaze on Alleyn and muttered she had mentioned that he wasn't forgotten.

'I let on,' he said, 'that I had no mind to pursue the matter.'

He waited for a moment and then said Alleyn would consider maybe that this was an ungracious response but he'd not like it to be thought he looked for anything of the sort from her. He became incoherent, shuffled his boots and finally burst out, 'To my way of thinking it wasna just the decent thing.'

'Did you say as much to Mrs Foster?'

'I did that.'

'How did she take it?'

'She fetched a laugh and said I'd no call to be sae squeamish.'

'And that was all?'

'Ou aye. I delivered the thing into the hand of Mrs Jim, having no mind to tak' it further and she told me she'd put it in the desk.'

'Was the envelope sealed?'

'No' sealed in the literal sense but licked up. The mistress wasna going to close it but I said I'd greatly prefer that she should.' He waited for a moment. 'It's no' that I wouldna have relished the acquisition of a wee legacy,' he said. 'Not a great outlandish wallop, mind, but a wee, decent amount. I'd like that. I would so. I'd like it fine and put it by, remembering the bonny giver. But I wouldna have it thowt or said I took any part in the proceedings.'

'I understand that,' said Alleyn. 'By the way, did Mrs Foster ask you to get the form for her?'

'The forrum? What forrum would that be, sir?'

'The Will. From a stationer's shop?'

'Na, na,' he said, 'I ken naething o' that.'

'And while we're on the subject, did she ask you to bring things in for her? When you visited her?'

It appeared that he had from time to time fetched things from Quintern to Greengages. She would make a list and he would give it to Mrs Jim. 'Clamjampherie', mostly, he thought, things from her dressing-table. Sometimes, he believed, garments. Mrs Jim would put them in a small case so that he wasn't embarrassed by impedimenta unbecoming to a man. Mrs Foster would repack the case with things to be laundered. Alleyn gathered that the strictest decorum was observed. If he was present at these exercises he would withdraw to the window. He was at some pains to make this clear, arranging his mouth in a prim expression as he did so.

A picture emerged from these recollections of an odd, rather cosy relationship, enjoyable, one would think, for both parties. Plans had been laid, pontifications exchanged. There had been, probably, exclamatory speculation as to what the world was coming to, consultations over nurserymen's catalogues, strolls round the rose-garden and conservatory. Bruce sustained an air of rather stuffy condescension in letting fall an occasional reference to these observances and still he gave, as Mrs Jim in her own fashion had given, an impression of listening for somebody or something.

Behind him in the side wall was a ramshackle closed door leading, evidently, into the main stables. Alleyn saw that it had gaps between the planks and had dragged its course through loose soil and what was left of the floor.

He made as if to go and then looking at Bruce's preparations asked if this was in fact to be the proposed mushroom bed. He said it was.

'It was the last request she made,' he said. 'And I prefer to carry it out.' He expanded a little on the techniques of mushroom culture and then said, not too pointedly, if that was all he could do for Alleyn he'd better get on with it and reached for his long-handled shovel.

'There was one other thing,' Alleyn said. 'I almost forgot. You did actually go over to Greengages on the day of her death, didn't you?'

'I did so. But I never saw her,' he said and described how he had waited in the hall with his lilies and how Prunella – 'the wee lassie' he predictably called her – had come down and told him her mother was very tired and not seeing anybody that evening. He had left the lilies at the desk and the receptionist lady had said they would be attended to. So he had returned home by bus.

'With Mr Claude Carter?' asked Alleyn.

Bruce became very still. His hands tightened on the shovel. He stared hard at Alleyn, made as if to speak and changed his mind. Alleyn waited.

'I wasna aware, just,' Bruce said at last, 'that you had spoken to that gentleman.'

'Nor have I. Miss Preston mentioned that he arrived with you at Greengages.'

He thought that over. 'He arrived. That is so,' said Bruce, 'but he did not depart with me.' He raised his voice. 'I wish it to be clearly understood,' he said. 'I have no perrsonal relationship with that gentleman.' And then very quietly and with an air of deep resentment, 'He attached himself to me. He wurrumed the information out of me as to her whereabouts. It was an indecent performance and one that I cannot condone.'

He turned his head fractionally towards the closed door. 'And that is the total sum of what I have to say in the matter,' he almost shouted.

'You've been very helpful. I don't think I need pester you any more. Thank you for co-operating.'

'There's no call for thanks. I'm a law-abiding man,' Bruce said, 'and I canna thole mysteries. Guid day to you, sir.'

'This is a lovely old building,' Alleyn said. 'I'm interested in Georgian domestic architecture. Do you mind if I have a look around?'

Without waiting for an answer he passed between Bruce and the closed door, dragged it open and came face to face with Claude Carter.

'Oh, hullo,' said Claude. 'I thought I heard voices.'

Chapter Four

ROUTINE

The room was empty and smelt of rats with perhaps an under-tone of long-vanished fodder. There was a tumbledown fire-place in one corner and in another a litter of objects that looked as if they had lain there for a century: empty tins, a sack that had rotted, letting out a trickle of cement, a brick-layer's trowel, rusted and handleless, a heap of empty manure bags. The only window was shuttered. Claude was a dim figure.

He said, 'I was looking for Bruce. The gardener. I'm afraid I don't know—?'

The manner was almost convincing, almost easy, almost that of a son of the house. Alleyn thought the voice was probably pitched a little above its normal level but it sounded quite natural. For somebody who had been caught red-eared in the act of eavesdropping, Claude displayed considerable aplomb.

Alleyn shut the door behind him. Bruce Gardener, already plying his long-handled shovel, didn't look up.

'And I was hoping to see you,' said Alleyn. 'Mr Carter, isn't it?'

'That's right. You have the advantage of me.'

'Chief Superintendent Alleyn.'

After a considerable pause, Claude said, 'Oh. What can I do for you, Chief Superintendent?'

As soon as Alleyn told him he seemed to relax. He answered all the questions readily. Yes, he had spoken to Miss Preston and Prue Foster but had not been allowed to visit his step-mother. He had gone for a stroll in the grounds, had missed the return bus and had walked into the village and picked up a later one there.

'A completely wasted afternoon,' he complained. 'And I must say I wasn't wildly enthusiastic about the reception I got. Particularly in the light of what happened. After all, she was my stepmother.'

'When was the last time you saw her?'

'When? I don't know when. Three – four years ago.'

'Before you went to Australia?'

He shot a sidelong look at Alleyn. 'That's right,' he said, and after a pause, 'You seem to be very well informed of my movements, Chief Superintendent.'

'I know you returned as a member of the ship's complement in the *Poseidon*.'

After a much longer pause, Claude said, 'Oh yes?'

'Shall we move outside and get a little more light and air on the subject?' Alleyn suggested.

Claude opened a door that gave directly on the yard. As they walked into the sunshine a clock in the stable turret tolled eleven very sweetly. The open front of the lean-to faced the yard. Bruce, shovelling vigorously, was in full view, an exemplar of ostentatious non-intervention. Claude stared resentfully at his stern and walked to the far end of the yard. Alleyn followed him.

'How long,' he asked cheerfully, 'had you been in that dark and rather smelly apartment?'

'How *long*? I don't know. No time at all really. Why?'

'I don't want to waste my breath and your time repeating myself, if you've already heard about the Will. And I think you must have heard it because, as I came up, the adjoining door in there was dragged shut.'

Claude gave a rather shrill titter. 'You *are* quick, aren't you?' he said. He lowered his voice. 'As I said,' he confided, 'I was looking for that gardener-man in there. As a matter of fact I thought he might be in the other room and then when you came in and began talking it was jolly awkward. I didn't want to intrude so I – I mean I – you know – it's difficult to explain—'

'You're making a brave shot at it, though, aren't you? Your sense of delicacy prompted you to remove into the next room, shut that same openwork door and remain close by it throughout our conversation. Is that it?'

'Not at all. You haven't understood.'

'You'd seen us arrive in a police car, perhaps, and you left the house in a hurry for the rose-garden and thence proceeded round the left wing to the stables?'

'I don't know,' said Claude, with a strange air of frightened effrontery, 'why you're taking this line with me, Superintendent, but I must say I resent it.'

'Yes, I thought you might be a bit put out by our appearance. Because of an irregularity in your departure from the *Poseidon*.'

Claude began feverishly to maintain that there had been some mistake and the police had had to climb down and he was thinking of lodging a complaint only it didn't seem worthwhile.

Alleyn let him talk himself to a standstill and then said his visit had nothing to do with any of this and that he only wanted to be told if Claude did in fact know of a recent Will made by Mrs Foster shortly before her death.

An elaborate shuffling process set in, hampered, it seemed, by the proximity of the ever-industrious Bruce. By means of furtive little nods and becks Claude indicated the desirability of a remove. Alleyn disregarded these hints and continued on a loudish, cheerful note.

'It's a perfectly simple question,' he said. 'Nothing private about it. Have you, in fact, known of such a Will?'

Claude made slight jabs with his forefinger, in the direction of Bruce's rear elevation.

'As it happens, yes,' he mouthed.

'You have? Do you mind telling me how it came to your knowledge?'

'It's – I – it just so happened—'

'What did?'

'I mean to say –'

'*Havers!*' Bruce suddenly roared out. He became upright and faced them. 'What ails you, man?' he demanded. 'Can you no' give a straight answer when you're speired a straight question? Oot wi' it, for pity's sake. Tell him and ha' done. There's nothing wrong wi' the facts o' the matter.'

'Yes, well, all right, all right,' said the wretched Claude and added with a faint show of grandeur, 'And you may as well keep a civil tongue in your head.'

Bruce spat on his hands and returned to his shovelling.

'Well, Mr Carter?' Alleyn asked.

By painful degrees it emerged that Claude had happened to be present when Bruce came into the house with the Will and had happened to see him hand it over to Mrs Jim and had happened to notice what it was on account of the word Will being written in large letters on the envelope.

'And had happened,' Bruce said, without turning round but with a thwack of his shovel on the heap of earth he had raised, 'to enquire with unco' perrrsistence as to the cirrrcumstances.'

'Look here, Gardener, I've had about as much of you as I can take,' said Claude, with a woeful show of spirit.

'You can tak' me or leave me, Mr Carter, and my preference

85

would be for the latter procedure.'

'Do you know the terms of the Will?' Alleyn cut in.

'No, I don't. I'm not interested. Whatever they are, they don't affect me.'

'How do you mean?'

'My father provided for me. With a trust fund or whatever it's called. Syb couldn't touch that and she's not bloody likely to have added to it,' said Claude with a little spurt of venom.

Upon this note Alleyn left them and returned deviously, by way of a brick-walled vegetable garden, to Fox. He noticed two newly made asparagus beds, and a multitude of enormous cabbages and wondered where on earth they all went and who consumed them. Fox, patient as ever, awaited him in the car.

'Nothing to report,' Fox said. 'I took a walk round but no signs of anyone.'

'The gardener's growing mushrooms in the stables and the stepson's growing butterflies in the stomach,' said Alleyn and described the scene.

'Miss Preston,' he said, 'finds Bruce's Scots a bit hard to take.'

'Phoney?'

'She didn't say that. More, "laid on with a trowel". She might have said with a long-handled shovel if she'd seen him this morning. But – I don't know. I'm no expert on dialects, Scots or otherwise, but it seemed to me he uses it more in the manner of someone who has lived with the genuine article long enough to acquire and display it inconsistently and inaccurately. His last job was in Scotland. He may think it adds to his charm or pawkiness or whatever.'

'What about the stepson?'

'Oh, quite awful, poor devil. Capable of anything if he had the guts to carry it through.'

'We move on?'

'We do. Hark forrard, hark forrard away to Greengages and the point marked x if there is one. Shall I drive and you follow the map?'

'Fair enough, if you say so, Mr Alleyn. What do I look for?'

'Turn right after Maidstone and follow the road to the village of Greenvale. Hence "Greengages", no doubt.'

'Colicky sort of name for a hospital.'

'It's not a hospital.'

'Colicky sort of a name for whatever it is.'

'There's no suggestion that the lady in question died of that, at least.'

'Seeing I've only just come in, could we re-cap on the way? What've we got for info?'

'We've got the lady who is dead. She was in affluent circumstances, stinking rich in fact, and probably in the early stages of Parkinson's disease but unaware of it, and we've got the medical incumbent of an expensive establishment that is neither hospital nor nursing home but a hotel that caters for well-to-do invalids, whose patient the lady was, and who did not spot the disease. We've got a local doctor called Field-Innis and a police pathologist who did. We've got the lady's daughter who on the afternoon of her mother's death announced her engagement to a rich young man who did not meet with the lady's approval. We've got the rich young man's millionaire papa who coveted the lady's house, failed to buy it but will now live in it when his son marries the daughter.'

'Hold on,' said Fox, after a pause. 'OK, I'm with you.'

'We've got an elderly Scottish gardener, possible pseudo-ish, to whom the lady has left twenty-five thousand deflated quid in a recent Will. The rest of her fortune is divided between her daughter if she marries a peer called Swingletree and the medical incumbent who didn't diagnose Parkinson's disease. If the daughter doesn't marry Swingletree the incumbent gets the lot.'

'That would be Dr Schramm?'

'Certainly. The rest of the cast is made up of the lady's step-son by her first marriage who is the archetype of all remittance-men and has a police record. Finally, we have a nice woman of considerable ability called Verity Preston.'

'That's the lot?'

'Give and take a trained nurse and a splendid lady called Mrs Jim who obliges in Upper Quintern, that's the lot.'

'What's the score where we come in? Exactly, I mean?'

'The circumstances are the score really, Br'er Fox. The Will and the *mise-en-scène*. The inquest was really adjourned because everybody says the lady was such an unlikely subject for suicide and had no motive. An extended autopsy seemed to be advisable. Sir James Curtis performed it. The undelicious results of Dr Schramm's stomach pump had been preserved and Sir James confirms that they disclosed a quantity of the barbiturate found in the remaining tablets on the bedside table and in the throat and at the back of the tongue. The assumption had been that she stuffed down enough of the things to become so far doped as to prevent her swallowing the last lot she put in her mouth.'

'Plausible?'

'Dr Schramm thought so. Sir James won't swallow it but says she would have – if you'll excuse a joke in bad taste, Br'er Fox. He points out that there's a delay of anything up to twenty minutes before the barbiturate in question, which is soluble in alcohol, starts to work and it's hard to imagine her waiting until she was too far under to swallow before putting the final lot in her mouth.'

'So what do we wonder about?'

'Whether somebody else put them there. By the way, Sir James looked for traces of cyanide.'

'Why?' Mr Fox asked economically.

'There'd been a smell of almonds in the room and in the contents of the stomach but it turned out that she used sweet almond oil in one of those glass-slipper things they put over lamp bulbs and that she'd wolfed quantities of marzipan petits-fours from the "Marquise de Sévigné" in Paris. The half-empty box was on her bedside table along with the vanity box and other litter.'

'Like – the empty bottle of scotch?'

'And the overturned glass. Exactly.'

'Anybody know how much there'd been in the bottle? That day, for instance?'

'Apparently not. She kept it in a cupboard above the hand-basin. One gathers it lasted her a good long time.'

'What about dabs?'

'The local chaps had a go before calling us in. Bailey and Thompson are coming down to give the full treatment.'

'Funny sort of set-up though, isn't it?' Fox mused.

The funniest bit is yet to come. Cast your mind back, however reluctantly, to the contents of the stomach as examined by Doctor Field-Innis and Schramm.'

'Oodles of barbiturate?'

'According to Schramm. But according to Sir James an appreciable amount but not enough, necessarily, to have caused death. You know how guarded he can be. Even allowing for what he calls "a certain degree of excretion" he would not take it as a matter of course that death would follow. He could find nothing to suggest any kind of susceptibility or allergy that might explain why it did.'

'So now we begin to wonder about the beneficiaries in the recent and eccentric Will?'

'That's it. And who provided her with the printed form. Young Mr Rattisbon allowed me to see it. It looks shop-new – fresh creases, sharp corners and edges.'

'And all in order?'

'He's afraid so. Outrageous though the terms may be. I gather, by the way, that Miss Prunella Foster would sooner trip down the aisle with a gorilla than with the Lord Swingletree.'

'So her share goes to this Dr Schramm?'

'In addition to the princely dollop he would get in any case.'

'It scarcely seems decent,' said Fox primly.

'You should hear the Rattisbons, *père et fils*, on the subject.'

'It's twenty to one,' Fox said wistfully as they entered a village, 'there's a nice-looking little pub ahead.'

'So there is. Tell me your thoughts.'

'They seem to dwell upon Scotch eggs, cheese and pickle sandwiches and a pint of mild-and-bitter.'

'So be it,' said Alleyn and pulled in.

2

Prunella Foster arrived from London at Quintern Place on her way to lunch with her fiancé and his father at Mardling. At Quintern Mrs Jim informed her of Alleyn's visit earlier in the morning. As a *raconteuse*, Mrs Jim was strong on facts and short on atmosphere. She gave a list of events in order of occurrence, answered Prunella's questions with the greatest possible economy and expressed no opinion of any sort whatsoever. Prunella was flustered.

'And he was a *policeman*, Mrs Jim?'

'That's what he said.'

'Do you mean there was any doubt about it?'

'Not to say doubt. It's on his card.'

'Well – what?'

Cornered, Mrs Jim said Alleyn had seemed a bit on the posh side for it. 'More after the style of one of your friends, like,' she offered and added that he had a nice way with him.

Prunella got her once more to rehearse the items of the visit, which she did with accuracy.

'So he asked about—?' Prunella cast her eyes and jerked her

head in the direction, vaguely, of that part of the house generally frequented by Claude Carter.

'That's right,' Mrs Jim conceded. She and Prunella understood each other pretty well on the subject of Claude. 'But it was only to remark he'd noticed him dodging up and down in the rose-garden. He went out, after, to the stables. The gentleman did.'

'To find Bruce?'

'That's right. Mr Claude, too, I reckon.'

'Oh?'

'Mr Claude come in after the gentleman had gone and went into the dining-room.'

This, Prunella recognized, was a euphemism for 'helped himself to a drink'.

'Where is he now?' she asked.

Mrs Jim said she'd no idea. They'd come to an arrangement about his meals, it emerged. She prepared a hot luncheon for one o'clock and laid the table in the small morning-room. She then beat an enormous gong and left for home. When she returned to Quintern in two days' time she would find the *disjecta membra* of this meal together with those of any subsequent snacks, unpleasantly congealed upon the table.

'How difficult everything is,' Prunella muttered. 'Thank you, Mrs Jim. I'm going to Mardling for lunch. We're making plans about Quintern – you know, arranging for Mr Gideon's father to have his own quarters with us. He's selling Mardling, I think. After all that he'd done to it! Imagine! And keeping the house in London for his headquarters.'

'Is that right, miss?' said Mrs Jim, and Prunella knew by the wooden tone she employed that she was deeply stimulated. 'We'll be hearing wedding-bells one of these days, then?' she speculated.

'Well – not yet, of couse.'

'No,' Mrs Jim agreed. 'That wouldn't be the thing. Not just yet.'

'I'd really rather not have a "wedding", Mrs Jim. I'd rather be just married early in the morning in Upper Quintern with hardly anyone there. But he – Gideon – wants it the other way, so I suppose my aunt – Auntie Boo –' she whispered her way into inaudibility and her eyes filled with tears. She looked helplessly at Mrs Jim and thought how much she liked her. For the first time since her mother died it occurred to Prunella that, apart of course from Gideon, she was very much alone in the world. She had never been deeply involved with her mother and had indeed found her deviousness and vanities irritating when not positively comical and even that degree of tolerance had been shaken by the preposterous terms of this wretched Will. And yet now, abruptly, when she realized that Sybil was not and never would be there to be laughed at or argued with, that where she had been there was – nothing, a flood of desolation poured over Prunella and she broke down and cried with her face in Mrs Jim's cardigan which smelt of floor polish.

Mrs Jim said, 'Never mind, then. It's been a right shock and all. We know that.'

'I'm so sorry,' Prunella sobbed. 'I'm awfully sorry.'

'You have your cry out, then.'

This invitation had the opposite result to what had been intended. Prunella blew her nose and pulled herself together. She returned shakily to her wedding arrangements. 'Somebody will have to give me away,' she said.

'As long as it's not that Mr Claude,' said Mrs Jim loudly.

'God forbid. I wondered – I don't know – can one be given away by a woman? I could ask the vicar.'

'Was you thinking of Miss Verity?'

'She *is* my godmother. Yes, I was.'

'Couldn't do better,' said Mrs Jim.

'I must be off,' said Prunella, who did not want to run into Claude. 'You don't happen to know where those old plans of Quintern are? Mr Markos wants to have a look at them. They're in a sort of portfolio thing.'

'Library. Cupboard near the door. Bottom shelf.'

'How clever of you, Mrs Jim.'

'Your mother had them out to show Bruce. Before she went to that place. She left them out and *he*—' the movement of the head they both used to indicate Claude – 'was handling them and leaving them all over the place so I put them away.'

'Good for you. Mrs Jim – tell me. Does he – well – does he sort of peer and prowl? Do you know what I mean? Sort of?'

'Not my place to comment,' said Mrs Jim, 'but as you've brought it up, yes, he do. I can tell by the way things have been interfered with – shifted, like.'

'Oh dear.'

'Yes. Specially them plans. He seemed to fancy them particular. I seen him looking at that one of the grounds through the magnifying glass in the study. He's a proper nosey-parker if you ask me and don't mind my mentioning it,' said Mrs Jim rapidly. She brought herself up with a jerk. 'Will I fetch them, then? Put out your washing,' said Mrs Jim as an afterthought.

'Bless you. I'll just collect some things from my room.'

Prunella ran up a lovely flight of stairs and across a first-floor landing to her bedroom – a muslin and primrose affair with long windows opening over terraces, rose-gardens and uncluttered lawns that declined to the ha-ha, meadows, hay-fields, spinneys and the tower of St Crispin-in-Quintern. A blue haze veiled the more distant valleys and hills and turned the chimneys of a paper-making town into minarets. Prunella was glad that after she had married she would still live in this house.

She bathed her eyes, repacked her suitcase and prepared to leave. On the landing she ran into Claude.

There was no reason why he should not be on the landing or that she should have been aware that he had arrived there but there was something intrinsically furtive about Claude that gave her a sensation of stealth.

He said, 'Oh, hullo, Prue, I saw your car.'

'Hullo, Claude. Yes. I just looked in to pick up some things.'

'Not staying, then?'

'No.'

'I hope I'm not keeping you away,' he said, and looked at his feet and smiled.

'Of course not. I'm mostly in London these days.'

He stole a glance at her left hand.

'Congratulations are in order, I see.'

'Yes. Thank you.'

'When's it to be?'

She said it hadn't been decided and began to move towards the stairs.

'Er—' said Claude, 'I was wondering—'

'Yes?'

'Whether I'm to be handed the push.'

Prunella made a panic decision to treat this as a joke.

'Oh,' she said jauntily, 'you'll be given plenty of notice.'

'Too kind. Are you going to live here?'

'As a matter of fact, yes. After we've made some changes. You'll get fair warning, I promise.'

'Syb said I could be here, you know.'

'I know what she said, Claude. You're welcome to stay until the workmen come in.'

'Too kind,' he repeated, this time with an open sneer. 'By the way, you don't mind my asking, do you? I would like to know when the funeral is to be.'

Prunella felt as if winter had come into the house and closed about her heart. She managed to say, 'I don't – we won't know until after the inquest. Mr Rattisbon is going to arrange everything. You'll be let know, Claude, I promise.'

'Are you going to this new inquest?'

'I expect so. I mean, yes. Yes, I am.'

'So am I. Not that it affects me, of course.'

'I really must go. I'm running late.'

'I never wrote to you. About Syb.'

'There was no need. Goodbye.'

'Shall I carry your case down?'

'No, thanks. Really. It's quite light. Thank you very much, though.'

'I see you've got the old plans out. Of Quintern.'

'Goodbye,' Prunella said desperately and made a business of getting herself downstairs.

She had reached the ground floor when his voice floated down to her. 'Hi!'

She wanted to bolt but made herself stop and look up to the first landing. His face and hands hung over the balustrade.

'I suppose you realize we've had a visit from the police,' said Claude. He kept his voice down and articulated pedantically.

'Yes, of couse.'

One of the dangling hands moved to cup the mouth. 'They seem to be mightily interested in your mother's horticultural favourite,' Claude mouthed. 'I wonder why.'

The teeth glinted in the moon-face.

Prunella bolted. She got herself and her baggage through the front door and into her car and drove, much too fast, to Mardling.

'Honestly,' she said ten minutes later to Gideon and his father, 'I almost feel we should get in an exorcizer when Claude goes. I wonder if the vicar's any good on the bell, book and candle lay.'

'You enchanting child,' said Mr Markos in his florid way and raised his glass to her. 'Is this unseemly person really upsetting you? Should Gideon and I advance upon him with threatening gestures? Can't he be dispensed with?'

'I must say,' Gideon chimed in, 'I really do think it's a bit much he should set himself up at Quintern. After all, darling, he's got no business there, has he? I mean, no real family ties or anything. Face it.'

'I suppose not,' she agreed. 'But my mama did feel she ought not to wash her hands of him completely, awful though he undoubtedly is. You see, she was very much in love with his father.'

'Which doesn't, if one looks at it quite cold-bloodedly, give his son the right to impose upon her daughter,' said Mr Markos.

Prunella had noticed that this was a favourite phrase – 'quite cold-bloodedly' – and was rather glad that Gideon had not inherited it. But she liked her father-in-law-to-be and became relaxed and expansive in the atmosphere (anything, she reflected, but 'cold-blooded') that he created around himself and Gideon. She felt that she could say what she chose to him without being conscious of the difference in their ages, and that she amused and pleased him.

They sat out of doors on swinging seats under canopies. Mr Markos had decided that it was a day for pre-prandial champagne – 'a sparkling, venturesome morning', he called it. Prunella, who had skipped breakfast and was unused to such extravagance, rapidly expanded. She downed her drink and accepted another. The horrors, and lately there really had been moments of horror, slipped into the background. She became perfectly audible and began to feel that this was the life for her and was meant for her and she for it, that she blossomed in the company of the exotic Markoses, the one so delightfully mundane, the other so enchantingly in love with her. Eddies of relief, floating on champagne, lapped over her and if they were vaguely disturbed by little undertows of guilt (for after all she had a social conscience) that, however reprehensively, seemed merely to add to her exhilaration. She took a vigorous pull at her champagne and Mr Markos refilled her glass.

'Darling,' said Gideon, 'what *have* you got in that monstrous compendium or whatever it is in your car?'

'A surprise,' cried Prunella, waving her hand. 'Not for you, love. For Pil.' She raised her glass to Mr Markos and drank to him.

'For *whom*?' asked the Markoses in unison.

'For my papa-in-law-to-be. I've been too shy to know what to call you,' said Prunella. 'Not for a moment, that you *are* a Pill. Far from it. *Pillycock sat on Pillycock hill*,' she sang before she could stop herself. She realized she had shaken her curls at Nikolas, like one of Dickens's more awful little heroines and was momentarily ashamed of herself.

'You shall call me whatever you like,' said Mr Markos and kissed her hand. Another Dickens reference swam incontinently into Prunella's dizzy ken, '*Todgers were going it.*' For a second or two she slid aside from herself and saw herself 'going it' like mad in a swinging chair under a canopy and having her hand kissed. She was extravagantly pleased with life.

'Shall I fetch it?' Gideon asked.

'Fetch what?' Prunella shouted recklessly.

'Whatever you've brought for your papa-in-law-to-be.'

'Oh, *that*. Yes, darling, do, and I think perhaps no more champagne.'

Gideon burst out laughing. 'And I think perhaps you may be right,' he said and kissed the top of her head. He went to her car and took out the portfolio.

Prunella said to Mr Markos, 'I'm tightish. How awful.'

'Are you? Eat some olives. Stuff down lots of those cheese things. You're not really very tight.'

'Promise? All right, I will,' said Prunella and was as good as her word. A car came up the avenue.

'Here is Miss Verity Preston,' said Mr Markos. 'Did we tell you she was lunching?'

'No!' she exclaimed and blew out a little shower of cheese straws. 'How too frightful, she's my godmother.'

'Don't you like her?'

'I adore her. But *she* won't like to see *me* flown with fizz so early in the day. Or ever. And as a matter of fact it's not my form at all, by and large,' said Prunella, swallowing most of an enormous mouthful of cheese straws and helping herself to more. 'I'm a sober girl.'

'You're a divine girl. I doubt if Gideon deserves you.'

'You're absolutely right. The cheese straws and olives are doing the trick. I shan't go on about being drunk. People who do that are such a bore always, don't you feel? And anyway I'm rapidly becoming sober.' As if to prove it, she had begun to whisper again.

The Markoses went to meet Verity. Prunella thought of following them but compromised by getting up from her swinging seat, which she did in a quickly controlled flounder.

'Godma V,' she said. And when they were close enough to each other she hung herself about Verity's neck and was glad to do so

'Hullo, young party,' said Verity, surprised by this effusion and not knowing what to do about it. Prunella sat down abruptly and inaccurately on the swinging chair.

The Markoses, father and son, stood one on each side of her, smiling at Verity, who thought that her godchild looked like a briar rose between a couple of succulent exotics. They will absorb her, Verity thought, into their own world and one doesn't know what that may be. Was Syb by any chance right? And ought I to take a hand? What about her Aunt Boo? Boo was Syb's flighty sister. I'd better talk to Prue and I suppose write to Boo, who ought to have come back and taken some responsibility, instead of sending vague cables from Acapulco. She realized that Nikolas Markos was talking to her.

'– hope you approve of champagne at this hour.'

'Lovely,' Verity said hastily, 'but demoralizing.'

'That's what I found, Godma V,' whispered Prunella, lurching about in her swinging chair.

For Heaven's sake, thought Verity, the child's tipsy.

But when Mr Markos had opened the portfolio, tenderly drawn out its contents and laid them on the garden table, which he dusted with his handkerchief, Prunella had so far recovered as to give a fairly informed comment on them.

'They're the original plans, I think. He was meant to be rather a grand architect. The house was built for my I-don't-know-how-many-times-great grandfather. You can see the date is 1780. He was called Lord Rupert Passcoigne. My mama was the last Passcoigne of that family and inherited Quintern from her father. I hope I've got it right. The plans are rather pretty, aren't they, with the coat-of-arms and all the trimmings and nonsense?'

'My dear child,' said Mr Markos, poring over them, 'they're exquisite. It's – I really can't tell you how excited I am to see them.'

'There are some more underneath.'

'We mustn't keep them too long in this strong light. Gideon, put this one back in the portfolio. Carefully. Gently. No, let me do it.'

He looked up at Verity. 'Have you seen them?' he asked. 'Come and look. Share my gloat, do.'

Verity had seen them, as it happened, many years ago, when Sybil had first married her second husband, but she joined the party round the table. Mr Markos had arrived at a plan for the gardens at Quintern and dwelt on it with greedy curiosity.

'But this has never been carried out,' he said. 'Has it? I mean, nicest possible daughter-in-law-to-be, the gardens today bear little resemblance in concept to this exquisite *schema*. Why?'

'Don't ask me,' said Prunella. 'Perhaps they ran out of cash or something. I rather think Mummy and Bruce were cooking up a grand idea about carrying out some of the scheme but decided we couldn't afford it. If only they hadn't lost the Black Alexander Claude could have done it.'

'Yes, indeed,' said Verity.

Mr Markos looked up quickly. 'The Black Alexander!' he said. 'What can you mean? You can't mean—'

'Oh, yes, of course. You're a collector.'

'I am indeed. Tell me.'

She told him and when she had done so he was unusually quiet for several seconds.

'But how immensely rewarding it would be—' he began at last and then pulled himself up. 'Let us put the plans away,' he said. 'They arouse insatiable desires. I'm sure you understand, don't you, Miss Preston? I've allowed myself to build – not castles in Spain but gardens in Kent, which is much more reprehensible. Haven't I?'

How very intelligent, Verity thought, finding his black eyes focused on hers, this Mr Markos is. He seems to be making all sorts of assumptions and I seem to be liking it.

'I don't remember that I saw the garden plan before,' she said. 'It would have been a perfect marriage, wouldn't it?'

'Ah. And you have used the perfect phrase for it.'

'Would you like to keep the plans here,' asked Prunella, 'to have another gloat?'

He thanked her exuberantly and, luncheon having been announced, they went indoors.

Since that first dinner-party, which now seemed quite a long time ago, and the visit to Greengages on the day of Sybil's death, Verity had not seen much of the Markoses. She had been twice asked to Mardling for cocktail-parties and on each occasion had been unable to go and one evening Markos Senior had paid an unheralded visit to Keys House, having spotted her, as he explained, in her garden and acted on the spur of the moment. They had got on well, having tastes in common and he showing a pretty acute appreciation of the contemporary theatre. Verity had been quite surprised to see the time when he finally took his stylish leave of her. The next thing

that she had heard of him was that he had 'gone abroad', a piece
of information conveyed by village telegraph through Mrs Jim.
And 'abroad', as far as Verity knew, he had remained until this
present reappearance.

They had their coffee in the library, now completely finished.
Verity wondered what would happen to all the books if, as
Mrs Jim had reported, Mr Markos really intended to sell Mardling. This was by no means the sterile, unhandled assembly
made by a moneyed person more interested in interior decora-
tion than the written word.

As soon as she came in she saw above the fireplace the painting called 'Several Pleasures' by Troy.

'So you did hang it there,' she said. 'How well it looks.'

'Doesn't it?' Mr Markos agreed. 'I dote on it. Who would
think it was painted by a policeman's missus.'

Verity said, 'Well, I can't see why not. Although, I suppose
you'd say a rather exceptional policeman.'

'So you know him?'

'I've met him, yes.'

'I see. So have I. I met him when I bought the picture. I
should have thought him an exotic in the Force, but perhaps
the higher you go at the Yard the rarer the atmosphere.'

'He visited me this morning.'

Prunella said, 'You don't tell me!'

'But I do,' said Verity.

'And me. According to Mrs Jim.'

Gideon said, 'Would it be about the egregious Claude?'

'No,' said Verity. 'It wouldn't. Not so far as I was concerned.
Not specifically, anyway. It seemed to be—' she hesitated – 'as
much about this new Will as anything.'

And in the silence that followed the little party in the library
quietly collapsed. Prunella began to look scared and Gideon
put his arm round her.

Mr Markos had moved in front of his fireplace. Verity
thought she saw a change in him – the subtle change that
comes over men when something has led a conversation into
their professional field – a guarded attentiveness.

Prunella said, 'I've been pushing things off. I've been pre-
tending to myself nothing is really very much the matter. It's
not true. Is it?' she insisted, appealing to Verity.

'Perhaps not quite, darling,' Verity said, and for a moment
it seemed to her that she and Prunella were, in some inexplic-
able way, united against the two men.

It was half past two when Alleyn and Fox arrived at Green-gages. The afternoon being clement, some of the guests were taking their post-prandial ease in the garden. Others, presumably, had retired to their rooms. Alleyn gave his professional card in at the desk and asked if they might have a word with Dr Schramm.

The receptionist stared briefly at Alleyn and hard at Mr Fox. She tightened her mouth, said she would see, appeared to relax slightly and left them.

'Know us when she sees us again,' said Fox placidly. He put on his spectacles and, tilting back his head, contemplated an emaciated water-colour of Canterbury Cathedral. 'Airy-fairy,' he said. 'Not my notion of the place at all,' and moved to a view of the Grand Canal.

The receptionist returned with an impeccably dressed man who had Alleyn's card in his hand and said he was the manager of the hotel. 'I hope,' he added, 'that we're not in for any further disruption.' Alleyn cheerfully assured him that he hoped so too and repeated that he would like to have a word or two with Dr Schramm. The manager retired to an inner office.

Alleyn said to the receptionist, 'May I bother you for a moment? Of course you're fussed we're here to ask tedious questions and generally make nuisances of ourselves about the death of Mrs Foster.'

'You said it,' she returned, 'not me.' But she touched her hair and she didn't sound altogether antagonistic.

'It's only a sort of tidying-up job. But I wonder if you remember anything about flowers that her gardener left at the desk for her.'

'I wasn't at the desk at the time.'

'Alas!'

'Pardon? Oh yes. Well, as a matter of fact I *do* happen to remember. The girl on duty mentioned that the electrical repairs man had taken them up when I was off for a minute or two.'

'When would that be?'

'I really couldn't say.'

'Is the repairs man a regular visitor?'

'Not that I know. He wasn't called in from the desk, that I can tell you.'

'Could you by any merciful chance find out when, where and

why he was here?'

'Well, I must say!'

'It would be *very* kind indeed. Really.'

She said she would see what she could do and retired into her office. Alleyn heard the whirr of a telephone dial. After a considerable interlude a highly starched nurse of opulent proportions appeared.

'Dr Schramm will see you now,' she said in a clinical voice. Only the copies of *Punch*, Alleyn felt, were missing.

The nurse rustled them down a passage to a door bearing the legend: 'Dr Basil Schramm, MB. Hours 3 – 5 p.m. and by appointment.'

She ushered them into a little waiting-room and there, sure enough, were the copies of *Punch* and the *Tatler*. She knocked at an inner door, opened it and motioned them to go in.

Dr Schramm swivelled round in his desk chair and rose to greet them.

A police officer of experience and sensibility may come to recognize mannerisms common to certain persons with whom he has to deal. If he is wise he will never place too much reliance on this simplification. When, for instance, he is asked by the curious layman if the police can identify certain criminal types by looking at them, he will probably say no. Perhaps he will qualify this denial by adding that he does find that certain characteristics tend to crop up – shabby stigmata – in sexual offenders. He is not referring to raincoats or to sidelong lurking but to a look in the eyes and about the mouth, a look he is unable to define.

To Alleyn it seemed that there were traits held in common by men who, in Victorian times, were called ladykillers – a display, covert or open, of sexual vainglory that sometimes, not always, made less heavily endowed acquaintances want, they scarcely knew why, to kick the possessors.

If ever he had recognized this element he did so now in Dr Basil Schramm. It declared itself in the brief, perfectly correct but experienced glance which he gave his nurse. It was latent in the co-ordinated ease with which he rose to his feet and extended his hand, in the boldish glance of his widely separated eyes and in the folds that joined his nostrils to the corners of his mouth. Dr Schramm was not unlike a better-looking version of King Charles II.

As a postscript to these observations he thought that Dr

Schramm looked like a heavy, if controlled, drinker.

The nurse left them.

'I'm so sorry to keep you waiting,' said Dr Schramm. 'Do sit down.' He glanced at Alleyn's card and then at him. 'Should I say Superintendent or Mr or just plain Alleyn?'

'It couldn't matter less,' said Alleyn. 'This is Inspector Fox.'

'Sit, sit, sit, do.'

They sat.

'Well, now, what's the trouble?' asked Dr Schramm. 'Don't tell me it's more about this unhappy business of Mrs Foster?'

'I'm afraid I do tell you. It's just that, as I'm sure you realize, we have to tidy up rather exhaustively.'

'Oh yes. That – of course.'

'The local Force has asked us to come in on the case. I'm sorry, but this does entail a tramp over ground that I dare say you feel has already been explored *ad nauseam*.'

'Well—' He raised his immaculately kept hands and let them fall. 'Needs must,' he said and laughed.

'That's about it,' Alleyn agreed. 'I believe her room has been kept as it was at the time of her death? Locked up and sealed.'

'Certainly. Your local people asked for it. To be frank it's inconvenient, but never mind.'

'Won't be long now,' said Alleyn cheerfully.

'I'm glad to hear it. I'll take you up to her room.'

'If I could have a word before we go.'

'Oh? Yes, of course.'

'I really wanted to ask you if you were at all, however slightly, uneasy about Mrs Foster's general health and spirits?'

Schramm started to make an instantly controlled gesture. 'I've stated repeatedly, to her solicitors, to the Coroner and to the police, that Mrs Foster was in improved health and in good spirits when I last saw her before I went up to London.'

'And when you returned she was dead.'

'Precisely.'

'You didn't know, did you, that she had Parkinson's disease?'

'That is by no means certain.'

'Dr Field-Innis thought so.'

'And is, of course, entitled to his opinion. In any case, it is not a positive diagnosis. As I understand it, Dr Field-Innis merely considers it a possibility.'

'So does Sir James Curtis.'

'Very possibly. As it happens I have no professional experience of Parkinson's disease and am perfectly ready to bow to their opinion. Of course, if Mrs Foster had been given any inkling—'

'Dr Field-Innis is emphatic that she had not—'

'—there would certainly have been cause for anxiety, depression—'

'Did she strike you as being anxious or depressed?'

'No.'

'On the contrary?'

'On the contrary. Quite. She was—'

'Yes?'

'In particularly good form,' said Dr Schramm.

'And yet you are persuaded it was suicide?'

An ornate little clock on Dr Schramm's desk ticked through some fifteen seconds before he spoke. He raised his clasped hands to his pursed lips and stared over them at Alleyn. Mr Fox, disregarded, coughed slightly.

With a definitive gesture – abrupt and incisive, Dr Schramm clapped his palms down on the desk and leant back in his chair.

'I had hoped,' he said, 'that it wouldn't come to this.'

Alleyn waited.

'I have already told you she was in particularly good form. That was an understatement. She gave me every reason to believe she was happier than she had been for many years.'

He got to his feet, looked fixedly at Alleyn and said loudly, 'She had become engaged to be married.'

The lines from nostril to mouth tightened into a smile of sorts.

'I had gone up to London,' he said, 'to buy the ring.'

4

'I knew, of course, that it would probably have to come out,' said Dr Schramm, 'but I hoped to avoid that. She was so very anxious that we should keep our engagement secret for the time being. The thought of making a sort of – well, posthumous announcement at the inquest was indescribably distasteful. One knew how the Press would set about it and the people in this place – I loathed the whole thought of it.'

He took one or two steps about the room. He moved with short strides, holding his shoulders rigid like a soldier. 'I don't offer this as an excuse. The thing has been a – an unspeakable shock to me. I can't believe it was suicide. Not when I remember – Not unless something that I can't even guess at happened between the time when I said goodbye to her and my return.'

'You checked with the staff, of course.'

'Of course. She had dinner in bed and watched television. She was perfectly well. No doubt you've seen the report of the inquest and know all this. The waiter collected her tray round about eight-thirty. She was in her bathroom and he heard her singing to herself. After that – nothing. Nothing, until I came back. And found her.'

'That must have been a terrible shock.'

Schramm made the brief sound that usually indicates a sort of contempt. 'You may say so,' he said. And then, suddenly: 'Why have you been called in? What's it mean? Look here, do you people suspect foul play?'

'Hasn't the idea occurred to you?' Alleyn asked.

'The *idea* has. Of course it has. Suicide being inconceivable, the *idea* occurred. But that's inconceivable, too. The circumstances. The evidence. Everything. She had no enemies. Who would want to do it? It's—' He broke off. A look of – what? sulkiness? derision? – appeared. It was as if he sneered at himself.

'But she wouldn't,' he said. 'I'm sure she didn't—'

'Didn't—?'

'It doesn't matter. It's silly.'

'Are you wondering if Mrs Foster did, after all, confide in somebody about your engagement?'

He stared at Alleyn. 'That's right,' he said. 'And then, there were visitors that afternoon, as of course you know.'

'Her daughter and the daughter's fiancé and Miss Preston.'

'And the gardener.'

'Didn't he leave his flowers with the receptionist and go away without seeing Mrs Foster?' Alleyn asked.

'That's what he says, certainly.'

'It's what your receptionist says, too, Dr Schramm.'

'Yes. Very well, then. Nothing in that line of thinking. In any case the whole idea is unbelievable. Or ought to be.'

Mr Fox, using a technique that Alleyn was in the habit of alluding to as his disappearing act, had contrived to make his large person unobservable. He had moved as far away from Alleyn as possible and to a chair behind Dr Schramm. Here he palmed a notebook and his palm was vast. He used a stub of pencil and kept his work on his knee and his eyes respectfully on nothing in particular. Alleyn and Fox made a point of not looking at each other but at this juncture he felt sure Fox contemplated him, probably with that air of bland approval that generally meant they were both thinking the same thing.

'When you say "or ought to be",' Alleyn said, 'are you thinking about motive?'

Schramm gave a short meaningless laugh. His manner, unexpected in a doctor, seemed to imply that nothing under discussion was of importance. Alleyn wondered if he treated his patients to this sort of display. 'I don't want to put ideas in your head,' Schramm said, 'but to be quite, quite frank that did occur to me. Motive.'

'I'm resistant to ideas,' said Alleyn. 'Could you explain?'

'It's probably a lot of bumph but it does seem to me that our engagement wouldn't have been madly popular in certain quarters. Her family, to make no bones about it.'

'Are you thinking of Mrs Foster's stepson?'

'You said it. I didn't.'

'Motive?'

'I know of no motive, but I do know he sponged on her and pestered her and has a pretty disgraceful record. She was very much upset at the thought of his turning up here and I gave orders that if he did he must not be allowed to see her. Or speak to her on the telephone. I tell you this,' Dr Schramm said, 'as a fact. I don't for a moment pretend that it has any particular significance.'

'But I think you have something more than this in mind, haven't you?'

'If I have, I wouldn't want too much weight to be given to it.'

'I shall not give too much weight to it, I hope.'

Dr Schramm thumbed up the ends of his moustache. 'It's just that it does occur to me that he might have expectations. I've no knowledge of any such thing. None.'

'You know, do you, that Carter was on the premises that afternoon?'

'I do not!' he said sharply. 'Where did you get that from?'

'From Miss Verity Preston,' said Alleyn.

Again the shadow of a smile, not quite a sneer, not entirely complacent.

'Verity Preston?' he said. 'Oh yes? She and Syb were old friends.'

'He arrived in the same bus as Bruce Gardener. I gather he

was ordered off seeing Mrs Foster.'

'I should bloody well hope so,' said Dr Schramm. 'Who by?'

'By Prunella Foster.'

'Good for her.'

'Tell me,' said Alleyn, 'speaking as a medical man, and supposing, however preposterously, that there was foul play, how would you think it could be accomplished?'

'There you are again! Nothing to indicate it! Everything points to the suicide I can't believe in. Everything. Unless,' he said sharply, 'something else has been found.'

'Nothing as I understand it.'

'Well then—!' He made a dismissive, rather ineloquent gesture.

'Dr Schramm, there's one aspect of her death I wanted to ask you about. Knowing, now, the special relationship between you I am very sorry to have to put this to you – it can't be anything but distressing to go over the circumstances again.'

'Christ Almighty!' he burst out. 'Do you suppose I don't "go over" them day in, day out? What d'you think I'm made of?' He raised his hand. 'I'm sorry!' he said. 'You're doing your job. What is it you want to ask?'

'It's about the partly dissolved tablets found in the throat and on the tongue. Do you find any inconsistency there? I gather the tablets take some twenty minutes to dissolve in water but are readily soluble in alcohol. It was supposed, wasn't it, that the reason they were not swallowed was because she became unconscious after putting them in her mouth? But – I suspect this is muddled thinking – would the tablets she had already taken have had time to induce insensibility? And anyway she couldn't have been insensible when she put these last ones in her mouth. I don't seem able to sort it out.'

Dr Schramm put his hand to his forehead, frowned and moved his head slowly from side to side.

'I'm sorry,' he said. 'Touch of migraine. Yes. The tablets. She took them with whisky, you know. As you say, they dissolve readily in alcohol.'

'Then wouldn't you think these would have dissolved in her mouth?'

'I would think that she didn't take any more whisky with them. Obviously, or she would have swallowed them.'

'You mean that she was conscious enough to put these four in her mouth but not conscious enough to drink or to swallow

105

them? Yes,' said Alleyn. 'I see.'

'Well,' Dr Schramm said loudly, 'what else? What do you suppose?'

'I? I don't go in for supposing – we're not allowed to. Oh, by the way, do you know if Mrs Foster had made a Will – recently, I mean?'

'Of that,' said Dr Schramm, 'I have no idea.' And after a brief pause, 'Is there anything else?'

'Do you know if there are members of the staff here called G. M. Johnson and Marleena Biggs?'

'I have not the faintest idea. I have nothing to do with the management of the hotel.'

'Of course you haven't. Stupid of me. I'll ask elsewhere. If it's convenient, could we look at the room?'

'I'll take you up.' He pressed a buzzer on his desk.

'Please don't bother. Tell me the number and we'll find our way.'

'No, no. Wouldn't dream of it.'

These protestations were interrupted by the entrance of the nurse. She stood inside the door, her important bosom, garnished with its professional badge, well to the fore. A handsome, slightly florid lady, specifically plentiful.

'Oh, Sister,' said Dr Schramm, 'would you be very kind and hold the fort? I'm just going to show our visitors upstairs. I'm expecting that call from New York.'

'Certainly,' she said woodenly.

Alleyn said, 'You must be Sister Jackson, mustn't you? I'm very glad to see you. Would you be very kind and give us a moment or two?'

She looked fixedly at Dr Schramm, who said grudgingly, 'Chief Superintendent Alleyn.'

'And Inspector Fox,' said Alleyn. 'Perhaps, as Dr Schramm expects his long-distance call, it won't be troubling you too much to ask you to show us the way to Mrs Foster's room?'

She still looked at Dr Schramm who began, 'No, that's all right, I'll—' when the telephone rang. Sister Jackson made a half move as if to answer it but he picked up the receiver.

'Yes. Yes. Speaking. Yes, I accept the call.'

Alleyn said, 'Shall we?' to Sister Jackson and opened the door.

Schramm nodded to her and with the suggestion of a bridle she led the way back to the hall.

'Do we take the lift?' Alleyn asked. 'I'd be very much obliged if you would come. There are one or two points about the room that I don't quite get from the reports. We've been asked by the local Force to take a look at the general picture. A formality, really, but the powers-that-be are always rather fussy in these sorts of cases.'

'Oh yes?' said Sister Jackson.

In the lift it became apparent that she used scent.

For all her handsome looks, she was a pretty tough lady, Alleyn thought. Black, sharp eyes and a small hard mouth, set at the corners. It wouldn't be long before she settled into the battleaxe form.

The room, No. 20, was on the second floor at the end of a passage and at a corner of the building. The Quintern police had put a regulation seal on the door and had handed the key over to Alleyn. They had also taken the precaution of slipping an inconspicuous morsel of wool between door and jamb. Sister Jackson looked on in silence while Mr Fox, who wore gloves, dealt with these obstructions.

The room was dark, the closed window curtains admitting only a sliver or two of daylight. It smelt thickly of material, carpet, stale scent, dust and of something indefinable and extremely unpleasant. Sister Jackson gave out a short hiss of distaste. Fox switched on the light. He and Alleyn moved into the centre of the room. Sister Jackson remained by the door.

The room had an air of suspended animation. The bed was unmade. Its occupant might have just left it to go into the bathroom. One of the pillows and the lower sheet were stained as if something had been spilt on them. Another pillow lay, face down, at the foot of the bed. The whisky bottle, glass and tablets were all missing and were no doubt still in the custody of the local police, but an unwrapped parcel, obviously a book, together with a vanity box and the half-empty box of marzipan confections lay on the table alongside a lamp. Alleyn peered down the top of a rose-coloured shade and saw the glass slipper in place over the bulb. He took it off and examined it. There was no oil left but it retained a faint reek of sweet almonds. He put it aside.

The dressing-table carried, together with an array of bottles and pots, three framed photographs all of which he had seen that morning on and in Sybil Foster's desk at Quintern: her pretty daughter, her second husband and the regimental group with her handsome young first husband prominent among the officers. This was a less faded print and Alleyn looked closely at it, marvelling that such an Adonis could have sired the undelicious Claude. He peered at an enormous corporal in the back row who squinted amicably back at him. Alleyn managed to make out the man's badge – antlers enclosed by something – what? – a heather wreath? Wasn't there some nickname? 'The Spikes'? That was it. 'The Duke of Montrose's' nicknamed 'The Spikes'. Alleyn wondered how soon after this photograph was taken Maurice Carter had died. Claude would have been a child of three or four, he supposed, and remembered Verity Preston's story of the lost Black Alexander stamp. What the hell is it, he thought, still contemplating the large corporal, that's nagging on the edge of my memory?

He went into the bathrom. A large bunch of dead lilies lay in the hand-basin. A dirty greenish stain showed where water had drained away. A new and offensive smell rose from the basin. ' "Lilies that fester," ' he reminded himself, ' "smell far worse than weeds." '

He returned to the bedroom and found Fox, placid in attendance, and Sister Jackson looking resentful.

'And this,' Alleyn said, 'is how it was when you were called in?'

'The things on the table have been removed. And there's no body,' she pointed out sourly.

'No more there is.'

'It's disgusting,' said Sister Jackson. 'Being left like this.'

'Horrid, isn't it? Could you just give us a picture of how things were when you arrived on the scene?'

She did so, eyeing him closely and with a certain air of appraisal. It emerged that she had been in her room and thinking of retiring when Dr Schramm telephoned her asking her to come at once to No. 20. There she found him stooping over the bed on which lay Mrs Foster, dead and cooling. Dr Schramm had drawn her attention to the table and its contents and told her to go to the surgery and fetch the equipment needed to empty the stomach. She was to do this without saying anything to anyone she met.

'We knew it was far too late to be of any use,' she said, 'but we did it. Dr Schramm said the contents should be kept and they were. In a sealed jar. We had to move the table away from the bed but nothing else was disturbed. Dr Schramm was very particular about that. Very.'

'And then?'

'We informed Mr Delaware, the manager. He was upset, of

course. They don't like that sort of thing. Then we got Dr Field-Innis to come over from Upper Quintern and he said the police should be informed. We couldn't see why but he said he thought they ought to be. So they were.'

Alleyn noticed the increased usage of the first person plural in this narrative and wondered if he only imagined that it sounded possessive.

He thanked Sister Jackson warmly and handed her a glossy photograph of Mr Fox's Aunt Elsie which was kept for this purpose. Auntie Elsie had become a kind of code-person between Alleyn and Fox and was sometimes used as a warning signal when one of them wished to alert the other without being seen to do so. Sister Jackson failed to identify Aunt Elsie and was predictably intrigued. He returned the photograph to its envelope and said they needn't trouble her any longer. Having dropped his handkerchief over his hand, he opened the door to her.

'Pay no attention,' he said. 'We do these things hoping they give us the right image. Goodbye, Sister.'

In passing between him and Fox her hand brushed his. She rustled off down the passage, one hundred and fifty pounds of active femininity if she was an ounce.

'Cripes,' said Fox thoughtfully.

'Did she establish contact?'

'*En passant*,' he confessed in his careful French. 'What about you, Mr Alleyn?'

'*En passant, moi aussi.*'

'Do you reckon,' Mr Fox mused, 'she knew about the engagement?'

'Do you?'

'If she did, I'd say she didn't much fancy it,' said Fox.

'We'd better push on. You might pack up that glass slipper, Fox. We'll get Sir James to look at it.'

'In case somebody put prussic acid in it?'

'Something like that. After all, there was and *is* a strong smell of almonds. Only "Oasis", you'll tell me and I'm afraid you'll be right.'

On their way out the receptionist said she had made enquiries as to the electrical repairs man. Nobody knew anything about him except the girl who had given him Mrs Foster's flowers. He told her he had been sent to repair a lamp in No. 20 and the lady had asked him to collect her flowers when he went down to his car to get a new bulb for the bedside lamp. She couldn't really describe him except that he was slight, short and well-spoken and didn't wear overalls but did wear spectacles.

'What d'you make of that?' said Alleyn when they got outside.

'Funny,' said Fox. 'Sussy. Whatever way you look at it, not convincing.'

'There wasn't a new bulb in the bedside lamp. Old bulb, murky on top. Ready to conk out.'

'Lilies in the basin, though.'

'True.'

'What now, then?'

Alleyn looked at his watch. 'I've got a date with the Coroner,' he said. 'In one hour. At Upper Quintern. In the meantime, Bailey and Thompson had better give these premises the full treatment. Every inch of them.'

'Looking for what?'

'All the usual stuff. Latent prints, including Sister J's on Aunt Elsie, of course. Schramm's will be on the book wrapping and Prunella Foster's and her mother's on the vanity box. We've got to remember the room was done over in the morning by the housemaids, so anything that crops up will have been established during the day. We haven't finished with that sickening little room, Br'er Fox. Not by a long bloody chalk.'

Chapter Five

GREENGAGES (II) ROOM 20

'—In view of which circumstances, members of the jury,' said the Coroner, 'you may consider that the appropriate decision would be again to adjourn these proceedings *sine die*.'

Not surprisingly, the jury embraced this suggestion and out into the age-old quietude of Upper Quintern village walked the people who, in one way or another, were involved, or had been obliged to concern themselves in the death of Sybil Foster: her daughter, her solicitor, her oldest friend, her gardener, the doctor she had disregarded and the doctor who had become her fiancé. And her stepson who by her death inherited the life interest left by her first husband. Her last and preposterous Will and Testament could not upset this entailment nor, according to Mr Rattisbon, could this Will itself be upset. G. M. Johnson and Marleena Biggs, chambermaids on the second floor of the hotel, confessed with uneasy giggles that they had witnessed Mrs Foster's signature a week before she died.

This Will provided the only sensation of the inquest. Nobody seemed to be overwhelmingly surprised at Bruce Gardener's legacy of £25,000 but the Swingletree clause and the sumptuous inheritance of Dr Schramm caused a sort of stupefaction in court. Three reporters from the provincial press were seen to be stimulated. Verity Preston, who was there because her goddaughter seemed to expect it, had a horrid foreboding of growing publicity.

The inquest had again been held in the parish hall. The spire of St Crispin-in-Quintern cast its shadow over an open space at the foot of steps that led up to the church. The local people referred to this area as the 'green' but it was little more than a rough lateral bulge in the lane. Upper Quintern was really a village only by virtue of its church and was the smallest of its kind; hamlet would have seemed a more appropriate title.

Sunlight, diffused by autumnal haze, the absence of wind and, until car engines started up, of other than countrified sounds, all seemed to set at a remove any process other than the rooted habit of the Kentish soil. Somehow or another, Verity thought, whatever the encroachments, continuity survives. And then she thought that it had taken this particular encroachment to put the idea into her head.

She wondered if Young Mr Rattisbon would expect a repetition of their former conviviality and decided to wait until he emerged. People came together in desultory groups and broke up again. They had the air of having been involved in some social contretemps.

Prunella came out between the two Markos men. Clearly she was shaken, Gideon held her hand and his father, with his elegant head inclined, stooped over her. Again, Verity had the feeling that they absorbed Prunella.

Prunella saw her godmother, said something to the men and came to Verity.

'Godma V,' she said. 'Did you know? I meant to let you know. It's the day after the day after tomorrow – Thursday – they're going to – they say we can—'

'Well, darling,' said Verity, 'that's a good thing, isn't it? What time?'

'Three o'clock. Here. I'm telling hardly anyone – just very old friends like you. And bunches of flowers out of our garden, don't you think?'

'I do indeed. Would you like me to bring you? Or – are you – ?'

Prunella seemed to hesitate and then said, 'That's sweet of you, Godma V. Gideon and Papa M are – coming with me but – could we sit together, please?'

'Of course, we could,' Verity said and kissed her.

The jury had come out. Some straggled away to the bus stop, some to a car. The landlord of the Passcoigne Arms was accompanied into the pub by three of his fellow jurors. The Coroner appeared with Mr Rattisbon. They stood together in the porch, looking at their feet and conversing. They were joined by two others.

Prunella, who still held Verity's hand, said, 'Who's that, I wonder? Do you know? The tall one?'

'It's the one who called on me. Superintendent Alleyn.'

'I can see what you mean about him,' said Prunella.

The three representatives of the provincial press slid up to Alleyn and began to speak to him. Alleyn looked over their heads towards Verity and Prunella and as if he had signalled to her Verity moved to hide Prunella from the men. At the same instant Bruce Gardener came out of the hall and at once the three men closed round him.

Alleyn came over to Verity and Prunella.

'Good morning, Miss Preston,' he said. 'I wondered if you'd be here.' And to Prunella, 'Miss Foster? I expect your splendid Mrs Jobbin told you I'd called. She was very kind and let me come into your house. *Did* she tell you?'

'Yes. I'm sorry I was out.'

'There wasn't any need, at that juncture, to bother you. *I'm* sorry you're having such a horrid time. Actually,' Alleyn said, 'I may have to ask you to see me one of these days but only if it's really necessary. I promise.'

'OK,' Prunella said. 'Whenever you like. OK.'

'My dear Alleyn!' said a voice behind Verity. 'How very nice to meet you again.'

Mr Markos had come up, with Gideon, unnoticed by the others. The temper of the little scene changed with their appearance. He put his arm round Prunella and told Alleyn how well Troy's picture looked. He said Alleyn really ought to come and see it. He appealed to Verity for support and by a certain change in his manner seemed to attach a special importance to her answer. Verity was reminded of poor Syb's encomium before she took against the Markoses. She had said that Nikolas Markos was 'ultra-sophisticated' and 'a complete man of the world'. He's a man of a world I don't belong to, Verity thought, but we have things in common, nevertheless.

'Miss Preston will support me,' Mr Markos said, 'won't you?'

Verity pulled herself together and said the picture was a triumph.

Alleyn said, 'The painter will be delighted,' and to all of them, 'The gentlemen of the Press look like heading this way. I suggest it might be as well if Miss Foster escaped.'

'Yes, of course,' said Gideon quickly. 'Darling, let's go to the car. Quick.'

But a stillness had fallen on the people who remained at the scene. Verity turned and saw that Dr Schramm had come out into the sunshine. The reporters fastened on him.

A handsome car was parked nearby. Verity thought, that's got to be his car. He'll have to come past us to get to it. We can't break up and bolt.

He said something – 'No comment,' Verity supposed, to the Press and walked briskly towards the group. As he passed them he lifted his hat. 'Good morning, Verity,' he said. 'Hullo, Markos, how are you? 'Morning, Superintendent.' He paused, looked at Prunella, gave a little bow and continued on his way.

It had been well done, Verity thought, if you had the nerve to do it, and she was filled with a kind of anger that he had included her in his performance.

Mr Markos said, 'We all of us make mistakes. Come along, children.'

Verity, left with Alleyn, supposed Mr Markos had referred to his dinner-party.

'I must be off,' she said. She thought, death creates social contretemps. One doesn't say, 'See you the day after tomorrow' when the meeting will be at a funeral.

Her car was next to Alleyn's and he walked beside her. Dr Schramm drove past them and lifted a gloved hand as he did so.

'That child's surviving all this pretty well, isn't she?' Alleyn asked. 'On the whole, wouldn't you say?'

'Yes. I think she is. She's sustained by her engagement.'

'To young Markos? Yes. And by her godmama, too, one suspects?'

'Me! Not at all. Or anyway, not as much as I'd like.'

He grunted companionably, opened her car door for her and stood by while she fastened her safety-belt. She was about to say goodbye but changed her mind. 'Mr Alleyn,' she said, 'I gather that probate has been granted or passed or whatever it is? On the second Will?'

'It's not a *fait accompli* but it will be. Unless, of course, she made yet another and later one, which doesn't seem likely. Would it be safe to tell you something in confidence?'

Verity, surprised, said, 'I don't break confidences but if it's anything that I would want to speak about to Prunella, you'd better not tell me.'

'I don't think you would want to but I'd make an exception of Prunella. Dr Schramm and Mrs Foster were engaged to be married.'

In the silence that she was unable to break Verity thought that it really was not so very surprising, this information. There was even a kind of logic about it. Given Syb and given Basil Schramm.

Alleyn said, 'Rather staggering news, perhaps?'

'No, no,' she heard herself saying. 'Not really. I'm just – trying to assimilate it. Why did you tell me?'

'Partly because I thought there was a chance that she might have confided it to you that afternoon but mostly because I had an idea it might be disagreeable for you to learn of it accidentally.'

'Will it be made known, then? Will *he* make it known?'

'Well,' said Alleyn, 'I'm not sure. If it's anything to go by, he did tell *me*.'

'I suppose it explains the Will?'

'That's the general idea, of course.'

Verity heard herself say, 'Poor Syb.' And then, 'I hope it doesn't come out. Because of Prue.'

'Would she mind so much?'

'Oh, I think so. Don't you? The young mind terribly if they believe their parents have made asses of themselves.'

'And would any woman engaging herself to Dr Schramm make an ass of herself?'

'Yes,' said Verity. 'She would. I did.'

2

When Alleyn had gone Verity sat inert in her car and wondered what had possessed her to tell him something that for twenty-odd years she had told nobody. A policeman! More than that, a policeman who must, in the way things had gone, take a keen professional interest in Basil Schramm, might even – no, almost certainly did – think of him as a 'suspect'. And she turned cold when she forced herself to complete the sequence – a suspect in what might turn out to be a case of foul play – of, very well then, use the terrible soft word, of murder.

He had not followed up her statement or pressed her with questions nor, indeed, did he seem to be greatly interested. He merely said, 'Did you? Sickening for you,' made one or two remarks of no particular significance and said goodbye. He drove off with a large companion who could not be anything that was not constabulary. Mr Rattisbon, too, looking gravely preoccupied, entered his own elderly car and quitted the scene.

Still Verity remained, miserably inert. One or two locals sauntered off. The vicar and Jim Jobbin, who was part-time sexton, came out of the church and surveyed the weathered company of headstones. The vicar pointed to the right and they made off in that direction, round the church. Verity knew, with a jolt, that they discussed the making of a grave. Sybil's remotest Passcoigne forebears lay in the vault but there was a family plot among the trees beyond the south transept.

Then she saw that Bruce Gardener, in his Harris tweed suit, had come out of the hall and was climbing up the steps to the church. He followed the vicar and Jim Jobbin and disappeared. Verity had noticed him at the inquest. He had sat at the back, taller than his neighbours, upright, with his gardener's hands on his thighs, very decorous and solemn. She thought that perhaps he wanted to ask about the funeral, about flowers from Quintern Place, it might be. If so, that was nice of Bruce. She herself, she thought, must offer to do something about flowers. She would wait a little longer and speak to the vicar.

'Good morning,' said Claude Carter, leaning on the passenger's door.

Her heart seemed to leap into her throat. She had been looking out of the driver's window and he must have come up from behind the car on her blind side.

'Sorry,' he said, and grinned. 'Made you jump, did I?'

'Yes.'

'My mistake. I just wondered if I might cadge a lift to the turn-off. If you're going home, that is.'

There was nothing she wanted less but she said yes, if he didn't mind waiting while she went up to the church. He said he wasn't in a hurry and got in. He had removed his vestigial beard, she noticed and had his hair cut to a conservative length. He was tidily dressed and looked less hang-dog than usual. There was even a hint of submerged jauntiness about him.

'Smoking allowed?' he asked.

She left him lighting his cigarette in a guarded manner as if he was afraid someone would snatch it out of his mouth.

At the head of the steps she met the vicar returning with Bruce and Jim. To her surprise Jim, a bald man with a loud voice, was now bent double. He was hovered over by the vicar.

'It's a fair bugger,' he shouted. 'Comes over you like a bloody thunderclap. Stooping down to pull up them bloody teazles and now look at me. Should of minded me own business.'

'Yes, well, jolly bad luck,' said the vicar. 'Oh, hullo, Miss Preston. We're in trouble, as you see. Jim's smitten with lumbago.'

'Will he be able to negotiate the descent?' Bruce speculated anxiously. 'That's what I ask myself. Awa' wi' ye, man, and let us handle you doon the steps.'

'No, you don't. I'll handle myself if left to myself, won't I?'

'Jim!' said Verity. '*What* a bore for you. I'll drive you home.'

'No, ta all the same, Miss Preston. It's happened before and it'll happen again. I'm best left to manage myself and if you'll excuse me that's what I'll do. I'll use the handrail. Only,' he added with a sudden shout of agony, 'I'd be obliged if I wasn't watched.'

'Perhaps,' said the vicar, 'we'd better—?'

Jim, moving like a gaffer in a Victorian melodrama, achieved the handrail and clung to it. He shouted, 'I won't be able to do the job now, will I?'

There was an awkward silence broken by Bruce. 'Dinna fash yourself,' he said. 'No problem. With the Minister's kind permission I'll dig it mysel' and think it an honour. I will that.'

'The full six foot, mind.'

'Ou aye,' Bruce agreed. 'All of it. I'm a guid hand at digging,' he added.

'Fair enough,' said Jim and began to ease himself down the steps.

'This is a most fortunate solution, Bruce,' said the vicar. 'Shall we just leave Jim as he wishes?' and he ushered them into the church.

St Crispin-in-Quintern was one of the great company of parish churches that stand as milestones in rural history; obstinate resisters of the ravages of time. It had a magnificent peal of bells, now unsafe to ring, one or two brasses, a fine east window and a surprising north window in which – strange conceit – a walrus-moustachioed Passcoigne, looking startlingly like Sir Arthur Conan Doyle, was depicted in full plate armour, an Edwardian St Michael without a halo. The legend indicated that he had met his end on the African veld. The familiar ecclesiastical odour of damp held at bay by paraffin heaters greeted Verity and the two men.

Verity explained that she would like to do anything that would help about the flowers. The vicar said that custody of all brass vases was inexorably parcelled out among the Ladies Guild, five in number. She gathered that any attempt to disrupt this procedure would trigger off a latent pecking order.

'But they would be grateful for flowers,' he added.

Bruce said that there were late roses up at Quintern Place and he'd thought it would be nice to have her ain favourites to see her off. He muttered in an uneven voice that the name was appropriate – Peace. 'They endure better than most oot o' watter,' he added and blew his nose. Verity and the vicar warmly supported this suggestion and Verity left the two men to complete, she understood, the arrangements for digging Sybil's grave.

When she returned to the top of the steps she found that Jim Jobbin had reached the bottom on his hands and knees and was being manipulated through the lych-gate by his wife. Verity joined them. Mrs Jim explained that she was on her way to get dinner and had found Jim crawling backwards down the last four steps. It was no distance, they both reminded Verity, along the lane to their cottage. Jim got to his feet by swarming up his wife as if she was a tree.

'It'll ease off once he straightens himself,' she said. 'It does him good to walk.'

'That's what you think,' her husband groaned but he straightened up and let out an oath as he did so. They made off in slow motion.

Verity returned to her car and to Claude, lounging in the passenger's seat. He made a token shuffle with his feet and leant over to open the door.

'That was as good as a play,' he said. 'Poor old Jobbin. Did you see him beetling down the steps? Fantastic!' He gave a neighing laugh.

'Lumbago's no joke to the person who's got it,' Verity snapped.

'It's hysterical for the person who hasn't, though.'

She drove as far as the corner where the lane up to Quintern Place branched off to the left.

'Will this suit you?' she asked, 'or would you like me to run you up?'

He said he wouldn't take her out of her way but when she pulled up he didn't get out.

'What did you make of the inquest?' he asked. 'I must say I thought it pretty off.'

'Off?'

'Well, you know. I mean what does that extraordinary detective person think he's on about? And a further postponement. Obviously they suspect something.'

Verity was silent.

'Which isn't exactly welcome news,' he said. 'Is it? Not for this medico, Schramm. Or for Mr Folksy Gardener if it comes to that?'

'I don't think you should make suggestions, Claude.'

'Suggestions! I'm not suggesting anything, but people are

sure to look sideways. I know I wouldn't feel comfortable if I were in those gentlemen's boots, that's all. Still they're getting their lovely legacies, aren't they, which'll be a great consolation. I could put up with plenty of funny looks for twenty-five thousand of the best. Even more for Schramm's little lot.'

'I must get home, Claude.'

'Nothing can touch my bit, anyway. God, can I use it! Only thing, that old relic Rattisbon says it won't be available until probate is allowed or passed or whatever. I suppose I can borrow on my prospects, wouldn't you think?'

'I'm running late.'

'Nobody seems to think it's a bit off colour her leaving twenty-five thousand of the best to a jobbing gardener she'd only hired a matter of months ago. It's pretty obvious he'd got round her in a big way. I could tell you one or two things about Mr gardener-Gardener.'

'I must go, Claude.'

'Yes. OK.'

He climbed out of the car and slammed the door. 'Thanks for the lift anyway,' he said. 'See you at the funeral. Ain't we got fun?'

Glad to be rid of him but possessed by a languor she could not understand, Verity watched him turn up the lane. Even seen from behind there was a kind of furtive jauntiness in his walk, an air of complacency that was out of character. He turned a corner and was gone.

I wonder, she thought, what he'll do with himself.

She drove on up her own lane into her own little avenue and got her own modest luncheon. She found she hadn't much appetite for it.

The day was gently sunny but Verity found it oppressive. The sky was clear but she felt as if it would almost be a relief if bastions of cloud shouldered each other up from beyond the horizon. It occurred to her that writers like Ibsen and Dickens – unallied in any other respect – were right to make storms, snow, fog and fire the companions of human disorders. Shakespeare too, she thought. We deprive ourselves aesthetically when we forgo the advantages of symbolism.

She had finished the overhaul of her play and had posted it off to her agent. It was not unusual when work in hand had been dealt with and she was cleaned out for her to experience a nervous impulse to start off at once on something new. As now, when she found herself wondering if she could give a fresh look to an old, old theme: that of an intelligent woman enthralled by a second-rate charmer, a 'bad lot' in Verity's dated jargon, for whom she had no respect but was drawn to by an obstinate attraction. If she could get such a play successfully off her chest, would she scotch the bogey that had returned to plague her?

When at that first Markos dinner-party she found that Basil Schramm's pinchbeck magnetism had evaporated, the discovery had been a satisfaction to Verity. Now, when a shadow crept towards him, how did she feel? And why, oh why, had she bleated out her confession to Alleyn? He won't let it rest, she thought, her imagination bolting with her. He'll want to know more about Basil. He may ask if Basil ever got into trouble and what'll I say to that?

And Alleyn, returning with Fox to Greengages via Maidstone, said, 'This case is getting nasty. She let it out without any pushing or probing and I think she amazed herself by doing so. I wouldn't mind betting there was more to it than the predatory male jilt and the humiliated woman, though there was all of that, too, I dare say.'

'If it throws any light on his past?'

'We may have to follow it up, of course. Do you know what I think she'll do about it?'

'Refuse to talk?'

'That's it. There's not much of the hell-knows-no-fury in Verity Preston's make-up.'

'Well,' said Fox reasonably, 'seeing how pretty he stands, we have to make it thorough. What comes first?'

'Get the background. Check up on the medical side. Qualified at Lausanne, or wherever it was. Find out the year and the degree. See if there was any regular practice in this country. Or in the USA. So much waste of time, it may be, but it'll have to be done, Br'er Fox. And, on a different lay – here comes Maidstone again. Call at stationers and bookshops and see if anyone's bought any Will forms lately. If not, do the same in villages and towns and in the neighbourhood of Greengages.'

'Hoping we don't have to extend to London?'

'Fervently. But courage, comrade, we may find that in addition to witnessing the Will, G. M. Johnson or Marleena Biggs or even that casket of carnal delights Sister Jackson, was detailed to pop into a stationer's shop on her day off.'

When they reached Greengages, this turned out to be the answer. Johnson and Biggs had their days off together and a week before Mrs Foster died they had made the purchase at a stationer's in Greenvale. Mrs Foster had given them a present and told them to treat themselves to the cinema and tea.

'That's fine,' said Alleyn. 'We just wanted to know. Was it a good film?'

They fell into an ecstasy of giggles.

'I see. One of those?'

'Aw!'

'Anybody else know about the shopping?'

'Aw, no,' said G. M. Johnson.

'Yes they did, you're mad,' said Marleena Biggs.

'They never.'

'They did, too. The doctor did. He come in while she told us.'

'Dr Schramm came in and heard all about it?' said Alleyn casually.

They agreed and were suddenly uninterested.

'There you are, both of you. Treat yourselves to another shocker and a blow-out of cream buns.'

This interview concluded, Alleyn was approached by the manager of the hotel, who evidently viewed their visit with minimal enthusiasm. He hustled them into his office, offered drinks and looked apprehensive when these were declined.

'It's just about the room,' he said. 'How much longer do you people want it? We're expecting a full house by next week and it's extremely inconvenient, you know.'

'I hope this will be positively our last appearance,' said Alleyn cheerfully.

'Without being uncivil, so do I. Do you want someone to take you up?'

'We'll take ourselves, thank you all the same. Come along, Br'er Fox,' said Alleyn. '*En avant*. You're having one of your dreamy spells.'

He led the way quickly to the lifts.

The second floor seemed to be deserted. They walked soundlessly down the carpeted passage to No. 20. The fingerprint and photography men had called and gone and their seal was still on the door. Fox was about to break it when Alleyn said, 'Half a jiffy. Look at this.'

Opposite the bedroom door was a curtained alcove. He had lifted the curtain and disclosed a vacuum-cleaner. 'Handy little hidey-hole, isn't it?' he said. 'Got your torch on you?'

'As it happens,' Fox said and gave it to him. He went into

the alcove and closed the curtain.

The lift at the far end of the long passage whined to a stop. Sister Jackson and another lady emerged. Fox, with a movement surprisingly nippy for one of his bulk, joined his superior in the alcove.

'Herself,' he whispered. Alleyn switched off his torch.

'See you?'

'Not to recognize.'

'Impossible. Once seen.'

'She had somebody with her.'

'No need for you to hide, you fathead. Why should you?'

'She flusters me.'

'You're bulging the curtain.'

But it was too late. The curtain was suddenly withdrawn and Sister Jackson discovered. She screamed.

'Good morning, Sister,' Alleyn said and flashed his torch-light full in her face. 'Do forgive us for startling you.'

'What,' she panted, her hand on her spectacular bosom, 'are you doing in the broom-cupboard?'

'Routine procedure. Don't give it another thought.'

'And you, don't shine that thing in my face. Come out.'

They emerged.

In a more conciliatory tone and with a sort of huffy come-to-ishness, she said, 'You gave me a shock.'

'So did you us,' said Mr Fox. 'A nice one,' he roguishly added.

'I dare say.'

She was between them. She flashed upward glances first at one, then the other. Her bosom slightly heaved. Alleyn was reminded of Mr Dick Emery and expected to be told he was awful.

'We really do apologize,' he said.

'I should hope so.' She laid her hand, which was plump, on his closed one. He was surprised to feel a marked tremor and to see that the colour had ebbed out of her face. She kept up the flirtatious note, however, though her voice was unsteady. 'I suppose I'll have to forgive you,' she said. 'But only if you tell me why you were there.'

'I caught sight of something.'

He turned his hand over, opened it and exposed the crumpled head of a pink lily. It was very dead and its brown pollen had stained his palm.

'I think,' he said, 'it will team up with the one in Mrs Foster's last bouquet. I wondered what the electrician was doing in the broom-cupboard.'

She gaped at him. 'Electrician?' she said. 'What electrician?'

'Don't let it worry you. Excuse us, please. Come on, Fox. Goodbye, Sister.'

When she had starched and bosomed herself away he said, 'I'm going to take another look at that broom-hide. Don't spring any more confrontations this time. Stay here.'

He went into the alcove, drew the curtains on himself and was away for some minutes. When he rejoined Fox he said, 'They're not so fussy about housework in there. Quite a lot of dust on the floor. Plenty of prints – housemaids' no doubt, but at the far end, in the corner away from the vacuum-cleaner where nobody would go normally, there are prints, left and right, side by side, with the heels almost touching the wall. Men's crêpe-soled shoes, and beside them – guess.'

He opened his hand and disclosed another dead lily-head. 'Near the curtain I could just find the prints again but overlaid by the housemaids' and some regulation-type extras. Whose do you think?'

'All right, all right,' said Fox. 'Mine.'

'When we go down we'll look like sleuths and ask the desk lady if she noticed the electrician's feet.'

'That's a flight of fancy, if you like,' said Fox. 'And she won't have.'

'In any case Bailey and Thompson will have to do their stuff. Come on.'

When they were inside No. 20 he went to the bathroom where the fetid bouquet still mouldered in the basin. It was possible to see that the finds matched exactly and actually to distinguish the truss from which they had been lost.

'So I make a note – "Find the electrician"?' asked Fox.

'You anticipate my every need.'

'How do you fancy this gardener? Gardener?'

'Not much!' said Alleyn. 'Do you?'

'You wouldn't fancy him sneaking back with the flowers when Miss Foster and party had gone?'

'Not unless he's had himself stretched. The reception girl said slight, short and bespectacled. Bruce Gardener's six foot three and big with it. He doesn't wear spectacles.'

'He'd be that chap in the Harris tweed suit at the inquest?'

'He would. I meant to point him out to you.'

'I guessed,' said Fox heavily.

'Claude Carter, on the contrary, is short, slight, bespectacled and in common with the electrician and several million other males doesn't wear overalls.'

'Motive? No. Hang on. He gets Mrs Foster's bit from her first husband.

'Yes.'

'Ask if anyone knows about electricians? And nobody will,' Fox prophesied.

'Ask about what bus he caught back to Quintern and get a dusty answer.'

'Ask if anyone saw him any time, anywhere.'

'With or without lilies. In the meantime, Fox, I seem to remember there's an empty cardboard box and a paper shopping-bag in the wardrobe. Could you put those disgusting lilies in the box? Keep the ones from the broom-cupboard separate. I want another look at her pillows.'

They lay as they had lain before – three of them, luxuriant pillowcases in fine lawn with broderie-anglaise threaded with ribbon. Brought them with her, Alleyn thought. Even Greengages wouldn't run to these lengths.

The smallest of them carried a hollow made by her dead or alive head. The largest lay at the foot of the bed and was smooth. Alleyn turned it over. The under surface was crumpled, particularly in the centre – crumpled and stained as if it had been wet and, in two places, faintly pink with small, more positive indentations, one of them so sharp that it actually had broken the delicate fabric. He bent down and caught a faint nauseating reek. He went to the dressing-table and found three lipsticks, all of them, as was the fashion at that time, very pale. He took one of them to the pillow. It matched.

3

During the remaining sixty hours before Sybil Foster's burial in the churchyard of St Crispin-in-Quintern the police investigations, largely carried out over the telephone, multiplied and accelerated. As is always the case, much of what was unearthed turned out to be of no relevance, much was of a doubtful or self-contradictory nature and only a scanty winnowing found to be of real significance. It was as if the components of several jigsaw puzzles had been thrown down on the table and before the one required picture could be assembled the rest would have to be discarded.

The winnowings, Alleyn thought, were for the most part suggestive rather than definitive. A call to St Luke's Hospital established that Basil Smythe, as he then was, had indeed been a first-year medical student at the appropriate time and had not completed the course. A contact of Alleyn's in Swiss police headquarters put through a call to a hospital in Lausanne confirming that Dr Basile Schramm had graduated from a teaching hospital in that city. Basile, Alleyn was prepared to accept, might well have been a Swiss shot at Basil. Schramm had accounted to Verity Preston for the change from Smythe. They would have to check if this was indeed his mother's maiden name.

So far nothing had been found in respect of his activities in the United States.

Mrs Jim Jobbin had, at Mrs Foster's request and a week before she died, handed a bottle of sleeping-pills over to Bruce Gardener. Mrs Foster had told Bruce where they would be found – in her writing-desk. They had been bought some time ago from a Maidstone chemist and were a proprietary brand of barbiturate. Mrs Jim and Bruce had both noticed that the bottle was almost full. He had duly delivered it that same afternoon.

Claude Carter had what Mr Fox called a sussy record. He had been mixed up, as a very minor figure, in the drug racket. In his youth he had served a short sentence for attempted blackmail. He was thought to have brought a small quantity of heroin ashore from *SS Poseidon*. If so, he had got rid of it before he was searched at the Customs.

Verity Preston had remembered the august name of Bruce Gardener's latest employer. Discreet enquiries had confirmed the authenticity of Bruce's references and his unblemished record. The head gardener, named McWhirter, was emphatic in his praise and very, very Scotch.

This, thought Alleyn, might tally with Verity Preston's theory about Bruce's dialectical vagaries.

Enquiries at appropriate quarters in the City elicited the opinion that Nikolas Markos was a millionaire with a great number of interests of which oil, predictably, was the chief. He was also the owner of a string of luxury hotels in Switzerland, the South Pacific, and the Costa Brava. His origin was Greek. Gideon had been educated at a celebrated public school and at the Sorbonne and was believed to be in training for a responsible part in his father's multiple business activities.

Nothing further could be discovered about the 'electrician' who had taken Bruce's flowers up to Sybil Foster's room. The desk lady had not noticed his feet.

'We'll be having a chat with Mr Claude Carter, then?' asked Fox, two nights before the funeral. He and Alleyn were at the Yard having been separated during the day on their several occasions, Fox in and about Upper Quintern and Alleyn mostly on the telephone and in the City.

'Well, yes,' he agreed. 'Yes. We'll have to, of course. But we'd better walk gingerly over that particular patch, Br'er Fox. If he's in deep, he'll be fidgety. If he thinks we're getting too interested he may take off and we'll have to waste time and men on running him down.'

'Or on keeping obbo to prevent it. Do you reckon he'll attend the funeral?'

'He may decide we'd think it odd if he didn't. After his being so assiduous about gracing the inquests. There you are! We'll need to go damn carefully. After all, what have we got? He's short, thin, wears spectacles and doesn't wear overalls.'

'If you put it like that.'

'How would you put it?'

'Well,' said Fox, scraping his chin, 'he'd been hanging about the premises for we don't know how long and, by the way, no joy from the bus scene. Nobody remembers him or Gardener. I talked to the conductors on every return trip that either of them might have taken but it was a Saturday and there was a motor rally in the district and they were crowded all the way. They laughed at me.'

'Cads.'

'There's the motive, of course,' Fox continued moodily. 'Not that you can do much with that on its own. How about the lilies in the broom-cupboard?'

'How about them falling off in the passage and failing to get themselves sucked up by the vacuum-cleaner?'

'You make everything so difficult,' Fox sighed.

'Take heart. We have yet to see his feet. And him, if it comes to that. Bailey and Thompson may have come up with something dynamic. Where are they?'

'Like they say in theatrical circles. Below and awaiting your pleasure.'

'Admit them.'

Bailey and Thompson came in with their customary air of being incapable of surprise. Using the minimum quota of words, they laid out for Alleyn's inspection an array of photographs: of the pillowcase *in toto*, of the stained area on the front in detail and of one particular tiny indentation blown up to the limit which had actually left a cut in the material. Over this, Alleyn and Fox concentrated.

'Well, you two,' Alleyn said at last, 'what do you make of this lot?'

It was by virtue of such invitations that his relationship with his subordinates achieved its character. Bailey, slightly more communicative than his colleague, said, 'Teeth. Like you thought, Governor. Biting the pillow.'

'All right. How about it?'

Thompson laid another exhibit before him. It was a sort of macabre triptych: first a reproduction of the enlargement he had already shown and beside it, corresponding in scale, a photograph of all too unmistakably human teeth from which the lips had been retracted in a dead mouth.

'We dropped in at the morgue,' said Bailey. 'The bite could tally.'

The third photograph, one of Thompson's montages, showed the first superimposed upon the second. Over this, Thompson had ruled vertical and horizontal lines.

'Tallies,' Alleyn said.

'Can't fault it,' said Bailey dispassionately.

He produced a further exhibit: the vital section of the pillowcase itself mounted between two polythene sheets and set it beside Thompson's display of photographs.

'Right,' Alleyn said. 'We send this to the laboratory, of course, and in the meantime, Fox, we trust our reluctant noses. People who are trying to kill themselves with an overdose of sleeping-pills may vomit but they don't bite holes in the pillow-case.'

'It's nice to know we haven't been wasting our time,' said Fox.

'You are,' said Alleyn, staring at him, 'probably the most remorseless realist in the service.'

'It was only a passing thought. Do we take it she was smothered, then?'

'If Sir James concurs, we do. He'll be cross about the pillow-case.'

'You'd have expected the doctors to spot it. Well,' Fox amended, 'you'd have expected the Field-Innis one to, anyway.'

'At that stage their minds were set on suicide. Presumably the great busty Jackson had got rid of the stomach-pumping impedimenta after she and Schramm, as they tell us, had seen to the bottling of the results. Field-Innis says that by the time he got there, this had been done. It was he, don't forget, who said the room should be left untouched and the police informed. The pillow was face downwards at the foot of the bed but in any case only a very close examination reveals the mark of the tooth. The stains, which largely obscure it, could well have been the result of the overdose. What about dabs, Bailey?'

'What you'd expect. Dr Schramm's, the nurse Jackson's. Deceased's of course, all over the shop. The other doctor's – Field-Innis. I called at his surgery and asked for a take. He wasn't all that keen but he obliged. The girl Foster's on the vanity box and her mother's like you indicated.'

'The tumbler?'

'Yeah,' said Bailey, with his look of mulish satisfaction. 'That's right. That's the funny bit. Nothing. Clean. Same goes for the pill bottle and the whisky bottle.'

'Now we're getting somewhere,' said Fox.

'Where do we get to, Br'er Fox?'

'Gloves used but only after she lost consciousness.'

'What I reckoned,' said Bailey.

'Or after she'd passed away?' Fox speculated.

'No, Mr Fox. Not if smothering's the story.'

Alleyn said, 'No dabs on the reverse side of the pillow?'

'That's the story,' said Thompson.

Bailey produced, finally, a polythene bag containing the back panel of the pretty lawn pillowcase, threaded with ribbon. 'This,' he said, 'is kind of crushed on the part opposite to the tooth print and stains. Crumpled up, like. As if by hands. No dabs, but crumpled. What I reckon – hands.'

'Gloved. Like the Americans say, it figures. Anything else in the bedroom?'

'Not to signify.'

The telephone rang. It was a long-distance call from Berne. Alleyn's contact came through loud and clear.

'M. le Superintendant? I am calling immediately to make an amendment to our former conversations.'

'An amendment, *mon ami*?'

'An addition, perhaps more accurately. In reference to the Doctor Schramm at the Sacré-Coeur, you recollect?'

'Vividly.'

'M. le Superintendant, I regret. My contact at the bureau has made a further search. It is now evident that the Doctor Schramm in question is deceased. In effect, since 1952.'

During the pause of the kind often described as pregnant Alleyn made a face at Fox and said, 'Dead.' Fox looked affronted.

'At the risk,' Alleyn said into the telephone, 'of making the most intolerable nuisance of myself, dare I ask if your source would have the very great kindness to find out if, over the same period, there is any record of an Englishman called Basil Smythe having qualified at Sacré-Coeur. I should explain, my dear colleague, that there is now the possibility of a not unfamiliar form of false pretence.'

'But of course. You have but to ask. And the name again?'

Alleyn spelt it out, and was told he could expect a return call within the hour. It came through in twelve minutes. An Englishman called Basil Smythe had attended the courses at the time in question but had failed to complete them. Alleyn thanked his expeditious confrère profusely. There was a further interchange of compliments and he hung up.

4

'It's not only in the story-books,' observed Fox on the following morning as they drove once more to Greengages, 'that you get a surplus of suspects but I'll say this for it – it's unusual. The dates tally, don't they?'

'According to the records at St Luke's, he was a medical student in London in 1950. It would seem he didn't qualify there.'

'And now we begin to wonder if he qualified anywhere at all?'

'Does the doctor practise to deceive, in fact?' Alleyn suggested.

'Perhaps if he was at the hospital and knew the real Schramm he might have got hold of his diploma when he died. Or am I being fanciful?' asked Fox.

'You are being fanciful. And yet I don't know. It's possible.'

'Funnier things have happened.'

'True,' said Alleyn and they fell silent for the rest of the drive.

They arrived at Greengages under the unenthusiastic scrutiny of the receptionist. They went directly to No. 20 and found it in an advanced stage of unloveliness.

'It's not the type of case I like,' Fox complained. 'Instead of knowing who the villain is and getting on quietly with routine until you've collected enough to make a charge, you have to go dodging about from one character to another like the chap in the corner of a band.'

'Bang, tinkle, crash?'

'Exactly. Motive,' Fox indignantly continued. 'Take motive. There's Bruce Gardener who gets twenty-five thousand out of it and the stepson who gets however much his father entailed on him after his mother's death and there's a sussy-looking quack who gets a fortune. Not to mention Mr Markos who fancied her house and Sister Jackson who fancies the quack. You can call them fringe characters. *I* don't know! Which of the lot can we wipe? Tell me that, Mr Alleyn.'

'I'm sorry too many suspects makes you so cross, Br'er Fox, but I can't oblige. Let's take a look at an old enemy, *modus operandi*, shall we? Now that Bailey and Thompson have done their stuff what do we take out of it? *You* tell *me* that, my Foxkin.'

'Ah!' said Fox. 'Well now, what? What happened, eh? I reckon – and you'll have to give me time, Mr Alleyn – I reckon something after this fashion. After deceased had been bedded down for the night by her daughter and taken her early dinner, a character we can call the electrician, though he was nothing of the kind, collected the lilies from the reception desk and came up to No. 20. While he was still in the passage he heard or saw someone approaching and stepped into the curtained alcove.'

'As you did, we don't exactly know why.'

'With me it was what is known as a reflex action,' said Fox modestly. 'While in the alcove two of the lilies got their heads knocked off. The electrician (*soi-disant*) came out and entered No. 20. He now – don't bustle me—'

'I wouldn't dream of it. He now?'

'Went into the bedroom and bathroom,' said Fox and himself suited the action to the word, raising his voice as he did so, 'and put the lilies in the basin. They don't half stink now. He returned to the bedroom and kidded to the deceased.'

'Kidded?'

'Chatted her up,' Fox explained. He leant over the bed in a beguiling manner. 'She tells him she's not feeling quite the thing and he says why not have a nice drink and a sleeping-pill. And, by the way, didn't the young lady say something about putting the pill bottle out for her mother? She did? Right! So this chap gets her the drink – scotch and water. Now comes the nitty-gritty bit.'

'It did, for her at any rate.'

'He returns to the bathroom, which I shan't bother to do. Ostensibly,' said Fox, looking his superior officer hard in the eye, 'ostensibly to mix the Scotch and water but he slips in a couple, maybe three, maybe four pills. Soluble in alcohol, remember.'

'There's a water jug on her table.'

'I thought you'd bring that up. He says it'll be stale. The water. Just picks up the whisky and takes it into the bathroom.'

'Casual-like?'

'That's it.'

'Yes. I'll swallow that, Br'er Fox. Just.'

'So does she. She swallows the drink knowing nothing of the tablets and he gives her one or maybe two more which she takes herself thinking they're the first, with the Scotch and water.'

'How about the taste, if they do taste?'

'It's a strong Scotch. And,' Fox said quickly, 'she attributes the taste, if noticed, to the one or maybe two tablets she's given herself. She has now taken, say, six tablets.'

'Go on. If you've got the nerve.'

'He waits. He may even persuade her to have another drink. With him. And puts more tablets in it.'

'What's he drink out of? The bottle?'

'Let that be as it may. He waits, I say, until she's dopey.'

'Well?'

'And he puts on his gloves and smothers her,' said Fox suddenly. 'With the pillow.'

'I see.'

'You don't buy it, Mr Alleyn?'

'On the contrary, I find it extremely plausible.'

'You do? I forgot to say,' Fox added, greatly cheered, 'that he put the extra tablets in her mouth after she was out. Gave them a push to the back of the tongue. That's where he overdid it. One of those fancy touches you're so often on about. Yerse. To make suicide look convincing he got rid of a lot more down the loo.'

'Was the television going all this time?'

'Yes. Because Dr Schramm found it going when he got there. Blast,' said Fox vexedly. 'Of course if *he's* our man—'

'He got home much earlier than he makes out. The girl at reception would hardly mistake him for an itinerant electrician. So someone else does that bit and hides with the vacuum-cleaners and puts the lilies in the basin and goes home as clean as a whistle.'

'Yerse,' said Fox.

'There's no call for you to be crestfallen. It's a damn good bit of barefaced conjecture and may well be right if Schramm's not our boy.'

'But if this Claude Carter is?'

'It would fit.'

'Ah! And Gardener? Well,' said Fox, 'I know he's all wrong if the receptionist girl's right. I know that. Great hulking cross-eyed lump of a chap,' said Fox crossly.

There followed a discontented pause at the end of which Fox said, with a touch of diffidence, 'Of course, there is another fringe character, isn't there? Perhaps two. I mean to say, by all accounts the deceased *was* dead set against the engagement, wasn't she?'

Alleyn made no reply. He had wandered over to the dressing-table and was gazing at its array of Sybil Foster's aids to beauty and at the regimental photograph in a silver frame. Bailey had dealt delicately with them all and scarcely disturbed the dust that had settled on them or upon the looking-glass that reflected her altered face.

After another long silence Alleyn said, 'Do you know, Fox, you have, in the course of your homily, proved me, to my own face and full in my own silly teeth, to be a copybook example of the unobservant investigating officer.'

'You don't say!'

'But I do say. Grinding the said teeth and whipping my cat, I do say.'

'It would be nice,' said Fox mildly, 'to know why.'

'Let's pack up and get out of this and I'll tell you on the way.'

'On the way to where?' Fox reasonably enquired.

'To the scene where I was struck down with sand-blindness

or whatever. To the source of all our troubles. To our patch. To the point marked bloody x.'

'Upper Quintern, would that be?'

'Upper Quintern it is. And I think, Fox, we'd better find ourselves rooms at a pub. Better to be there than here. Come on.'

Chapter Six

POINT MARKED X

Prunella was at home at Quintern Place. Her car was in the drive and she herself answered the door, explaining that she was staying at Mardling and had merely called in to pick up her mail. She took Alleyn and Fox into the drawing-room. It was a room of just proportions with appointments that had occurred quietly over many years rather than by any immediate process of collective assembly. The panelling and ceiling were graceful. It was a room that seemed to be full of gentle light.

Alleyn exclaimed with pleasure.

'Do you like it?' Prunella said. 'Most people seem to like it.' 'I'm sure you do, don't you?'

'I expect so. It always feels quite nice to come back to. It's not exactly riveting, of course. Too predictable. I mean, it doesn't *send* one, does it? I don't know, though. It sends my father-in-law-to-be up like a rocket. Do sit down.'

She herself sat between them. She arranged her pretty face in a pout almost as if she parodied some Victorian girl. She was pale and, Alleyn thought, very tense.

'We won't be long about this,' he said. 'There are one or two bits and pieces we're supposed to tidy up. Nothing troublesome, I hope.'

'Oh,' said Prunella. 'I see. I thought that probably you'd come to tell me my mother was murdered. Officially tell me, I mean. I know, of course, that you thought so.'

Until now she had spoken in her customary whisper but this was brought out rapidly and loudly. She stared straight in front of her and her hands were clenched in her lap.

'No,' Alleyn said. 'That's not it.'

'But you think she was, don't you?'

'I'm afraid we do think it's possible. Do you?'

Prunella darted a look at him and waited a moment before she said, 'I don't know. The more I wonder the less I can make up my mind. But then, of course, there are all sorts of things the police dig up that other people know nothing about. Aren't there?'

'That's bound to happen,' he agreed. 'It's our job to dig, isn't it?'

'I suppose so.'

'My first reason for coming is to make sure you have been properly consulted about the arrangements for tomorrow and to ask if there is anything we can do to help. The service is at half past three, isn't it? The present suggestion is that your mother will be brought from Maidstone to the church, arriving about two o'clock, but it has occurred to me that you might like her to rest there tonight. If so, that can easily be arranged.'

Prunella, for the first time looked directly at him. 'That's kind,' she said. 'I'd like that, I think. Please.'

'Good. I'll check with our chaps in Maidstone and have a word with your vicar. I expect he'll let you know.'

'Thank you.'

'All right then.'

'Super,' said Prunella with shaking lips. Tears trickled down her cheeks. 'I'm sorry,' she said. 'I thought I'd got over all this. I thought I was OK.' She knuckled her eyes and fished a handkerchief out of her pocket. Mr Fox rose and walked away to the furthest windows through which he contemplated the prospect.

'Never mind,' Alleyn said. 'That's the way delayed shock works. Catches you on the hop when you least expect it.'

'Sickening of it,' Prunella mumbled into her handkerchief. 'You'd better say what you wanted to ask.'

'It can wait a bit.'

'No!' said Prunella and stamped like an angry child. 'Now.'

'All right. I'd better say first what we always say. Don't jump to conclusions and read all sorts of sinister interpretations into routine questions. You must realize that in a case of this sort everyone who saw anything at all of your mother or had contact, however trivial, with her during the time she was at Greengages, and especially on the last day, has to be crossed off.'

'All except one.'

'Perhaps not excepting even one then we *do* look silly.'

Prunella sniffed. 'Go ahead,' she said.

'Do you know a great deal about your mother's first husband?'

Prunella stared at him.

'*Know*? Me? Only what everyone knows. Do you mean about how he was killed and about the Black Alexander stamp?'

'Yes. We've heard about the stamp. And about the unfinished

letter to your mother.'

'Well then. There's nothing else that I can think of.'

'Do you know if she kept that letter? And any other of his letters?'

Prunella began, 'If I did I wouldn't—' and pulled herself up. 'Sorry,' she said, 'yes, she did. I found them at the back of a drawer in her dressing-table. It's a converted sofa-table and it's got a not terribly secret, secret drawer.'

'And you have them still?'

She waited for a second or two and then nodded. 'I've read them,' she said. 'They're fantastic, lovely letters. They can't possibly have anything at all to do with any of this. Not possibly.'

'I've seen the regimental group photograph.'

'Mrs Jim told me.'

'He was very good-looking, wasn't he?'

'Yes. They used to call him Beau Carter. It's hard to believe when you see Claude, isn't it? He was only twenty-one when his first wife died. Producing Claude. Such an awful waste, I've always thought. Much better if it'd been the other way round, though of course in that case I would have been – just not. Or would I? How muddling.'

She glanced down the long room to where Mr Fox, at its furthest extreme, having put on his spectacles, was bent over a glass-topped curio table. 'What's he doing?' she whispered.

'Being tactful.'

'Oh. I see.'

'About your mother – did she often speak of her first husband?'

'Not often. I think she got out of the way of it when my papa was alive. I think he must have been jealous, poor love. He wasn't exactly a heart-throb to look at himself. You know – pink and portly. So I think she kept things like pre-papa photographs and letters discreetly out of circulation. Sort of. But she did tell me about Maurice – that was his name.'

'About his soldiering days? During the war when I suppose that photograph was taken?'

'Yes. A bit about him. Why?'

'About his brother officers, for instance? Or the men under him?'

'Why?' Prunella insisted. 'Don't be like those awful pressmen who keep bawling out rude questions that haven't got anything to do with the case. Not,' she added hastily, 'that you'd really do that because you're not at all that kind. But, I mean what on *earth* can my Mum's first husband's brother officers and men have to do with his wife's murder when most of them are dead, I dare say, themselves?'

'His soldier-servant, for instance? Was there anything in the letters about *him*? The officer-batman relationship can be, in its way, quite a close one.'

'Now you mention it,' said Prunella on a note of impatience, 'there were jokey bits about somebody he called the Corp, who I suppose might have been his servant but they weren't anything out of the way. In the last letter, for instance. It was written here. He'd got an unexpected leave and come home but Mummy was with her WRNS in Scotland. It says he's trying to get a call through to her but will leave the letter in case he doesn't. It breaks off abruptly saying he's been recalled urgently to London and has just time to get to the station. I expect you know about the train being bombed.'

'Yes. I know.'

'Well,' said Prunella shortly, 'it was a direct hit. On his carriage. So that's all.'

'And what about the Corp? In the letter?'

'What? Oh. There's a very effing bit about – sorry,' said Prunella. ' "Effing" is family slang for "affecting" or kind of "terribly touching". This bit is about what she's to do if he's killed and how much – how he feels about her and she's not to worry and anyway the Corp looks after him like a nanny. He must have been rather a super chap, Maurice, I always think.'

'Anything about the Black Alexander?'

'Oh, that! Well – actually, yes, there is something. He says he supposes she'll think him a fusspot but, after all, his London bank's in the hottest blitz area and he's taken the stamp out and will store it elsewhere. There's something about its being in a waterproof case or something. It was at that point he got the urgent recall to London. So he breaks off – and – says goodbye. Sort of.'

'And the stamp was never to be found.'

'That's right. Not for want of looking. But obviously he had it on him.'

'Miss Foster, I wouldn't ask you this if it wasn't important and I hope you won't mind very much that I do ask. Will you let me see those letters?'

Prunella looked at her own hands. They were clenched

G.M.–F

tightly on her handkerchief and she hurriedly relaxed them. The handkerchief lay in a small damply crumpled heap in her lap. Alleyn saw where a fingernail had bitten into it.

'I simply can't imagine *why*,' she said. 'I mean, it's fantastic. Love letters, pure and simple, written almost forty years ago and concerning nothing and nobody but the writer. And Mummy, of course.'

'I know. It seems preposterous, doesn't it? But I can't tell you how "professional" and detached I shall be about it. Rather like a doctor. Please let me see them.'

She glanced at the distant Fox, still absorbed in the contents of the curio table. 'I don't want to make a fuss about nothing,' she said. 'I'll get them.'

'Are they still in the not-so-secret secret drawer of the converted sofa-table?'

'Yes.'

'I should like to see it.'

They had both risen.

'Secret drawers,' said Alleyn lightly, 'are my speciality. At the Yard they called me Peeping Tom Alleyn.' Prunella compressed her lips. 'Fox,' Alleyn said loudly, 'may I tear you away?'

'I beg your pardon, Mr Alleyn,' Fox said, removing his spectacles but staying where he was. 'I beg *your* pardon, Miss Foster. My attention was caught by this – should I call it specimen table? My aunt, Miss Elsie Smith, has just such another in her shop in Brighton.'

'Really?' said Prunella and stared at him.

Alleyn strolled down to the other end of the room and leant over the table. It contained a heterogeneous collection of medals, a vinaigrette, two miniatures, several little boxes in silver or cloisonné and one musical box, all set out on a blue velvet base.

'I'm always drawn to these assemblies,' Alleyn said. 'They are family history in hieroglyphics. I see you've rearranged them lately.'

'No, I haven't. Why?' asked Prunella, suddenly alerted. She joined them. It was indeed clear from indentations in the velvet that a rearrangement had taken place. 'Damn!' she said. 'At it again! No, it's too much.'

'At it?' Alleyn ventured. 'Again? Who?'

'Claude Carter. I suppose you know he's staying here. He – does so fiddle and pry.'

'What does he pry into?'

'All over the place. He's always like that. The old plans of this house and garden. Drawers in tables. He turns over other people's letters when they come. I wouldn't put him past reading them. I'm not living here at the moment so I dare say he's having field days. I don't know why I'm talking about it.'

'Is he in the house at this moment?'

'I don't know. I've only just come in myself. Never mind. Forget it. Do you want to see the letters?'

She walked out of the room, Alleyn opened the door for her. He followed her into the hall and up the staircase.

'How happy Mr Markos will be,' he remarked, 'climbing up the golden stairs. They *are* almost golden, aren't they? Where the sun catches them?'

'I haven't noticed.'

'Oh, but you should. You mustn't allow ownership to dull the edge of appetite. One should always know how lucky one is.'

Prunella turned on the upper landing and stared at him.

'Is it your habit,' she asked, 'to go on like this? When you're on duty?'

'Only if I dare hope for a sympathetic reception. What happens now? Turn right, proceed in a westerly direction and effect an entrance?'

Since this was in fact what had to be done, Prunella said nothing and led the way into her mother's bedroom.

A sumptuous room. There was a canopied bed and a silken counterpane with a lacy nightgown case topped up by an enormous artificial rose. A largesse of white bearskin rugs. But for all its luxury the room had a depleted air as if the heart had gone out of it. One of the wardrobe doors was open and disclosed complete emptiness.

Prunella said rapidly, 'I sent everything, all the clothes, away to the nearest professional theatre. They can sell the things they don't use – fur hats and coats and things.'

There were no photographs or feminine toys of any kind on the tables and chimney-piece and Sybil's sofa-cum-dressing-table with its cupid-encircled looking-glass, had been bereft of all the pots, bottles and jars that Alleyn supposed had adorned it.

Prunella said, following his look, 'I got rid of everything. Everything.' She was defiant.

'I expect it was the best thing to do.'

'We're going to change the room. Completely. My father-

139

in-law-to-be's fantastic about houses – an expert. He'll advise us.'

'Ah, yes,' said Alleyn politely.

She almost shouted at him, 'I suppose you think I'm hard and modern and over-reacting to everything. Well, so I may be. But I'll thank you to remember that Will. How she tried to bribe me, because that's what it was, into marrying a monster, because that's what he is, and punish me if I didn't. I never thought she had it in her to be so mean and despicable and I'm not going to bloody cry again and I don't in the least know why I'm talking to you like this. The letters are in the dressing-table and I bet you can't find the hidden bit.'

She turned her back on Alleyn and blew her nose.

He went to the table, opened the central drawer, slid his finger round inside the frame and found a neat little knob that released a false wall at the back. It opened and there in the 'secret' recess was the classic bundle of letters tied with the inevitable faded ribbon.

There was also an open envelope with some half-dozen sepia snapshots inside.

'I think,' he said, 'the best way will be for me to look at once through the letters and if they are irrelevant return them to you. Perhaps there's somewhere downstairs where Fox and I could make ourselves scarce and get it settled.'

Without saying anything further Prunella led the way downstairs to the 'boudoir' he had visited on his earlier call. They paused at the drawing-room to collect Mr Fox, who was discovered in contemplation of a portrait in pastel of Sybil as a young girl.

'If,' said Prunella, 'you don't take the letters away perhaps you'd be kind enough to leave them in the desk.'

'Yes, of course,' Alleyn rejoined with equal formality. 'We mustn't use up any more of your time. Thank you so much for being helpful.'

He made her a little bow and was about to turn away when she suddenly thrust out her hand.

'Sorry, I was idiotic. No bones broken?' Prunella asked.

'Not even a green fracture.'

'Goodbye then.'

They shook hands.

'That child,' said Alleyn when they were alone, 'turned on four entirely separate moods, if that's what they should be called, in scarcely more than as many minutes. Not counting the drawing-room comedy which was not a comedy. You and your Aunt Elsie!'

'Perhaps the young lady's put about by recent experience,' Fox hazarded.

'It's the obvious conclusion, I suppose.'

In the boudoir Alleyn divided the letters – there were eight – between them. Fox put on his spectacles and read with the catarrhal breathing that always afflicted him when engaged in that exercise.

Prunella had been right. They were indeed love letters, 'pure and simple' within the literal meaning of the phrase, and most touching. The young husband had been deeply in love and able to say so.

As his regiment moved from the Western Desert to Italy, the reader became accustomed to the nicknames of brother officers and regimental jokes. The Corp, who was indeed Captain Carter's servant, featured more often as time went on. Some of the letters were illustrated with lively little drawings. There was one of the enormous Corp being harassed by bees in Tuscany. They were represented as swarming inside his kilt and he was depicted with a violent squint and his mouth wide open. A balloon issued from it with a legend that said, 'It's no' saw much the ticklin', it's the imperrtinence, ye ken.'

The last letter was as Prunella had described it. The final sentences read: 'So my darling love, I shan't see you this time. If I don't stop I'll miss the bloody train. About the stamp – sorry, no time left. Your totally besotted husband, Maurice.'

Alleyn assembled the letters, tied the ribbon and put the little packet in the desk. He emptied out the snapshots: a desolate, faded company well on its slow way to oblivion. Maurice Carter appeared in all of them and in all of them looked like a near relation of Rupert Brooke. In one, he held by the hand a very small nondescript child: Claude, no doubt. In another he and a ravishingly pretty young Sybil appeared together. A third was yet another replica of the regimental group still in her desk drawer. The fourth and last showed Maurice kilted and a captain now, with his enormous 'Corp' stood to attention in the background.

Alleyn took it to the window, brought out his pocket lens and examined it. Fox folded his arms and watched him.

Presently he looked up and nodded.

'We'll borrow these four,' he said. 'I'll leave a receipt.'

He wrote it out, left it in the desk and put the snapshots in his pocket. 'Come on,' he said.

They met nobody on their way out. Prunella's car was gone. Fox followed Alleyn past the long windows of the library and the lower west flank of the house. They turned right and came at last to the stables.

'As likely as not, he'll still be growing mushrooms,' Alleyn said.

And so he was. Stripped to the waist, bronzed, golden-bearded and looking like a much younger man, Bruce was hard at work in the converted lean-to. When he saw Alleyn he grounded his shovel and arched his earthy hand over his eyes to shield them from the sun.

'Ou aye,' he said, 'so it's you again, Chief Superintendent. What can I do for you, the noo?'

'You can tell us, if you will, Corporal Gardener, the name of your regiment, and of its captain,' said Alleyn.

2

'I canna credit it,' Bruce muttered and gazed out of his non-aligned blue eyes at Alleyn. 'It doesna seem within the bounds of possibility. It's dealt me a wee shock, I'll say that for it.'

'You hadn't an inkling?'

'Don't be saw daft man,' Bruce said crossly. 'Sir, I should say. How would I have an inkling, will you tell me that? I doubt if her first husband was ever mentioned in my hearing and why would he be?'

'There was this stepson,' Fox said to nobody in particular. 'Name of Carter.'

'Be damned to that,' Bruce shouted. 'Carrrter! Carrrter! Why would he not be Carrrter? Would I be saw daft as to say my captain, dead nigh on forty years, was a man o' the name of Carrrter so you must be his son and he the bonniest lad you'd ever set eyes on and you, not to dra' it mild, a pure, sickly, ill-put-taegither apology for a man? Here, sir, can I have anither keek at them photies?'

Alleyn gave them to him.

'Ah,' he said, 'I mind it fine, the day that group was taken. I'd forgotten all about it but I mind it fine the noo.'

'But didn't you notice the replica of this one in her bedroom at the hotel?'

Bruce stared at him. His expression became prudish. He

half-closed his eyes and pursed his enormous mouth. He said, in a scandalized voice, 'Sir, I never set fut in her bedroom. It would have not been the thing at a'. Not at a'.'

'Indeed?'

'She received me in a wee private parlour upstairs or in the garden.'

'I see. I beg your pardon.'

'As for these ither ones: I never see them before.' He gazed at them in silence for some moments. 'My God,' he said quietly, 'look at the bairn, just. That'll be the bairn by the first wife. My God, it'll be this Claude. Who'd've thought it? And here's anither wi' me in the background. It's a strange coincidence, this, it is indeed.'

'You never came to Quintern or heard him speak of it?'

'If I did, the name didna stick in my mind. I never came here. What for would I? When we had leave and we only had but one before he was kilt, he let me gang awa' home. Aye, he was a considerate officer. *Christ!*'

'What's the matter?' Alleyn asked. Bruce had dealt his knees a devastating smack with his ginger-haired earthy hands.

'When I think of it,' he said. 'When I mind how me and her would have our bit crack of an evening when I came in for my dram. Making plans for the planting season and that. When I remember how she'd talk saw free and friendly and there, all unbeknownst, was my captain's wife that he'd let on to me was the sonsiest lass in the land. He had her picture in his wallet and liked fine to look at it. I took a wee keek mysel' one morning when I was brushing his tunic. She was bonny, aye, she was that. Fair as a flooer. She seems to have changed and why wouldn't she over the passage of years? Ou aye,' he said heavily. 'She changed.'

'We all do,' said Alleyn. 'You've changed yourself. I didn't recognize you at first, in the photographs.'

'That'd be the beard,' he said seriously and looked over his lightly sweating torso with the naïve self-approval of the physically fit male. 'I'm no' so bad in other respects,' he said.

'You got to know Captain Carter quite well, I suppose?'

'Not to say well, just. And yet you could put it like that. What's that spiel to the effect that no man's a hero to his valey? He can be so to his soldier-servant and the captain came near enough to it with me.'

'Did you get in touch with his wife after he was killed? Perhaps write to her?'

'Na, na. I wadna tak' the liberty. And forby I was back wi' the regiment that same night and awa' to the front. We didna get the news until after we landed.'

'When did you return to England?'

'After the war. I was taken at Cassino and spent the rest of the duration in a prison camp.'

'And Mrs Carter never got in touch? I mean, Captain Carter wrote quite a lot about you in his letters. He always referred to you as the Corp. I would have thought she would have liked to get in touch.'

'Did he? Did he, mention me, now?' said Bruce eagerly. 'To think o' that.'

'Look here, Gardener, you realize by this time, don't you, that we are considering the possibility of foul play in this business?'

Bruce arranged the photographs carefully like playing cards in his left fist and contemplated them as if they were all aces.

'I'm aware of that,' he said absently. 'It's a horrid conclusion but I'm aware of it. To think he made mention of me in his correspondence. Well, now!'

'Are you prepared to help us if you can? Do,' begged Alleyn, 'stop looking at those damn photographs. Here – give them to me and attend to what I say.'

Bruce, with every sign of reluctance, yielded up the photographs.

'I hear you,' he said. 'Ou aye, I am prepared.'

'Good. Now. First question. Did Captain Carter ever mention to you or in your hearing a valuable stamp in his possession?'

'He did not. Wait!' said Bruce dramatically. 'Aye. I mind it now. It was before he went on his last leave. He said it was in his bank in the City but he was no' just easy in his mind on account of the blitz and intended to uplift it.'

'Did he say what he meant to do with it?'

'Na, na. Not a wurrrd to that effect.'

'Sure?'

'Aye, I'm sure,' said Bruce indifferently.

'Oh, well,' Alleyn said after a pause and looked at Fox.

'You can't win all the time,' said Fox.

Bruce shook himself like a wet dog. 'I'll not deny this has been a shock to me,' he said. 'It's given me an unco' awkward feeling. As if,' he added, opening his eyes very wide and producing a flight of fancy that seemed to surprise him, 'as if time, in a manner of speaking, had got itself mixed. That's a gey weird notion, to be sure.'

'Tell me, Gardener. Are you a Scot by birth?'

'Me? Na, na, I'm naething of the sort, sir. Naething of the sort. But I've worked since I was a laddie in Scotland and under Scots instruction. I enlisted in Scotland. I served in a Scots regiment and I dare say you've noticed I've picked up a trick or two of the speech.'

'Yes,' said Alleyn. 'I had noticed.'

'Aye,' said Bruce complacently. 'I dare say I'd pass for one in a crowd and proud to do it.' As if to put a signature to his affirmation he gave Alleyn a look that he would have undoubtedly described as 'canny'. 'I ken weel enough,' he said, 'that I must feature on your short list if it's with homicide that you're concerning yourself, Superintendent. For the simple reason the deceased left me twenty-five thousand pounds. That's correct, is it not?'

'Yes,' Alleyn said. 'That's correct.'

'I didna reckon to be contradicted and I can only hope it won't be long before you eliminate me from the file. In the meantime, I can do what any guiltless man can do under the circumstances: tell the truth and hope I'm believed. For I have told you the truth, Chief Superintendent. I have indeed.'

'By and large, Bruce,' said Alleyn, 'I believe you have.'

'There's no "by" and there's no "large" in it,' he said seriously, 'and I don't doubt you'll come to acknowledge the fact.' He looked at his wristwatch, a Big Ben of its species, glanced at the sun, and said he ought to be getting down to the churchyard.

'At St Crispin's?'

'Aye. Did ye no' hear? Jim Jobbin has the lumbago on him and I'm digging the grave. It's entirely appropriate that I should do so.'

'Yes?'

'Aye, 'tis. I've done her digging up here and she'd have been well content I'd do it down there in the finish. The difference being we canna have our bit crack over the matter. So if you've no further requirements of me, sir, I'll bid you good day and get on with it.'

'Can we give you a lift?'

'I'm much obliged, sir, but I have my ain auld car. Mrs Jim has left a piece and a bottle ready and I'll take them with me. If it's a long job, and it may be that, I'll get a bite of supper at my sister's. She's a wee piece up Stile Lane, overlooking the kirk. When would the deceased be brought for burying, can you tell me that?'

"This evening. After dark, very likely.'

'And rest in the kirk overnight?'

'Yes.'

'Ou aye,' said Bruce on an indrawn breath. 'That's a very decent arrangement. Aweel, I've a long job ahead of me.'

'Thank you for your help.'

Alleyn went to the yard door of the empty room. He opened it and looked in. Nothing had changed.

'Is this part of the flat that was to be built for you?' he called out.

'Aye, that was the idea,' said Bruce.

'Does Mr Carter take an interest in it?'

'Ach, he's always peering and prying. You'd think,' said Bruce distastefully, 'it was him that's the lawful heir.'

'Would you so,' said Alleyn absently. 'Come along, Fox.'

They left Bruce pulling his shirt over his head in an easy workmanlike manner. He threw his jacket across his shoulder, took up his shovel and marched off.

'In his way,' said Fox, 'a remarkable chap.'

3

Verity, to her surprise, was entertaining Nikolas Markos to luncheon. He had rung her up the day before and asked her to 'take pity' on him.

'If you would prefer it,' he had said, 'I will drive you somewhere else, all the way to the Ritz if you like, and you shall be my guest. But I did wonder, rather wistfully, if we might have an egg under your lime trees. Our enchanting Prue is staying with us and I suddenly discover myself to be elderly. Worse, she, dear child, is taking pains with me.'

'You mean?'

'She laughs a little too kindly at my dated jokes. She remembers not to forget I'm there. She includes me, with scarcely an effort, in their conversations. She's even taken to bestowing the odd butterfly kiss on the top of my head. I might as well be bald,' said Mr Markos bitterly.

'I'll undertake not to do that, at least. But I'm not much of a cook.'

'My dear, my adorable lady, I said Egg and I meant Egg. I am,' said Mr Markos, 'your slave for ever and if you will allow me will endorse the declaration with what used to be called a bottle of the Widow. Perhaps, at this juncture I should warn you that I shall also present you with a problem. *A demain* and a thousand thanks.'

He gets away with it, Verity thought, but only just. And if he says eggs, eggs he shall have. On creamed spinach. And my standby: iced sorrel soup first and the Stilton afterwards.

And as it was a lovely day they did have lunch under the limes. Mr Markos, good as his word, had brought a bottle of champagne in an ice bucket and the slightly elevated atmosphere that Verity associated with him was quickly established. She could believe that he enjoyed himself as fully as he professed to do, but he was as much of an exotic in her not very tidy English garden as frangipani. His hair luxuriant but disciplined, his richly curved, clever mouth and large black eyes, his clothes that, while they avoided extravagance, were inescapably very, very expensive – all these factors reminded Verity of Sybil Foster's strictures.

The difference is, she thought, that I don't mind him being like this. What's more I don't think Syb would have minded either if he'd taken a bit more notice of her.

When they had arrived at the coffee stage and he at his Turkish cigarette, he said, 'I would choose, of course, to hear you talk about your work and this house and lovely garden. I should like you to confide in me and perhaps a little to confide in you myself.' He spread his hands. 'What am I saying! How ridiculous! Of course I am about to confide in you – that is my whole intention, after all. I think you are accustomed to confidences – they are poured into your lap and you are discreet and never pass them on. Am I right?'

'Well,' said Verity, who was not much of a hand at talking about herself and didn't enjoy it. 'I don't know so much about that.' And she thought how Alleyn, though without any Markosian floridity, had also introduced confidences. Ratsy too, she remembered, and thought irrelevantly that she had become quite a one for gentlemen callers over the last fortnight.

Mr Markos fetched from his car two large sheets of cardboard tied together. 'Do you remember,' he asked, 'when we examined Prunella's original plans of Quintern Place there was a smaller plan of the grounds that you said you had not seen before?'

'Yes, of course.'

'This is it.'

He put the cardboards on the table and opened them out. There was the plan.

'I think it is later than the others,' he said, 'and by a different hand. It is drawn on the scale of a quarter of an inch to the foot and is very detailed. Now. Have a close, a *very* close look. Can you find a minute extra touch that doesn't explain itself? Take your time,' Mr Markos invited, with an air of extraordinary relish. He took her arm and led her close to the table.

Verity felt that he was making a great build-up and that the climax had better be good but she obediently pored over the map.

Since it was a scheme for laying out the grounds, the house was shown simply as an outline. The stable block was indicated in the same manner. Verity, not madly engaged, plodded conscientiously over elaborate indications of water-gardens, pavilions, fountains, terraces and spinneys but although they suggested a prospect that Evelyn himself would have treasured, she could find nothing untoward. She was about to say so when she noticed that within the empty outline of the stables there was an interior line suggesting a division into two rooms, a line that seemed to be drawn freehand in pencil rather than ruled in the brownish ink of the rest of the plan. She bent down to examine it more closely and found, in one corner of the indicated stable-room a tiny x, also, she was sure, pencilled.

Mr Markos, who had been watching her intently, gave a triumphant little crow. 'Aha!' he cried. 'You see! You've spotted it.'

'Well, yes,' said Verity. 'If you mean—' and she pointed to the pencilled additions.

'Of course, of course. And what, my dear Miss Preston-Watson, do you deduce? You know my methods. Don't bustle.'

'Only, I'm afraid, that someone at some time has thought of making some alteration in the old stable buildings.'

'A strictly Watsonian conclusion. I must tell you that at the moment a workman is converting the outer half of the amended portion – now an open-fronted broken-down lean-to, into a mushroom bed.'

'That will be Bruce, the gardener. Perhaps he and Sybil, in talking over the project, got out this plan and marked the place where it was to go.'

'But why "the point marked x"? It does not indicate the

mushroom bed. It is in a deserted room that opens off the mushroom shed.'

'They might have changed their minds.'

'It is crammed into a corner where there are the remains of an open fireplace. I must tell you that after making this discovery I strolled round the stable yard and examined the premises.'

'I can't think of anything else,' said Verity.

'I have cheated. I have withheld evidence. You must know, as Scheherezade would have said, meaning that you are to learn, that a few evenings after Prunella brought the plans to Mardling she found me poring over this one in the library. She remarked that it was strange that I should be so fascinated by it and then, with one of her nervous little spurts of confidence (she *is*, you will have noticed, unusually but Heaven knows, understandably, nervous just now) she told me that the egregious Claude Carter exhibited a similar interest in the plans and had been discovered examining this one through a magnifying glass. And I should like to know,' cried Mr Markos sparkling at Verity, 'what you make of all that!'

Verity did not make a great deal of it. She knew he expected her to enter into zestful speculation but, truth to tell, she found herself out of humour with the situation. There was something unbecoming in Nikolas Markos's glee over his discovery and if, as she suspected, he was going to link it in some way with Sybil Foster's death, she herself wanted no part in the proceedings. At the same time she felt apologetic – guilty even – about her withdrawal, particularly as she was sure he was very well aware of it. He really is, she thought, so remarkably sharp.

'To look at the situation quite cold-bloodedly,' he was saying, 'and of course that is the only sensible way to look at it, the police clearly are treating Mrs Foster's death as a case of homicide. This being so, anything untoward that has occurred at Quintern either before or after the event should be brought to their notice. You agree?'

Verity pulled herself together. 'I suppose so. I mean, yes of course. Unless they've already found it out for themselves. What's the matter?'

'If they have not, we have, little as I welcome the intrusion, an opportunity to inform them. Alas, you have a visitor, dear Verity,' said Mr Markos and quickly kissed her hand.

Alleyn, in fact, was walking up the drive.

'I'm sorry,' he said, 'to come at such an unlikely time of day but I'm on my way back from the Quintern Place and I thought perhaps you might like to know about the arrangements for this evening and tomorrow.'

He told them. 'I dare say the vicar will let you know,' he said, 'but in case he doesn't, that's what will happen.'

'Thank you,' Verity said. 'We were to do flowers first thing in the morning. It had better be this afternoon, hadn't it? Nice of you to think of it.'

She told herself she knew precisely why she was glad Alleyn had arrived. Idiotically it was because of Mr Markos's manner which had become inappropriately warm. Old hand though she was, this had flustered Verity. He had made assumptions. He had been too adroit. Quite a long time had gone by since assumptions had been made about Verity and still longer since she had been ruffled by them. Mr Markos made her feel clumsy and foolish.

Alleyn had spotted the plan. He said Prunella had mentioned the collection. He bent over it, made interested noises, looked closer and finally took out a pocket lens. Mr Markos crowed delightedly. 'At last!' he cried, 'we can believe you are the genuine article.' He put his arm round Verity and gave her a quick little squeeze. 'What is he going to look at?' he said. 'What do you think?'

And when Alleyn used his lens over the stable buildings, Mr Markos was enraptured.

'There's an extra bit pencilled in,' Alleyn said. 'Indicating the room next the mushroom bed.'

'So, my dear Alleyn, what do you make of *that*?'

'Nothing very much, do you?'

'Not of the "point marked x"? No buried treasure, for instance? Come!'

'Well,' said Alleyn, 'you can always dig for it, can't you? Actually it marks the position of a dilapidated fireplace. Perhaps there was some thought of renovating the rooms. A flat for the gardener, for instance.'

'Do you know,' Verity exclaimed, 'I believe I remember Sybil said something about doing just that. Setting him up on the premises because his room at his sister's house was tiny and he'd nowhere to put his things and they didn't hit it off anyway.'

'No doubt you are right, both of you,' admitted Mr Markos, 'but what a dreary solution. I am desolate.'

'Perhaps I can cheer you up with news of an unexpected development,' said Alleyn. 'It emerges that Bruce Gardener was Captain Maurice Carter's soldier-servant during the war.'

After a considerable interval Mr Markos said, 'The *gardener*. You mean the local man? Are you saying that this was known to Sybil Foster? And to Prunella? No. No, certainly not to Prunella.'

'Not, it seems, even to Gardener himself.'

Verity sat down abruptly. 'What *can* you mean?' she said.

Alleyn told her.

'I have always,' Mr Markos said, 'regarded stories of coincidence in a dubious light. My invariable instinct is to discredit them.'

'Is it?' said Verity. 'I always believe them and find them boring. I am prepared to acknowledge, since everyone tells me so, that life is littered with coincidences. I don't much mind. But this,' she said to Alleyn, 'is something else again. This takes a hell of a lot of acceptance.'

'Is that perhaps because of what has happened? If Mrs Foster hadn't died and if one day in the course of conversation it had emerged that her Maurice Carter had been Bruce Gardener's Captain Carter what would have been the reaction?'

'I can tell you what Syb's reaction would have been. She'd have made a big tra-la about it and said she'd always sensed there was "something".'

'And you?'

Verity thought it over. 'Yes,' she said. 'You're right. I'd have said, Fancy! Extraordinary coincidence, but wouldn't have thought much more about it.'

'If one may ask?' said Mr Markos, already asking. 'How did you find out? You or whoever it was?'

'I recognized him in an old photograph of the regiment. Not at first. I was shamefully slow. He hadn't got a beard in those days but he had got his squint.'

'Was he embarrassed?' Verity asked. 'When you mentioned it, I mean?'

'I wouldn't have said so. Flabbergasted is the word that springs to mind. From there he passed quickly to the "what a coincidence" bit and then into the realms of misty Scottish sentiment on "who would have thought it" and "had I but known" lines.'

'I can imagine.'

'Your Edinburgh Castle guide would have been brassy in comparison.'

'Castle?' asked Mr Markos. 'Edinburgh?'

Verity explained.

'What's he doing now?' Mr Markos sharply demanded. 'Still cultivating mushrooms? Next door, by yet another coincidence —' he tapped the plan – 'to the point marked x.'

'When we left him he was going to the church.'

'To the *church*! Why?'

Verity said, 'I know why.'

'You do?'

'Yes. Oh,' said Verity, 'this is all getting too much. Like a Jacobean play. He's digging Sybil's grave.'

'Why?' asked Mr Markos.

'Because Jim Jobbin has got lumbago.'

'Who is – no,' Mr Markos corrected himself, 'it doesn't matter. My dear Alleyn, forgive me if I'm tiresome, but doesn't all this throw a very dubious light upon the jobbing Gardener?'

'If it does, he's not the only one.'

'No? No, of course. I am forgetting the egregious Claude. By the way – I'm sorry, but you may slap me back if I'm insufferable – where does all this information come from?'

'In no small part,' said Alleyn, 'from Mrs Jim Jobbin.'

Mr Markos flung up his hands. 'These Jobbins!' he lamented and turned to Verity. 'Come to my rescue. Who *are* the Jobbins?'

'Mrs Jim helps you out once a week at Mardling. Her husband digs drains and graves and mows lawns. I dare say he mows yours if the truth were known.'

'Odd-job Jobbins, in fact,' said Alleyn and Verity giggled.

'Gideon would know,' his father said. 'He looks after that sort of thing. In any case, it doesn't matter. Unless – I suppose she's – to be perfectly cold-blooded about it – trustworthy?'

'She's a long-standing friend,' said Verity, 'and the salt of the earth. I'd sooner suspect the vicar's wife of hanky-panky than Mrs Jim.'

'Well, of course, my dear Verity' (Damn, thought Verity. I wish he wouldn't), 'that disposes of her, no doubt.' He turned to Alleyn. 'So the field is, after all, not extensive. Far too few

152

suspects for a good read.'

'Oh, I don't know,' Alleyn rejoined. 'You may have over-looked a candidate.'

In the pause that followed a blackbird somewhere in Verity's garden made a brief statement and traffic on the London motorway, four miles distant, established itself as a vague rumour.

Mr Markos said, 'Ah, yes. Of course. But I hadn't overlooked him. You're talking about my acquaintance, Dr Basil Schramm.'

'Only because I was going to ring up and ask if I might have a word with you about him. I think you introduced him to the Upper Quintern scene, didn't you?'

'Well – fleetingly, I suppose I did.'

Verity said, 'Would you excuse me? I've got a telephone call I must make and I *must* see about the flowers.'

'Are you being diplomatic?' Mr Markos asked archly.

'I don't even know how,' she said and left them not, she hoped, too hurriedly. The two men sat down.

'I'll come straight to the point, shall I?' Alleyn said. 'Can you, and if so, will you, tell me anything of Dr Schramm's history? Where he qualified, for instance? Why he changed his name? Anything?'

'Are you checking his own account of himself? Or hasn't he given a satisfactory one? You won't answer that of course and very properly not.'

'I don't in the least mind answering. I haven't asked him.'

'As yet?'

'That's right. As yet.'

'Well,' said Mr Markos, airily waving his hand, 'I'm afraid I'm not much use to you. I know next to nothing of his background except that he took his degree somewhere in Switzerland. I had no idea he'd changed his name, still less why. We met when crossing the Atlantic in the QE2 and subsequently in New York at a cocktail-party given at the St Regis by fellow passengers. Later on that same evening at his suggestion we dined together and afterwards visited some remarkable clubs to which he had the entrée. The entertainment was curious. That was the last time I saw him until he rang me up at Mardling on his way to Greengages. On the spur of the moment I asked him to dinner. I have not seen him since then.'

'Did he ever talk about his professional activities – I mean whether he had a practice in New York or was attached to a hospital or clinic or what have you?'

'Not in any detail. In the ship going over he was the life and soul of a party that revolved round an acquaintance of mine – the Princess Palevsky. I rather gathered that he acquired her and two American ladies of considerable renown as – patients. I imagine,' said Mr Markos smoothly, 'that he is the happy possessor of a certain expertise in that direction. And, really, my dear Alleyn, that is the full extent of my acquaintance with Basil Schramm.'

'What do you think of him?' said Alleyn abruptly.

'*Think* of him? What can I say? And what exactly do you mean?'

'Did you form an opinion of his character, for instance? Nice chap? Lightweight? Man of integrity?'

'He is quite entertaining. A lightweight, certainly, but good value as a mixer and with considerable charm. I would trust him,' said Mr Markos, 'no further than I could toss a grand piano. A concert grand.'

'Where women are concerned?'

'Particularly where women are concerned.'

'I see,' said Alleyn cheerfully and got up. 'I must go,' he said, 'I'm running late. By the way, is Miss Foster at Quintern Place, do you happen to know?'

'Prunella? No. She and Gideon went up to London this morning. They'll be back for dinner. She's staying with us.'

'Ah yes. I must go. Would you apologize for me to Miss Preston?'

'I'll do that. Sorry not to have been more informative.'

'Oh,' Alleyn said, 'the visit has not been unproductive. Goodbye to you.'

Fox was in the car in the lane. When he saw Alleyn, he started up his engine.

'To the nearest telephone,' Alleyn said. 'We'll use the one at Quintern Place. We've got to lay on surveillance and be quick about it. The local branch'll have to spare a copper. Send him up to Quintern as a labourer. He's to dig up the fireplace and hearth and dig deep and anything he finds that's not rubble, keep it. And when he's finished tell him to board up the room and seal it. If anyone asks what he's up to he'll have to say he's under police orders. But I hope no one will ask.'

'What about Gardener?'

'Gardener's digging the grave.'

'Fair enough,' said Fox.

'Claude Carter may be there, though.'

'Oh,' said Fox. 'Aha. Him.'

But before they reached Quintern they met Mrs Jim on her way to do flowers in the church. She said Claude Carter had gone out that morning. 'To see a man about a car,' he had told her and he said he would be away all day.

'Mrs Jim,' Alleyn said. 'We want a telephone and we want to take a look inside the house. Miss Foster's out. Could you help us? Do you have a key?'

She looked fixedly at him. Her workaday hands moved uneasily.

'I don't know as I have the right,' she said. 'It's not my business.'

'I know. But it is, I promise you, very important. An urgent call. Look, come with us, let us in, follow us about if you like or we'll drive you back to the church at once. Will you do that? Please?'

There was another and a longer pause. 'All right,' said Mrs Jim and got into the car.

They arrived at Quintern and were admitted by Mrs Jim's key which she kept under a stone in the coal house.

While Fox rang the Upper Quintern police station from the staff sitting-room telephone, Alleyn went out to the stable yard. Bruce's mushroom beds were of course in the same shape as they had been earlier in the afternoon when he left them, taking his shovel with him. The ramshackle door into the deserted room was shut. Alleyn dragged it open and stood on the threshold. At first glance it looked and smelt as it had on his earlier visit. The westering sun shone through the dirty window and showed traces of his own and Carter's footprints on the dusty floorboards. Nobody else's, he thought, but more of Carter's than his own. The litter of rubbish lay undisturbed in the corner. With a dry-mouthed sensation of foreboding he turned to the fireplace.

Alleyn began to swear softly and prolifically, an exercise in which he did not often indulge.

He was squatting over the fireplace when Fox appeared at the window, saw him and looked in at the yard door.

'They're sending up a chap at once,' he said.

'Like hell they are,' said Alleyn. 'Look here.'

'Had I better walk in?'

'The point's academic.'

Fox took four giant strides on tiptoe and stopped over the hearth. 'Broken up, eh?' he said. 'Fancy that, eh?'

'As you say. But look at this.' He pointed a long finger. 'Do you see what I see?'

'Remains of a square hole. Something regular in shape like a box or tin's been dug out. Right?'

'I think so. And take a look here. And here. And in the rubble.'

'Crêpe soles, by gum.'

'So what do you say now to the point marked bloody x?'

'I'd say the name of the game is Carter. But why? What's he up to?'

'I'll tell you this, Br'er Fox. When I looked in here at about three o'clock this hearth was as it had been for Lord knows how long.'

'Gardener left when we left,' Fox mused.

'And is digging a grave and should continue to do so for some considerable time.'

'Anybody up here since then?'

'Not Mrs Jim, at all events.'

'So we're left,' Fox said—

'With the elusive Claude. We'll have to put Bailey and Thompson in but I bet you that's going to be the story.'

'Yes. And he's seeing a man about a car,' said Fox bitterly. 'It might as well be a dog.'

'And we might as well continue in our futile ways by seeing if there's a pick and shovel on the premises. After all, he couldn't have rootled up the hearth with his fingernails. Where's the gardener's shed?'

It was near at hand, hard by the asparagus beds. They stood in the doorway and if they had entered would have fallen over a pick that lay on the floor, an untidy note in an impeccably tidy interior. Bruce kept his tools as they should be kept, polished, sharpened and in racks. Beside the pick, leaning against a bench was a lightweight shovel and nearby a crowbar.

They all bore signs of recent and hard usage.

Alleyn stooped down and without touching, examined them.

'Scratches,' he said. 'Blunted. Chucked in here in a hurry. And take a look – crêpe-soled prints on the path.'

'Is Bob your Uncle, then?' said Fox.

'If you're asking whether Claude Carter came down to the stable yard as soon as Bruce Gardener and you and I left it, dug up the hearth and returned the tools to this shed, I suppose he *is*. But if you're asking whether this means that Claude Carter murdered his stepmother, I can't say it follows as the night the day.'

Alleyn reached inside the door and took a key from a nail. He shut and locked the door and put the key in his pocket.

'Bailey and Thompson can pick it up from the nick,' he said. 'They'd better get here as soon as possible.'

He led the way back to the car. Half way there he stopped. 'I tell you what, Br'er Fox,' he said. 'I've got a strong feeling of being just a couple of lengths behind and in danger of being beaten to the post.'

'What,' said Fox pursuing his own line of thought, 'would it be? What was it? That's what I ask myself.'

'And how do you answer?'

'I don't. I can't. Can you?'

'One can always make wild guesses, of course. Mr Markos was facetious about buried treasure. He might turn out to be right.'

'Buried treasure,' Fox echoed disgustedly. 'What sort of buried treasure?'

'How do you fancy a Black Alexander stamp?' said Alleyn.

Chapter Seven

GRAVEYARD (I)

Mr Markos had stayed at Keys for only a short time after Alleyn had gone. He had quietened down quite a lot and Verity wondered if she had turned into one of those dreadful spinsters of an all too certain age who imagine that any man who shows them the smallest civility is making a pass.

He had said goodbye with a preoccupied air. His black liquid gaze was turned upon her as if in speculation. He seemed to be on the edge of asking her something but, instead, thanked her for 'suffering' him to invite himself, took her hand, kissed his own thumb and left her.

Verity cut roses and stood them in scalding water for half an hour. Then she tidied herself up and drove down to St Crispin's.

It was quite late in the afternoon when she got there. Lengthening shadows stretched out towards gravestones lolling this way and that, in and out of the sunshine. A smell, humid yet earthy, hung on the air and so did the sound of bees.

As Verity, carrying roses, climbed the steps, she heard the rhythmic, purposeful squelch of a shovel at work. It came from beyond the church and of course she knew what it was: Bruce at his task. Suddenly she was filled with a liking for Bruce, for the direct way he thought about Sybil's death and his wish to perform the only service he could provide. It no longer seemed to matter that he so readily took to sentimental manifestations and she was sorry she had made mock of them. She thought that of all Sybil's associates, even including Prunella, he was probably the only one who honestly mourned her. I won't shy off, she thought. When I've done the flowers, little as I like graves, I'll go and talk to him.

The vicar's wife and Mrs Field-Innis and the Ladies Guild, including Mrs Jim, were in the church and well advanced with their flowers and brass vases. Verity joined Mrs Jim who was in charge of Bruce's lilies from Quintern and was being bossily advised by Mrs Field-Innis what to do with them.

An unoccupied black trestle stood in the transept – waiting for Sybil. The Ladies Guild, going to and fro with jugs of water, gave it a wide berth as if, thought Verity, they were cutting it dead. They greeted Verity and spoke in special voices.

'Come on, Mrs Jim,' said Verity cheerfully, 'let's do ours together.' So they put their lilies and red roses in two big jars on either side of the chancel steps, flanking the trestle. 'They'll be gay and hopeful there,' said Verity. Some of the ladies looked as if they thought she had chosen the wrong adjectives.

When Mrs Jim had fixed the final lily in its vase, she and Verity replaced the water-jugs in their cupboard.

'Police again,' Mrs Jim muttered with characteristic abruptness. 'Same two, twice today.'

'What time?' Verity asked, equally laconic.

'Two, about. And back again before three-thirty. Give me a lift up there. Got me to let them in, and the big one drove me back. I'll have to tell Miss Prunella, won't I?'

'Yes, I expect you must.'

They went out into the westering sunlight, golden now and shining full in their faces.

'I'm going round to have a word with Bruce,' said Verity. 'Are you coming?'

'I see him before. I'm not overly keen on graves. Give me the creeps,' said Mrs Jim. 'He's making a nice job of it, though. Jim'll be pleased. He's still doubled up and crabby with it. We don't reckon he'll make it to the funeral but you never know with lumbago. I'll be getting along, then.'

The Passcoigne plot was a sunny clearing in the trees. There was quite a company of headstones there, some so old that the inscriptions were hard to make out. They stood in grass that was kept scythed but were not formally tended. Verity preferred them like that. One day the last of them would crumble and fall. Earth to earth.

Bruce had got some way with Sybil's grave and now sat on the edge of it with his red handkerchief on his knee and his bread and cheese and bottle of beer beside him. To Verity he looked a timeless figure and the gravedigger's half-forgotten doggerel came into her head.

> *In youth when I did love, did love,*
> *Methought 'twas very sweet—*

His shovel was stuck in the heap of earth he had built up and behind him was a neat pile of small sticky pine branches, sharpened at the ends. Their resinous scent hung on the air.

'You've been hard at work, Bruce.'

'I have so. There's a vein of clay runs through the soil here and that makes heavy going of it. I've broken off to eat my piece and wet my whistle and then I'll set to again. It'll tak' me all my time to get done before nightfall and there's the pine branches forby to line it.'

'That's a nice thing to do. How good they smell.'

'They do that. She'd be well enough pleased, I dare say.'

'I'm sure of it,' said Verity. She hesitated for a moment and then said, 'I've just heard about your link with Captain Carter. It must have been quite a shock for you – finding out after all these years.'

'You may weel ca' it that,' he said heavily. 'And to tell you the truth, it gets to be more of a shock, the more I think about it. Ou aye, it does so. It's unco' queer news for a body to absorb. I don't seem,' said Bruce, scratching his head, 'to be able to sort it out. He was a fine man and a fine officer, was the Captain'.

'I'm sure he was.'

'Aweel,' he said, 'I'd best get on for I've a long way to go.'

He stood up, spat on his hands and pulled his shovel out of the heap of soil.

She left him hard at work and drove herself home.

Bruce dug through sunset and twilight and when it grew dark lit an acetylene lamp. His wildly distorted shadow leapt and gesticulated among the trees. He had almost completed his task when above him, the east window, representing the Last Supper, came to life and glowed like a miraculous apparition, above his head. He heard the sound of a motor drawing up. The vicar came round the corner of the church using a torch.

'They've arrived, Gardener,' he said. 'I thought you would like to know.'

Bruce put on his coat. Together they walked round to the front of the church.

Sybil, in her coffin, was being carried up the steps. The doors were open and light from the interior flooded the entrances. Even outside, the scent of roses and lilies was heavily noticeable. The vicar in his cassock welcomed his guest for the night and walked before her into her hostelry. When he came away, locking the door behind him, he left the light on in the sanctuary. From outside the church glowed faintly.

Bruce went back to her grave.

A general police search for Claude Carter had been set up.

In his room up at Quintern, Alleyn and Fox had completed an extremely professional exploration. The room, slapped up twice a week by Mrs Jim, was drearily disordered and smelt of cigarette smoke and of an indefinable and more personal staleness. They had come at last upon a japanned tin box at the bottom of a rucksack shoved away at the top of the wardrobe. It was wrapped in a sweater and submerged in a shirt, three pairs of unwashed socks and a windjacket. The lock presented no difficulties to Mr Fox.

Inside the box was a notebook and several papers.

And among these a rough copy of the plan of the room in the stable yard, the mushroom shed and the point marked x.

2

'Earth to earth,' said the vicar, 'ashes to ashes. In sure and certain hope—'

To Alleyn, standing a little apart from them, the people round the grave composed themselves into a group that might well have been chosen by the Douanier Rousseau: simplified persons of whom the most prominent were clothed in black. Almost, they looked as if they had been cut out of cardboard, painted and then endowed with a precarious animation. One expected their movements, involving the lowering of the coffin and the ritual handful of earth, to be jerky.

There they all were and he wondered how many of them had Sybil Foster in their thoughts. Her daughter, supported on either side by the two men, now become her guardians-in-chief? Verity Preston, who stood nearby and to whom Prunella had turned when the committal began? Bruce Gardener, in Harris tweed suit, black armband and tie, decently performing his job as stand-in sexton with his gigantic wee laddie in support? Young Mr Rattisbon, decorous and perhaps a little tired from standing for so long? Mrs Jim, bright-eyed and wooden-faced? Sundry friends in the county. And finally, taller than the rest, a little apart from them, impeccably turned-out and so handsome that he looked as if he had been type-cast for the role of distinguished medico – Dr Basil Schramm, the presumably stricken but undisclosed fiancé of the deceased and her principal heir.

Claude Carter, however, was missing.

Alleyn had looked for him in church. At both sittings of the inquest Claude had contrived to get himself into an inconspicuous place and might have been supposed to lurk behind a pillar or in a sort of no-man's-land near the organ but out here in the sunny graveyard he was nowhere to be seen. There was one large Victorian angel, slightly lopsided on its massive base but pointing, like Agnes in *David Copperfield*, upwards. Alleyn trifled with the notion that Claude might be behind it and would come sidling out when all was over, but no, there was no sign of him. This was not consistent. One would have expected him to put in a token appearance. Alleyn wondered if by any chance something further had cropped up about Claude's suspected drug-smuggling activities and he was making himself scarce, accordingly. But if anything of that sort had occurred Alleyn would have been informed.

It was all over. Bruce Gardener began to fill in the grave. He was assisted by the wee lad, the six-foot adolescent known to the village as Daft Artie, he being, as was widely acknowledged, no more than fifty p. in the pound.

Alleyn, who had kept in the background, withdrew still further and waited.

People now came up to Prunella, said what they could find to say and walked away, not too fast but with the sense of release and buoyancy that follows the final disposal of (however deeply loved) the dead. Prunella shook hands, kissed, thanked. The Markos pair stood behind her and Verity a little further off.

The last to come was Dr Schramm. Alleyn saw the fractional pause before Prunella touched his offered hand. He heard her say, 'Thank you for the beautiful flowers,' loudly and quickly and Schramm murmur something inaudible. It was to Verity that Prunella turned when he had gone.

Alleyn had moved further along the pathway from the grave to the church. It was flanked by flowers lying in rows on the grass, some in Cellophane wrappings, some picked in local gardens and one enormous professional bouquet of red roses and carnations. Alleyn read the card.

'From B.S. with love.'

'Mr Alleyn?' said Prunella, coming up behind him. He turned quickly. 'It was kind of you to come,' she said. 'Thank you.'

'What nice manners you have,' Alleyn said gently. 'Your mama must have brought you up beautifully.'

She gave him a surprised look and a smile.

'Did you hear that, Godma V?' she said and she and her three supporters went down the steps and drove away.

When the vicar had gone into the vestry to take his surplice off and there was nobody left in the churchyard, Alleyn went to the grave. Bruce said, 'She's laid to her rest, then, Superintendent, and whatever brought her to it, there's no disturbing her in the latter end.'

He spat on his hands. 'Come on, lad,' he said. 'What are you gawping at?'

Impossible to say how old Daft Artie was – somewhere between puberty and manhood – with an incipient beard and a feral look as if he would have little difficulty in melting into the landscape and was prepared to do so at a moment's alarm.

He set to, with excessive, almost frantic energy. With a slurp and a flump, shovelfuls of dark, friable soil fell rhythmically into Sybil Foster's grave.

'Do you happen,' Alleyn asked Bruce, 'to have seen Mr Claude Carter this morning?'

Bruce shot a brief glance at him. 'Na, na,' he said, plying his shovel, 'I have not, but there's nothing out of the ordinary in that circumstance. Him and me don't hit it off. And forby I don't fancy he's been just all that comfortable within himself. Nevertheless, it's a disgrace on his head not to pay his last respects. Aye, I'll say that for him: a black disgrace,' said Bruce, with relish.

'When *did* you last see him?'

'Ou now – when? I couldna say with any precision. My engagements take me round the district, ye ken. I'm sleeping up at Quintern but I'm up and awa' before eight o'clock. I take my dinner with my widowed sister, Mrs Black, pure soul, up in yon cottage on the hill there and return to Quintern in time for supper and my bed, which is in the chauffeur's old room above the garage. Not all that far,' said Bruce pointedly, 'from where you unearthed him, so to speak.'

'Ah yes, by the way,' said Alleyn, 'we're keeping observation on those premises. For the time being.'

'You are! For what purpose? Och!' said Bruce irritably, 'the Lord knows and you, no doubt, won't let on.'

'Oh,' said Alleyn airily, 'it's a formality really. Pure routine. I fancy Miss Foster hasn't forgotten that her mother was thinking of turning part of the buildings into a flat for you.'

'Has she not? I wouldna mind and that's a fact. I wouldna

say no for I'm crampit up like a hen in a wee coopie where I am and, God forgive me, I'm sick and tired of listening to the praises of the recently deceased.'

'The recently deceased!' Alleyn exclaimed. 'Do you mean Mrs Foster?'

Bruce grounded his shovel and glared at him. 'I am shocked,' he said at last, pursing up his mouth to show how shocked he was and using his primmest tones, 'that you should entertain such a notion. It comes little short of an insult. I referred to the fact that my sister Mrs Black is recently widowed.'

'I beg your pardon.'

'Och, well. It was an excusable misunderstanding. So there's some idea still of fixing the flat?' He paused and stared at Alleyn. 'That's not what you'd call a reason for having the premises policed, however,' he said drily.

'Bruce,' Alleyn said. 'Do you know what Mr Carter was doing in that room on the morning I first visited you?'

Bruce gave a ringing sniff. 'That's an easy one,' he said. 'I told you yesterday. Spying. Trying to catch what you were speiring. To me. Aye, aye, that's what *he* was up to. He'd been hanging about the premises, feckless-like, making oot he was interested in mushrooms and letting on the police were in the hoose. When he heard you coming he was through the door like a rabbit and dragging it to, behind him. You needna suppose I'm not acquainted with Mr Carter's ways, Superintendent. My lady telt me aboot him and Mrs Jim's no' been backward in coming forward on the subject. When persons of his class turn aside they make a terrible bad job of themsels. Aye, they're worse by a long march than the working-class chap with some call to slip from the paths of rectitude.'

'I agree with you.'

'You can depend on it.'

'And you can't think when you last saw him?'

Bruce dragged his hand over his beard. 'When would it have been now?' he mused. 'Not today. I left the premises before eight and I was hame for dinner and after that I washed myself and changed to a decent suit for the burying. I'll tell you when it was,' he said, brightening up. 'It was yesterday morning. I ran into him in the stable yard and he asked me if I knew how the trains run to Dover. He let on he has an acquaintance there and might pay him a visit some time.'

'Did you say anything about going to the funeral?'

'Did he now? Wait, now. I canna say for certain but I carry the impression he passed a remark that led me to suppose he'd be attending the obsequies. That,' said Bruce summing up, 'is the length and breadth of my total recollection.' He took up his shovel.

The wee laddie, who had not uttered nor ceased with frantic zeal to cast earth on earth, suddenly gave tongue.

'I seen 'im,' he said loudly.

Bruce contemplated him. 'You seen who, you pure daftie?' he asked kindly.

'Him. What you're talking about.'

Bruce slightly shook his head at Alleyn, indicating the dubious value of anything the gangling creature had to offer. 'Did ye noo?' he said tolerantly.

'In the village. It weren't 'alf dark, 'cept up here where you was digging the grave, Mr Gardener, and had your 'ceterlene lamp.'

'Where'd you been, then, young Artie, stravaging abroad in the night?'

'I dunno,' said Artie, showing the whites of his eyes.

'Never mind,' Alleyn intervened. 'Where were you when you saw Mr Carter?'

'Corner of Stile Lane, under the yedge, weren't I? And him coming down into Long Lane.' He began to laugh again: the age-old guffaw of the rustic oaf. 'I give him a proper scare, din' I?' He let out an eldritch screech. 'Like that. I was in the yedge and he never knew where it come from. Reckon he was dead scared.'

'What did he do, Artie?' Alleyn asked.

'I dunno,' Artie muttered, suddenly uninterested.

'Where did he go, then?'

'I dunno.'

'You must know,' Bruce roared out. 'Oot wi' it. Where did he go?'

'I never see. I was under the yedge, wasn' I? Up the steps then, he must of, because I yeard the gate squeak. When I come out 'e'd gone.'

Bruce cast his eyes up and shook his head hopelessly at Alleyn. 'What are you trying to tell us, Artie?' he asked patiently. 'Gone *wheer*? I never saw the man and there I was, was I no'? He never came my way. Would he enter the church and keep company wi' the dead?'

This produced a strange reaction. Artie seemed to shrink into himself. He made a movement with his right hand, almost as if to bless himself with the sign of the cross, an age-old self-defensive gesture.

'Did you know,' Alleyn asked quietly, 'that Mrs Foster lay in the church last night?'

Artie looked into the half-filled grave and nodded. 'I seen it. I seen them carry it up the steps,' he whispered.

'That was before you saw Mr Carter come down the lane?'

He nodded.

Bruce said, 'Come awa', laddie. Nobody's going to find fault with you. Where did Mr Carter go? Just tell us that now.'

Artie began to whimper. 'I dunno,' he whined. 'I looked out of the yedge, din' I? And I never saw 'im again.'

'Where *did* you go?' Alleyn asked.

'Nowhere.'

Bruce said, 'Yah!' and with an air of hardly controlled exasperation returned to his work.

'You must have gone somewhere,' Alleyn said. 'I bet you're quite a one for getting about the countryside on your own. A night bird, aren't you, Artie?'

A look of complacency appeared. 'I might be,' he said, and then with a sly glance at Bruce, 'I sleep out,' he said, 'of a night. Often.'

'Did you sleep out last night? It was a warm night, wasn't it?'

'Yeah,' Artie conceded off-handedly, 'it was warm. I slep' out.'

'Where? Under the hedge?'

'In the yedge. I got a place.'

'Where you stayed hid when you saw Mr Carter?'

'That's right.' Stimulated by the recollection he repeated his screech and raucous laugh.

Bruce seemed about to issue a scandalized reproof but Alleyn checked him. 'And after that,' he said, 'you settled down and went to sleep? Is that it?'

''Course,' said Artie haughtily and attacked his shovelling with renewed energy.

'When you caught sight of him,' Alleyn asked, 'did you happen to notice how he was dressed?'

'I never see nothing to notice.'

'Was he carrying anything? A bag or suitcase?' Alleyn persisted.

'I never see nothing,' Artie repeated morosely.

Alleyn jerked his head at Artie's back. 'Is he to be relied on?' he said quietly.

'Hard to say. Weak in the head but truthful as far as he goes and that's not far.' Bruce lowered his voice. 'There's a London train goes through at five past eleven: a slow train with a passenger carriage. Stops at Great Quintern. You can walk it in an hour,' said Bruce with a steady look at Alleyn.

'Is there indeed?' said Alleyn. 'Thank you, Bruce. I won't keep you any longer but I'm very much obliged to you.'

As he turned away Artie said in a sulky voice and to nobody in particular, 'He were carrying a pack. On his back. Pleased with the rhyme he improvised, 'Pack on 'is back and down the track,' and, as an inspired addition, ' 'E'd got the sack.'

'Alas, alack,' Alleyn said and Artie giggled. 'Pack on 'is back and got the sack,' he shouted.

'Och, *havers*!' said Bruce disgustedly. 'You're nowt but a silly, wanting kind of crittur. Haud your whist and get on with your work.'

'Wait a moment,' said Alleyn, and to Artie, 'Did you sleep out all night? When did you wake up?'

'When 'e went 'ome,' said Artie, indicating the indignant Bruce. 'You woke me up, Mr Gardener, you passed that close. Whistling. I could of put the wind up you, proper, couldn't I? I could of frown a brick at you, Mr Gardener. But I never,' said Artie virtuously.

Bruce made a sound of extreme exasperation.

'When was this, Artie? You wouldn't know, would you?' said Alleyn.

'Yes, I would, then. Twelve. Church clock sounded twelve, din' it?'

'Is that right?' Alleyn asked Bruce.

'He can't count beyond ten. It was nine when I knocked off.'

'Long job you had of it.'

'I did that. There's a vein of solid clay runs through, three-foot depth of it. And after that the pine boughs to push in. It was an unco' weird experience. Everybody in the village asleep by then and an owl overhead and bats flying in and out of the lamplight. And inside the kirk, the leddy herself, cold in her coffin and me digging her grave. Aye, it was, you may say, an awfu', uneasy situation, yon. In literature,' said Bruce, lecturing them, 'it's an effect known as Gothic. I was pleased enough to have done with it.'

Alleyn lowered his voice. 'Do you think he's got it right?'

'That he slept under the hedge and woke as I passed? I dare say. It might well be, pure daftie.'

'And that he saw Carter, earlier?'

'I'd be inclined to credit it. I didna see anything of the man mysel' but then I wouldn't, where I was.'

'No, of course not. Well, thanks again,' Alleyn said. He returned to the front of the church, ran down the steps and found Fox waiting in the car.

'Back to Quintern,' he said. 'The quest for Charmless Claude sets in with a vengeance.'

'Skedaddled?'

'Too soon to say. Bruce indicates as much.'

'Ah, to hell with it,' said Fox in a disgusted voice. 'What's the story?'

Alleyn told him.

'There you are!' Fox complained when he had finished. 'Scared him off, I dare say, putting our chap in. Here's a pretty kettle of fish.'

'We'll have to take up the Dover possibility, of course, but I don't like it much. If he'd considered it as a getaway port he wouldn't have been silly enough to ask Bruce about trains. Still, we'll check. He's thought to have some link with a stationer's shop in Southampton.'

'Suppose we do run him down, what's the charge?'

'You may well ask. We've got nothing to warrant an arrest unless we can hold him for a day or two on the drug business and that seems to have petered out. We can't run him in for grubbing up an old fireplace in a disused room in his stepmother's stable yard. Our chap's found nothing to signify, I suppose?'

'Nothing, really. You've had a better haul, Mr Alleyn?'

'I don't know, Foxkin, I don't know. In one respect I think perhaps I have.'

3

When Verity drove home from the funeral it was with the expectation of what she called 'putting her boots up' and relaxing for an hour or so. She found herself to be suddenly used up and supposed that the events of the past days must have been more exhausting, emotionally, than she had realized. And after further consideration, an inborn honesty prompted her to conclude that the years were catching up on her.

'Selfishly considered,' she told herself, 'this condition has its advantages. Less is expected of one.' And then she pulled herself together. Anyone would think she was involved up to her ears in this wretched business, whereas, of course, apart from being on tap whenever her god-daughter seemed to want her, she was on the perimeter.

She had arrived at this reassuring conclusion when she turned in at her own gate and saw Basil Schramm's car drawn up in front of her house.

Schramm himself was sitting at the iron table under the lime trees.

His back was towards her but at the sound of her car, he swung round and saw her. The movement was familiar.

When she stopped he was there, opening the door for her.

'You didn't expect to see me,' he said.

'No.'

'I'm sorry to be a bore. I'd like a word or two if you'll let me.'

'I can't very well stop you,' said Verity lightly. She walked quickly to the nearest chair and was glad to sit on it. Her mouth was dry and there was a commotion going on under her ribs.

He took the other chair. She saw him through a kind of mental double focus: as he had been when, twenty-five years ago, she made a fool of herself, and as he was now, not so much changed or aged as exposed.

'I'm going to ask you to be terribly, terribly kind,' he said and waited.

'Are you?'

'Of course you'll think it bloody cool. It is bloody cool but you've always been a generous creature, Verity, haven't you?'

'I shouldn't depend on it, if I were you.'

'Well – I can but try.' He took out his cigarette case. It was silver with a sliding action. 'Remember?' he said. He slid it open and offered it to her. She had given it to him.

Verity said, 'No, thank you, I don't.'

'You used to. How strong-minded you are. I shouldn't, of course, but I do.' He gave his rather empty social laugh and lit a cigarette. His hands were unsteady.

Verity thought, I know the line I ought to take if he says what I think he's come here to say. But can I take it? Can I avoid saying things that will make him suppose I still mind? I know this situation. After it's all over you think of how dignified and quiet and unmoved you should have been and remember how you gave yourself away at every turn. As I did when he degraded me.

He was preparing his armoury. She had often, even when she had been most attracted, thought how transparent and silly and predictable were his ploys.

'I'm afraid,' he was saying, 'I'm going to talk about old times. Will you mind very much?'

'I can't say I see much point in the exercise,' she said cheerfully. 'But I don't *mind*, really.'

'I hoped you wouldn't.'

He waited, thinking perhaps that she would invite him to go on. When she said nothing he began again.

'It's nothing, really. I didn't mean to give it a great build-up. It's just an invitation for you to preserve what they call "a masterly inactivity".' He laughed again.

'Yes?'

'About – well, Verity, I expect you've guessed what about, haven't you?'

'I haven't tried.'

'Well, to be quite honest and straightforward—' He boggled for a moment.

'Quite honest and straightforward?' Verity couldn't help repeating but she managed to avoid a note of incredulity. She was reminded of another stock phrase-maker – Mr Markos and his 'quite cold-bloodedly'.

'It's about that silly business a thousand years ago at St Luke's,' Schramm was saying. 'I dare say you've forgotten all about it.'

'I could hardly do that.'

'I know it looked bad. I know I ought to have – well – asked to see you and explain. Instead of – all right, then—'

'Bolting?' Verity suggested.

'Yes. All right. But you know there were extenuating circumstances. I was in a bloody bad jam for money and I would have paid it back.'

'But you never got it. The bank questioned the signature on the cheque, didn't they? And my father didn't make a charge.'

'Very big of him! He only gave me the sack and shattered my career.'

Verity stood up. 'It would be ridiculous and embarrassing to discuss it. I think I know what you're going to ask. You want me to say I won't tell the police. Is that it?'

'To be perfectly honest—'

'Oh, *don't*,' Verity said, and closed her eyes.

'I'm sorry. Yes, that's it. It's just that they're making nuisances of themselves and one doesn't want to present them with ammunition.'

Verity was painfully careful and slow over her answer. She said, 'If you are asking me not to go to Mr Alleyn and tell him that when you were one of my father's students I had an affair with you and that you used this as a stepping-stone to forging my father's signature on a cheque – no, I don't propose to do that.'

She felt nothing more than a reflected embarrassment when she saw the red flood into his face, but she did turn away.

She heard him say, 'Thank you for that, at least. I don't deserve it and I didn't deserve you. God, what a fool I was!'

She thought, I mustn't say 'in more ways than one'. She made herself look at him and said, 'I think I should tell you that I know you were engaged to Sybil. It's obvious that the police believe there was foul play and I imagine that as a principal legatee under the Will—'

He shouted her down, 'You can't – Verity, you would never think I – I – ? Verity?'

'Killed her?'

'My God!'

'No. I don't think you did that. But I must tell you that if Mr Alleyn finds out about St Luke's and the cheque episode and asks me if it was all true, I shan't lie to him. I shan't elaborate or make any statements. On the contrary I shall probably say I prefer not to answer. But I shan't lie.'

'By God,' he repeated, staring at her. 'So you haven't forgiven me, have you?'

'Forgiven? It doesn't arise.' Verity looked squarely at him. 'That's true, Basil. It's the wrong sort of word. It upsets me to look back at what happened, of course it does. After all, one has one's pride. But otherwise the question's academic. Forgiven you? I suppose I must have but – no, it doesn't arise.'

'And if you "prefer not to answer",' he said, sneering it seemed at himself as much as at her, 'what's Alleyn going to think? Not much doubt about that one, is there? Look here, has he been at you already?'

'He came to see me.'

'What for? Why? Was it about – that other nonsense? On Capri?'

'In the long vacation? When you practised as a qualified doctor? No, he said nothing about that.'

'It was a joke. A ridiculous old hypochondriac, dripping with jewels and crying out for it. What did it matter?'

'It mattered when they found out at St Luke's.'

'Bloody pompous lot of stuffed shirts. I knew a damn sight more medics than most of their qualified teachers' pets.'

'Have you *ever* qualified? No, don't tell me,' said Verity quickly.

'Has Nick Markos talked about me? To you?'

'No.'

'Really?'

'Yes, Basil, really,' she said and tried to keep the patient sound out of her voice.

'I only wondered. Not that he'd have anything to say that mattered. It's just that you seemed to be rather thick with him, I thought.'

There was only one thing now that Verity wanted and she wanted it urgently. It was for him to go away. She had no respect left for him and had had none for many years but it was awful to have him there, pussy-footing about in the ashes of their past and making such a shabby job of it. She felt ashamed and painfully sorry for him too.

'Was that all you wanted to know?' she asked.

'I think so. No, there's one other thing. You won't believe this but it happens to be true. Ever since that dinner-party at Mardling, when we met again, I've had – I mean I've not been able to get you out of my head. You haven't changed all that much, Verry. Whatever you may say, it was very pleasant. Us. Well, wasn't it? What? Come on, be honest. Wasn't it quite fun?'

He actually put his hand over hers. She was aghast. Something of her incredulity and enormous distaste must have appeared in her face. He withdrew his hand as if it had been scalded.

'I'd better get on my tin tray and slide off,' he said. 'Thank you for seeing me.'

He got into his car. Verity went indoors and gave herself a strong drink. The room felt cold.

Claude Carter had gone. His rucksack and its contents had disappeared and some of his undelicious garments. His room was in disorder. It had not been Mrs Jim's day at Quintern Place. She had shown Alleyn where her key was always hidden – under a stone in the coal house – and they had let themselves in with it.

There was a note scrawled on a shopping-pad in the kitchen. 'Away for an indefinite time. Will let you know if and when I return. C.C.' No date. No time.

And now, in his room, they searched again and found nothing of interest until Alleyn retrieved a copy of last week's local newspaper from the floor behind the unmade bed.

He looked through it. On the advertisement page under 'Cars for Sale' he found, half way down the column, a ring round an insertion that offered a 1964 Heron for £500 or nearest offer. The telephone number had been underlined.

'He gave it out,' Alleyn reminded Fox, 'that he was seeing a man about a car.'

'Will I ring them?'

'If you please, Br'er Fox.'

But before Fox could do so a distant telephone began to ring. Alleyn opened the door and listened. He motioned to Fox to follow him and walked down the passage towards the stairhead.

The telephone in the hall below could now be heard. He ran down the stairs and answered it, giving the Quintern number.

'Er yes,' said a very loud man's voice. 'Would this be the gentleman who undertook to buy a '64 Heron off of me and was to collect it yesterday evening? Name of Carter?'

'He's out at the moment, I'm afraid. Can I take a message?'

'Yes, you can. I'll be obliged if he'll ring up and inform me one way or the other. If he don't, I'll take it the sale's off and dispose of the vehicle elsewhere. He can collect his deposit when it bloody suits him. Thank *you*.'

The receiver was jammed back before Alleyn could reply.

'Hear that?' he asked Fox.

'Very put about, wasn't he? Funny that. Deposit paid down and all. Looks like something urgent cropped up to make him have it on the toes,' said Fox, meaning 'bolt'. 'Or it might be he couldn't raise the principal. What do you reckon, Mr Alleyn?

He's only recently returned from abroad so his passport ought to be in order.'

'Presumably.'

'Or he may be tucked away somewhere handy or gone to try and raise the cash for the car. Have we got anything on his associates?'

'Nothing to write home about. His contact in the suspected drug business is thought to be this squalid little stationer's shop in Southampton: one of the sort that provides an accommodation address. It's called 'The Good Read' and is in Port Lane.'

'Sussy on drugs,' Fox mused, 'and done for blackmail.'

'Attempted blackmail. The victim didn't play ball. He charged him and Claude did three months. Blackmail tends to be a chronic condition. He may have operated at other times with success.'

'What's our move, then?'

'Complete this search and then get down to the village again and see if we can find anything to bear out Artie's tale of Claude's nocturnal on-goings.'

When they arrived back at the village and inspected the hedgerow near the corner of Stile Lane and Long Lane they soon found what they sought, a hole in the tangle of saplings, blackthorn and weeds that could be crept into from the field beyond and was masked from the sunken lane below by grasses and wild parsnip. Footprints from a hurdle gate into the field led to the hole and a flattened depression within it where they found five cigarette butts and as many burnt matches. Clear of the hedge was an embryo fireplace constructed of a few old bricks and a crossbar of wood supported by two cleft sticks.

'Snug,' said Fox. 'And here's where sonny-boy plays Indian.'

'That's about the form.'

'And kips with the bunnies and tiggywinkles.'

'And down the lane comes Claude with his pack on his back.'

'All of a summer's night.'

'All right, all right. He must have passed more or less under Artie's nose.'

'Within spitting range,' Fox agreed.

'Come on.'

Alleyn led the way back into Long Lane and to the lych-gate at the foot of the church steps. He pushed it open and it squeaked.

'I wonder,' Alleyn said, 'how many people have walked up

those steps since nine o'clock last night. The whole funeral procession.'

'That's right,' said Fox gloomily.

'Coffin bearers, mourners. Me. After that, tidying-uppers, and the vicar, one supposes.'

He stooped down, knelt, peered. 'Yes, I think so,' he said. 'On the damp earth the near side of the gate and well to the left In the shelter of the lych, if that's the way to put it. Very faint but I fancy they're our old friends the crêpe-soled shoes. Take a look.'

Fox did so. 'Yes,' he said. 'By gum, I think so.'

'More work for Bill Bailey and until he gets here the local copper can undisguise himself and take another turn at masterly inactivity. So far it's one up to Artie.'

'Not a chance of anything on the steps.'

'I'm afraid, not a chance. Still – up we go.'

They climbed the steps, slowly and searchingly. Inside the church the organ suddenly blared and infant voices shrilled.

Through the night of doubt and sorrow—

'Choir practice,' said Alleyn. 'Damn. Not an inappropriate choice, though, when you come to think of it.'

The steps into the porch showed signs of the afternoon's traffic. Alleyn took a look inside. The vicar's wife was seated at the organ with five little girls and two little boys clustered round her. When she saw Alleyn her jaw dropped in the middle of 'Onward'. He made a pacifying signal and withdrew. He and Fox walked round the church to Sybil Foster's grave.

Bruce and Artie had taken trouble over finishing their job. The flowers – Bruce would certainly call them 'floral tributes', no longer lined the path but had been laid in meticulous order on the mound which they completely covered, stalks down, blossoms pointing up, in receding size. The Cellophane covers on the professional offerings glistened in the sun and looked, Alleyn thought, awful. On the top, as a sort of baleful *bonne-bouche*, was the great sheaf of red roses and carnations: 'From B.S. with love'.

'It's quite hopeless,' Alleyn said. 'There must have been thirty or more people tramping round the place. If ever his prints were here they've been trodden out. We'd better take a look but we won't find.'

And nor they did.

'Not to be fanciful,' Fox said. 'As far as the footsteps go it's like coming to the end of a trail. Room with the point marked x, gardener's shed, broom recess, lych-gate and – nothing. It would have been appropriate, you might say, if they'd finished up for keeps at the graveside.'

Alleyn didn't answer for a second or two.

'You do,' he then said, 'get the oddest flights of fancy. It *would* in a macabre sort of way have been dramatically satisfactory.'

'If he did her, that is.'

'Ah. If.'

'Well,' said Fox, 'it looks pretty good to me. How else do you explain the ruddy prints? He lets on he's an electrician, he takes up the lilies, he hides in the recess and when the coast's clear he slips in and does her. Motive: the cash – a lot of it. You *can't* explain it any other way.'

'Can't you?'

'Well, can you?'

'We mentioned his record, didn't we? Blackmail. Shouldn't we perhaps bestow a passing thought on that?'

'Here! Wait a bit – wait a bit,' said Fox, startled. He became broody and remained so all the way to Great Quintern.

They drove to the police station where Alleyn had established his headquarters and been given a sort of mini-office next door to the charge room. It had a table, three chairs, writing material and a telephone which was all he expected to be given and suited him very well.

The sergeant behind the counter in the front office was on the telephone when they came in. When he saw Alleyn he raised his hand.

'Just a minute, madam,' he said. 'The Chief Superintendent has come in. Will you hold on, please?' He put his enormous hand over the receiver. 'It's a lady asking for you, sir. She seems to be upset. Shall I take the name?'

'Do.'

'What name was it, madam? Yes, madam, he *is* here. What name shall I say? Thank you. Hold the line, please,' said the sergeant, re-stopping the receiver. 'It's a Sister Jackson, sir. She says it's very urgent.'

Alleyn gave a long whistle, pulled a face at Fox and said he'd take the call in his room.

Sister Jackson's voice, when it came through, was an extraordinary mixture of refinement and what sounded like sheer terror. She whispered, and her whisper was of the piercing kind. She gasped, she faded out altogether and came back with a rush. She apologized for being silly and said she didn't know what he would think of her. Finally, she breathed heavily into the receiver, said she was 'in shock' and wanted to see him. She could not elaborate over the telephone.

Alleyn, thoughtfully contemplating Mr Fox, said he would come to Greengages, upon which she gave an instantly muffled shriek and said no, no that would never do and that she had the evening off and would meet him in the bar parlour of the Iron Duke on the outskirts of Maidstone. 'It's quite nice, really,' she quavered.

'Certainly,' Alleyn said. 'What time?'

'About nayne?'

'Nine let it be. Cheer up, Sister. You don't feel like giving me an inkling as to what it's all about?'

When she answered she had evidently put her mouth inside the receiver.

'Blackmail,' she articulated and his eardrum tingled.

Approaching voices were to be heard. Sister Jackson came through from a normal distance. 'OK,' she cried, 'that'll be fantastic, cheery-bye,' and hung up.

'Blackmail,' Alleyn said to Fox. 'We've only got to mention it and up it rises.'

'Well!' said Fox. 'Fancy that! Would it be going too far to mention Claude?'

'Who can tell? But at least it's suggestive. I'll leave you to get things laid on up in the village. Where are Bailey and Thompson, by the way?'

'Doing the fireplace and the tool shed. They're to ring back here before leaving.'

'Right. Get the local copper to keep an eye on the lych-gate until B. and T. arrive. Having dealt with that and just to show zealous they may then go over the churchyard area and see if they can find a trace we've missed. And having turned them on, Fox, check the progress if any of the search for Claude Carter. Oh, and see if you can get a check on the London train from Great Quintern at eleven-five last night. I think that's the lot.'

'You don't require me at the Iron Duke?'

'No. *La belle Jackson* is clearly not in the mood. Sickening for you.'

'We'll meet at our pub, then?'

'Yes.'

'I shan't wait up,' said Fox.

'Don't dream of it.'

'In the meantime, I'll stroll down to the station hoping for better luck than I had with the Greengages bus.'

'Do. I'll bring my file up to date.'

'Were you thinking of taking dinner at the Iron Duke?'

'I was thinking of taking worm-coloured fish in pink sauce and athletic fowl at our own pub. Do join me.'

'Thanks. That's all settled then,' said Fox comfortably, and took himself off.

5

There were only seven customers in the bar parlour of the Iron Duke when Alleyn walked in at a quarter to nine: an amorous couple at a corner table and five city-dressed men playing poker.

Alleyn took a glass of a respectable port to a banquette at the furthest remove from the other tables and opened the evening paper. A distant roar of voices from the two bars bore witness to the Duke's popularity. At five to nine Sister Jackson walked in. He received the slight shock caused by an encounter with a nurse seen for the first time out of uniform. Sister Jackson was sheathed in clinging blue with a fairly reckless cleavage. She wore a velvet beret that rakishly shaded her face, and insistent gloves. He saw that her make-up was more emphatic than usual, especially about the eyes. She had been crying.

'How punctual we both are,' he said. He turned a chair to the table with its back to the room and facing the banquette. She sat in it without looking at him and with a movement of her shoulders that held a faint suggestion of what might have passed as provocation under happier circumstances. He asked her what she would have to drink and when she hesitated and bridled a little, proposed brandy.

'Well – thank you,' she said. He ordered a double one. When it came she took a sudden pull at it, shuddered and said she had been under a severe strain. It was the first remark of more than three words that she had offered.

'This seems quite a pleasant pub,' he said. 'Do you often come here?'

'No. Never. They – we – all use the Crown at Greenvale. That's why I suggested it. To be sure.'

'I'm glad,' Alleyn said, 'that whatever it's all about you decided to tell me.'

'It's very difficult to begin.'

'Never mind. Try. You said something about blackmail, didn't you? Shall we begin there?'

She stared at him for an awkwardly long time and then suddenly opened her handbag, pulled out a folded paper and thrust it across the table. She then took another pull at her brandy.

Alleyn unfolded the paper, using his pen and a fingernail to do so. 'Were you by any chance wearing gloves when you handled this?' he asked.

'As it happened. I was going out. I picked it up at the desk.'

'Where's the envelope?'

'I don't know. Yes, I do. I think. On the floor of my car. I opened it in the car.'

The paper was now spread out on the table. It was a kind as well known to the police as to a hand-bill: a piece of off-white commercial paper, long and narrow, that might have been torn from a domestic *aide-mémoire*. The message was composed of words and letters that had been cut from newsprint and gummed in two irregular lines.

'Post £500 fives and singles to C. Morris, 11 Port Lane Southampton otherwise will inform police your visit to room 20 Genuine.'

Alleyn looked at Sister Jackson and Sister Jackson looked like a mesmerized rabbit at him.

'When did it come?'

'Yesterday morning.'

'To Greengages?'

'Yes.'

'Is the envelope addressed in this fashion?'

'Yes. My name's all in one. I recognized it – it's from an advertisement in the local rag for Jackson's Drapery and it's the same with Greengages Hotel. Cut out of an advertisement.'

'You didn't comply, of course?'

'No. I didn't know what to do. I – nothing like that's ever happened to me – I – I was dreadfully upset.'

'You didn't ask anyone to advise you?'

She shook her head.

'Dr Schramm, for instance?'

He could have sworn that her opulent flesh did a little hop and that for the briefest moment an extremely vindictive look clicked on and off. She wetted her mouth. 'Oh no,' she whispered. 'No, *thank* you!'

'This is the only message you've received?'

'There's been something else. Something much worse. Last evening. Soon after eight. They fetched me from the dining-room!'

'What was it? A telephone call?'

'You knew!'

'I guessed. Go on, please.'

'When the waiter told me, I knew. I don't know why but I did. I knew. I took it in one of the telephone boxes in the hall. I think he must have had something over his mouth. His voice was muffled and peculiar. It said, "You got the message." I couldn't speak and then it said, "You did or you'd answer. Have you followed instructions?" I – didn't know what to say, so I said, "I will," and it said, "You better." It said something else, I don't remember exactly, something about the only warn-ing, I think. That's all,' said Sister Jackson, and finished her cognac. She held the unsteady glass between her white-gloved paws and put it down awkwardly.

Alleyn said, 'Do you mind if I keep this? And would you be kind enough to refold it and put it in here for me?' He took an envelope from his pocket and laid it beside the paper.

She complied and made a shaky business of doing so. He put the envelope in his breast pocket.

'What will he do to me?' asked Sister Jackson.

'The odds are: nothing effective. The police may get some-thing from him but you've anticipated that, haven't you? Or you will do so.'

'I don't understand.'

'Sister Jackson,' Alleyn said, 'don't you think you had better tell me about your visit to Room 20?'

She tried to speak. Her lips moved. She fingered them and then looked at the smudge of red on her glove.

'Come along,' he said.

'You won't understand.'

'Try me.'

'I can't.'

'Then why have you asked to see me? Surely it was to antici-pate whatever the concoctor of this message might have to say to us. You've got in first.'

'I haven't done anything awful. I'm a fully qualified nurse.'

'Of course you are. Now then, when did you pay this visit?'

She focused her gaze on the couple in the far corner, stiffened her neck and rattled off her account in a series of disjointed phrases.

It had been at about nine o'clock on the night of Mrs Foster's death (Sister Jackson called it her 'passing'). She herself walked down the passage on her way to her own quarters. She heard the television bawling away in No. 20. Pop music. She knew Mrs Foster didn't appreciate pop and she thought she might have fallen asleep and the noise would disturb the occupants of neighbouring rooms. So she tapped and went in.

Here Sister Jackson paused. A movement of her chin and throat indicated a dry swallow. When she began again her voice was pitched higher but not by any means louder than before.

'The patient,' she said, 'Mrs Foster, I mean, was as I thought she would be. Asleep. I looked at her and made sure she was – asleep. So I came away. *I came away.* I wasn't there for more than three minutes. That's all. All there is to tell you.'

'How was she lying?'

'On her side, with her face to the wall.'

'When Dr Schramm found her she was on her back.'

'I know. That proves it. Doesn't it. *Doesn't it?*'

'Did you turn off the television?'

'No. Yes! I don't remember. I think I must have. I don't know.'

'It was still going when Dr Schramm found her.'

'Well, I didn't then, did I? I didn't turn it off.'

'Why, I wonder?'

'It's no good asking me things like that. I've been shocked. I don't remember details.'

She beat on the table. The amorous couple unclinched and one of the card players looked over his shoulder. Sister Jackson had split her glove.

Alleyn said, 'Should we continue this conversation somewhere else?'

'No. I'm sorry.'

With a most uncomfortable parody of coquettishness she leant across the table and actually smiled or seemed to smile at him.

'I'll be all right,' she said.

Their waiter came back and looked enquiringly at her empty glass.

'Would you like another?' Alleyn asked.

'I don't think so. No. Well, a small one, then.'

The waiter was quick bringing it.

'Right. Now – how was the room? The bedside table? Did you notice the bottle of barbiturates?'

'I didn't notice. I've said so. I just saw she was asleep and I went away.'

'Was the light on in the bathroom?'

This seemed to terrify her. She said, 'Do you mean – ? Was he *there*? Whoever it was? Hiding? Watching? No, the door was shut, I mean – I think it was shut.'

'Did you see anybody in the passage? Before you went into the room or when you left it?'

'No.'

'Sure?'

'Yes.'

'There's that alcove, isn't there? Where the brooms and vacuum-cleaner are kept?'

She nodded. The amorous couple were leaving. The man helped the girl into her coat. They both looked at Alleyn and Sister Jackson. She fumbled in her bag and produced a packet of cigarettes.

Alleyn said, 'I'm sorry. I've given up and forget to keep any on me. At least I can offer you a light.' He did so and she made a clumsy business of using it. The door swung to behind the couple. The card players had finished their game and decided, noisily, to move into the bar. When they had gone Alleyn said, 'You realize, don't you – well, of course you do – that the concoctor of this threat must have seen you?'

She stared at him. 'Naturally,' she said, attempting, he thought, a sneer.

'Yes,' he said. 'It's a glimpse of the obvious, isn't it? And you'll remember that I showed you a lily-head that Inspector Fox and I found in the alcove?'

'Of course.'

'And that there were similar lilies in the hand-basin in Mrs Foster's bathroom?'

'Naturally. I mean – yes, I saw them afterwards. When we used the stomach pump. We scrubbed up under the bath taps. It was quicker than clearing away the mess in the basin.'

'So it follows as the night the day that the person who dropped the lily-head in the alcove was the person who put the flowers in the hand-basin. Does it also follow that this same person was your blackmailer?'

'I – yes. I suppose it might.'

'And does it also follow, do you think, that the blackmailer was the murderer of Mrs Foster?'

'But you don't know. You don't know that she was – *that*.'

'We believe we do.'

She ought, he thought, to be romping about like a Rubens lady in an Arcadian setting – all sumptuous flesh, no brains and as happy as Larry, instead of quivering like an over-dressed jelly in a bar parlour.

'Sister Jackson,' he said, 'why didn't you tell the Coroner or the police or anyone at all, that you went into Room 20 at about nine o'clock that night and found Mrs Foster asleep in her bed?'

She opened and shut her smudged lips two or three times, gaping like a fish.

'Nobody asked me,' she said. 'Why should I?'

'Are you sure Mrs Foster was asleep?'

Her lips formed the words but she had no voice. 'Of course I am.'

'She wasn't asleep, was she? She was dead.'

The swing door opened and Basil Schramm walked in. 'I thought I'd find you,' he said. 'Good evening.'

Chapter Eight

GRAVEYARD (II)

'May I join you?' asked Dr Schramm. The folds from his nostrils to the corners of his mouth lifted and intensified. It was almost a mephistophelian grin.

'Do,' said Alleyn and turned to Sister Jackson. 'If Sister Jackson approves,' he said.

She looked at nothing, said nothing and compressed her mouth.

'Silence,' Dr Schramm joked, 'gives consent, I hope.' And he sat down.

'What are you drinking?' he invited.

'Not another for me, thank you,' said Alleyn.

'On duty?'

'That's my story.'

'Dot?'

Sister Jackson stood up. 'I'm afraid I must go,' she said to Alleyn and with tolerable success achieved a social manner. 'I hadn't realized it was so late.'

'It isn't late,' said Schramm, 'sit down.'

She sat down. First round to the doctor, thought Alleyn.

'The bell's by you, Alleyn,' said Schramm. 'Do you mind?'

Alleyn pressed the wall bell above his head. Schramm had leant forward. Alleyn caught a great wave of whisky and saw that his eyes were bloodshot and not quite in focus.

'I happened to be passing,' he chatted. He inclined his head towards Sister Jackson. 'I noticed your car. And yours, Superintendent.'

'Sister Jackson has been kind enough to clear up a detail for us.'

'That's what's known as "helping the police in their investigations", isn't it? With grim connotations as a rule.'

'You've been reading the popular press,' said Alleyn.

The waiter came in. Schramm ordered a large scotch. 'Sure?' he asked them and then, to the waiter, 'Correction. Make that two large scotches.'

Alleyn said, 'Not for me. Really.'

'Two large scotches,' Schramm repeated on a high note. The waiter glanced doubtfully at Alleyn.

'You heard what I said,' Schramm insisted. 'Two large scotches.'

Alleyn thought, This is the sort of situation where one could do with the odd drop of omnipotence. One wrong move from me and it'll be a balls-up.

Complete silence set in. The waiter came and went. Dr Schramm downed one of the two double whiskies very quickly. The bar parlour clock ticked. He continued to smile and began on the second whisky slowly, with concentration, absorbing it and cradling the glass. Sister Jackson remained perfectly still.

'What's she been telling you?' Schramm suddenly demanded. 'She's an inventive lady. You ought to realize that. To be quite, quite frank and honest, she's a liar of the first water. Aren't you, sweetie?'

'You followed me.'

'It's some considerable time since I left off doing that, darling.'

Alleyn had the passing thought that it would be nice to hit Dr Schramm.

'I really must insist,' Schramm said. 'I'm sorry, but you have seen for yourself how things are, here. I realize, perf'ly well, that you will think I had a motive for this crime, if crime it was. Because I am a legatee I'm a suspect. So of course it's no good my saying that I asked Sybil Foster to marry me. *Not*,' he said wagging his finger at Alleyn, '*not* because I'd got my sights set on her money but because I loved her. Which I did, and that,' he added, staring at Sister Jackson, 'is precisely where the trouble lies.' His speech was now all over the place like an actor's in a comic drunken scene. 'You wouldn't have minded if it had been like that. You wouldn't have minded all that much if you believed I'd come back earlier and killed her for her money. You really are a bitch, aren't you, Dotty? My God, you even threatened to take to her yourself. Didn't you? Well, didn't you? Where's the bloody waiter?'

He got to his feet, lurched across the table and fetched up with the palms of his hands on the wall, the left supporting him and the right clamped down over the bell-push which could be heard distantly to operate. His face was within three inches of Alleyn's. Sister Jackson shrank back in her chair.

'Disgusting!' she said.

Alleyn detached Dr Schramm from the wall and replaced him in his chair. He then moved over to the door, anticipating the return of the waiter. When the man arrived Alleyn showed his credentials.

'The gentleman's had as much as is good for him,' he said. 'Let me handle it. There's a side door, isn't there?'

'Well, yes,' said the waiter, looking dubious. 'Sir,' he added.

'He's going to order another scotch. Can you cook up a poor single to look like a double? Here – this'll settle the lot and forget the change. Right?'

'Well, thank you very much, sir,' said the waiter, suddenly avid with curiosity and gratification, 'I'll do what I can.'

'Waiter!' shouted Dr Schramm. 'Same 'gain.'

'There's your cue,' said Alleyn.

'What'll I say to him?'

' "Anon, anon, sir" would do.'

'Would that be Shakespeare?' hazarded the waiter.

'It would, indeed.'

Waiter!

' "Anon, anon, sir," ' said the waiter self-consciously. He collected the empty glasses and hurried away.

' 'Strordinary waiter,' said Dr Schramm. 'As I was saying. I insist on being informed for reasons that I shall make 'bundantly clear. What's she said? 'Bout me?'

'You didn't feature in our conversation,' said Alleyn.

'That's what you say.'

Sister Jackson, with a groggy and terrified return to something like her habitual manner, said, 'I wouldn't demean myself.' She turned on Alleyn. 'You're mad,' she said, exactly as if there had been no break in their exchange. 'You don't know what you're talking about. She was asleep.'

'Why didn't you report your visit, then?' Alleyn said.

'It didn't matter.'

'Oh, nonsense. It would have established, if true, that she was alive at that time.'

With one of those baffling returns to apparent sobriety by which drunken persons sometimes bewilder us, Dr Schramm said, 'Do I understand, Sister, that you visited her in her room?'

Sister Jackson ignored him. Alleyn said, 'At about nine o'clock.'

'And didn't report it? Why? *Why?*' he appealed to Alleyn.

'I don't know. Perhaps because she was afraid. Perhaps because—'

Sister Jackson gave a strangulated cry. 'No! No, for God's

sake! He'll get it all wrong. He'll jump to conclusions. It wasn't like that. She was asleep. Natural sleep. There was nothing the matter with her.'

The waiter came back with a single glass, half full.

'Take that away,' Schramm ordered. 'I've got to have a clear head. Bring some ice. Bring me a lot of ice.'

The waiter looked at Alleyn, who nodded. He went out.

'I'm going,' said Sister Jackson.

'You'll stay where you are unless you want a clip over the ear.'

'And you,' said Alleyn, 'will stay where you are unless you want to be run in. Behave yourself.'

Schramm stared at him for a moment. He said something that sounded like, 'Look who's talking,' and took an immaculate handkerchief from his breast pocket, laid it on the table and began to fold it diagonally. The waiter reappeared with a jug full of ice.

'I really ought to mention this to the manager, sir,' he murmured. 'If he gets noisy again, I'll have to.'

'I'll answer for you. Tell the manager it's an urgent police matter. Give him my card. Here you are.'

'It – it wouldn't be about that business over at Greengages, would it?'

'Yes, it would. Give me the ice and vanish, there's a good chap.'

Alleyn put the jug on the table. Schramm, with shaking hands, began to lay ice on his folded handkerchief.

'Sister,' he said impatiently. 'Make a pack, if you please.'

To Alleyn's utter astonishment she did so in a very professional manner. Schramm loosened his tie and opened his shirt. It was as if they both responded like Pavlovian dogs to some behaviouristic prompting. He rested his forehead on the table and she placed the pack of ice on the back of his neck. He gasped. A trickle of water ran down his jawline. 'Keep it up,' he ordered and shivered.

Alleyn, watching this performance, thought how unpredictable the behaviour of drunken persons could be. Sister Jackson had been in the condition so inaccurately known as 'nicely, thank you'. Basil Schramm had been in an advanced stage of intoxication but able to assess his own condition and after a fashion deal with it. And there they were, both of them, behaving like automata and, he felt sure, frightened out of what wits they still, however precariously, commanded.

187

She continued to operate the ice packs. A pool of water enlarged itself on the table and began to drip to the carpet.

'That's enough,' Schramm said presently. Sister Jackson squeezed his handkerchief into the jug. Alleyn offered his own and Schramm mopped himself up with it. He fastened his shirt and reknotted his tie. As if by common consent he and Sister Jackson sat down simultaneously, facing each other across the table with Alleyn between them on the banquette – like a referee, he thought. This effect was enhanced when he took out his notebook. They paid not the smallest attention to him. They glared at each other. He with distaste and she with hatred. He produced a comb and used it.

'Now, then,' he said. 'What's the story? You went to her room at nine. You say she was asleep. And *you* – ' he jabbed a finger at Alleyn – 'say she was dead. Right?'

'I don't say so positively. I suggested it.'

'Why?'

'For several reasons. If Mrs Foster was sleeping, peacefully and naturally, it's difficult to see why Sister Jackson did not report her visit.'

'If there'd been anything wrong, I would have,' she said.

Schramm said, 'Did you think it was suicide?'

'She was asleep.'

'Did you see the tablets – spilled on the table?'

'No. *No.*'

'Did you think she'd been drugged?'

'She was asleep. Peacefully and naturally. Asleep.'

'You're lying, aren't you? Aren't you? Come on!'

She began to gabble at Alleyn. 'It was the shock you know. When he rang through and told me, I came and we did everything – such a shock – I couldn't remember anything about how the room had looked before. Naturally not.'

'It was no shock to you,' Dr Schramm said profoundly. 'You're an old hand. An experienced nurse. And you didn't regret her death, my dear. You gloated. You could hardly keep a straight face.'

'Don't listen to this,' Sister Jackson gabbled at Alleyn, 'it's all lies. Monstrous lies. Don't listen.'

'You'd better,' said Schramm. 'This is the hell-knows-no-fury bit, Superintendent, and you may as well recognize it. Oh, yes. She actually said when she heard about Sybil and me that she bloody well wished Syb was dead and she meant it. Fact, I assure you. And I don't mind telling you she felt the same about me. Still does. Look at her.'

Sister Jackson was hardly a classical figure of panic but she certainly presented a strange picture. The velvet beret had flopped forward over her left eye so that she was obliged to tilt her head back at an extravagant angle in order to see from under it. Oddly enough, and deeply unpleasant as the situation undoubtedly was, she reminded Alleyn momentarily of a grotesque lady on a comic postcard.

They began to exchange charge and countercharge, often speaking simultaneously. It was the kind of row that is welcome as manna from Heaven to an investigating officer. Alleyn noted it all down, almost under their noses, and was conscious, as often before, of a strong feeling of distaste for the job.

They repeated themselves *ad nauseam*. She used the stock phrases of the discarded mistress. He, as he became articulate, also grew reckless and made more specific his accusations about her having threatened to do harm to Sybil Foster and even hinted that on her visit to Room 20 she might well have abetted Sybil in taking an overdose.

At that point they stopped dead, stared aghast at each other and then, for the first time since the slanging match had set in, at Alleyn.

He finished his notes and shut the book.

'I could,' he said, 'and perhaps I should, ask you both to come to the police station and make statements. You would then refuse to utter or to write another word until you had seen your respective solicitors. A great deal of time would be wasted. Later on you would both state that you had been dead drunk and that I had brought about this pitiable condition and made false reports about your statements and taken them down in writing. All this would be very boring and unproductive. Instead, I propose that you go back to Greengages, think things over and then concoct your statements. You've been too preoccupied to notice, I fancy, but I've made pretty extensive notes and I shall make a report of the conversation and, in due course, invite you to sign it. And now, I expect you will like to go. If, that is, you are in a fit state to drive. If not, you'd better go to the lavatories and put your fingers down your throats. I'll be in touch. Good evening.'

He left them gaping and went out to his car where he waited

about five minutes before they appeared severally, walking with unnatural precision. They entered their cars and drove, very slowly, away.

2

Fox had not gone to bed at their pub. He and Alleyn took a nightcap together in Alleyn's room.

'Well, now,' said Fox, rubbing his hands on his knees. 'That was a turn-up for the books, wasn't it? I'd've liked to be there. How do you read it, then, Mr Alleyn? As regards the lady, now? Dropped in on the deceased round about nine p.m. and was watched by crêpe-soles from the alcove and is being black-mailed by him. Which gives us one more reason, if we'd needed it, for saying crêpe-soles is Claude?'

'Go on.'

'*But*,' said Fox opening his eyes wide, '*but* when the doctor (which is what he isn't, properly speaking, but never mind), when the doctor rings through an hour, or thereabouts, later and tells her to come to Room 20 and she does come and the lady's passed away, does she say – ' and here Mr Fox gave a sketchy impersonation of a female voice – ' "Oh, Doctor, I looked in at nine and she was as right as Christmas"? No. She does not. She keeps her tongue behind her teeth and gets cracking with the stomach pump. Now why? Why not mention it?'

'Schramm seemed to suggest that at some earlier stage, in a fit of jealous rage, that Jackson had threatened she'd do some mischief to Mrs Foster. And was now afraid he'd think that on this unmentioned visit she'd taken a hand in overdosing her with barbiturates.'

'Ah,' said Fox. 'But the catch in that is, Mrs Foster, according to our reading of the evidence, was first drugged and then smothered. So it looks as if he didn't realize she was smothered, which, if true, puts him in the clear. Any good?'

'I think so, Br'er Fox. I think it's quite a lot of good.'

'Would you say, now, that Sister J would be capable of doing the job herself – pillow and all?'

'Ah, there you have me. I think she's a jealous, slighted woman with a ferocious temper. Jealous, slighted women have murdered their supplanters before now but generally speaking they're more inclined to take to the man. And by George, judging by the way she shaped up to Schramm tonight I wouldn't put it past her.'

'By and large, then, these two are a bit of a nuisance. We'd got things more or less settled – well, *I* had,' said Mr Fox with a hard look at Alleyn, 'and it was just a matter of running Claude to earth. And now this silly lot crops up.'

'Very inconsiderate.'

'Yerse. And there's no joy from the Claude front, by the way. The Yard rang through. The search is what the Press likes to call nation-wide but not a squeak.'

'Southampton?'

'They sent a copper they don't reckon looks like it into "The Good Read", in Port Lane. It's an accommodation address-shop all right but there was nothing for "Morris". Very cagey the chap was – sussy for drugs but they've never collected enough to knock him off. The DI I talked to thinks it's possible Claude Carter off-loaded the stuff he brought ashore there. If he's thinking of slipping out by Southampton he could have fixed it to collect Sister J's blackmail delivery on the way.'

'Suppose she'd posted it today, first-class mail, it wouldn't arrive at the earliest until tomorrow,' said Alleyn.

'They've got the shop under the obbo non-stop. If he shows, they'll feel his collar, all right,' said Fox.

'If. It's an odd development, isn't it?' Alleyn said. 'There he is, large as life, mousing about up at Quintern Place and in and around the district until (according to Daft Artie) twelve o'clock or (according to Bruce) nine, last night. He comes down the lane with his pack on his back. He opens the squeaky lych-gate and leaves his prints there. And vanishes.'

'Now you see him, now you don't. Lost his nerve, d'you reckon?'

'We mustn't forget he left that note for Mrs Jim.'

'P'raps that's all there is to it. P'raps,' said Fox bitterly, 'he'll come waltzing back with a silly grin on his face having been to stay with his auntie. P'raps it was somebody else blackmailing Sister J, and we'll get egg all over our faces.'

'It's an occupational hazard,' Alleyn said vaguely and then to himself, ' "Into thin air" and but for the footprints at the lych-gate, leaving "not a wrack behind". *Why?* And then – where to, for pity's sake?'

'Not by the late train to London,' said Fox. 'They said at the station, nobody entered or left it at Great Quintern.'

'Hitched a lift?'

'Nice job for our boys, that'll be. Ads in the papers and what a hope.'

'You're in a despondent mood, my poor Foxkin.'

Mr Fox, who, although an occasional grumbler, was never known to succumb to the mildest hint of depression, placidly ignored this observation.

'I shall cheer you up,' Alleyn continued. 'You need a change of scene. What do you say to a moonlight picnic?'

'Now then!' said Fox guardedly.

'Well, not perhaps a picnic but a stroll in a graveyard? Bruce Gardener would call it a Gothic stroll, no doubt.'

'You don't mean this, I suppose, Mr Alleyn?'

'I do, though. I can *not* get Daft Artie's story out of my head, Fox. It isn't all moonshine, presumably, because there *are* those prints. Carter *has* disappeared and there *is* the layby in the hedge. I suggest we return to the scene and step it out. What's the time?'

'Eleven-ten.'

'The village ought to be asleep.'

'So ought we,' sighed Fox.

'We'd better give the "factory" a shout and ask if they can raise an acetylene lamp or its equivalent.'

'A reconstruction, then?'

'You find it a fanciful notion? A trifle *vieux-jeu*, perhaps?'

'I dare say it makes sense,' said Fox resignedly and went off to telephone.

Sergeant McGuiness on night duty at the station did produce an acetylene lamp, kept in reserve against power failures. He had it ready for them and handed it over rather wistfully. 'I'd've liked to be in on this,' he confided to Fox. 'It sounds interesting.'

Alleyn overheard him. 'Can you raise a copper to hold the desk for an hour?' he asked. 'We could do with a third man.'

Sergeant McGuiness brightened. He said, 'Our PC Dance was competing in the darts semi-finals at the local tonight. He'll be on his way home but if he's won he'll be looking in to tell me. I dare say if it's agreeable to you, sir, —'

'I'll condone it,' said Alleyn.

A scraping sound and a bobbing light on the window-blind announced the arrival of a bicycle. The sergeant excused himself and hurried to the door. A voice outside shouted, 'Done it, Sarge.'

'You never!'

'Out on the double seven.'

'That's the stuff.'

'Very near thing, though. Wait till I tell you.'

'Hold on.' The sergeant's voice dropped to a mumble. There was a brief inaudible exchange. He returned followed by a ginger-headed simpering colossus.

'PC Dance, sir,' said Sergeant McGuiness.

Alleyn congratulated PC Dance on his prowess and said he would be obliged if they could 'borrow' him. 'Borrow' is a synonym for 'arrest' in the Force and the disreputable pun, if pun it was, had an undeserved success. They left Dance telephoning in triumph to his wife.

On their way to the village Alleyn outlined the object of the exercise for the gratified McGuiness. 'We're trying to make sense of an apparently senseless situation,' he said. 'Item: could a walker coming down Stile Lane into Long Lane see much or anything of the light from Bruce Gardener's lamp? Item: can someone hidden in the hedge see the walker? Item: can the walker, supposing he climbs the steps to the church and goes into the church—'

'Which,' said the sergeant, 'excuse me, he can't. The church is locked at night, sir. By our advice. Possibility of vandals.'

'See how right we were to bring you in. Who locks it? The vicar?'

'That's correct, Mr Alleyn. And once the deceased lady was brought in that's what he'd do. Lock up the premises for the night.'

'Leaving the church in darkness?' Fox asked.

'I think not, Fox. I think he'd leave the sanctuary light on. We can ask.'

'So it's after the arrival of the deceased that Artie's story begins?'

'And our performance too for what it's worth. Do they keep early hours in the village, Sergeant?'

'Half an hour after the local closes they're all in bed.'

'Good.'

'Suppose,' Fox said, on a note of consternation, 'Daft Artie's sleeping out?'

'It'll be a bloody nuisance,' Alleyn grunted. 'If he is we'll have to play it by ear. I don't know, though. We might pull him in to demonstrate.'

'Would he co-operate?'

'God knows. Here we are. We make as little noise as possible.

Don't bang the doors. Keep your voices down.'

They turned a sharp corner through a stand of beech trees and entered the village; a double row of some dozen cottages on either side of Long Lane, all fast asleep: the church, high above, its towers silhouetted against the stars, the rest almost disappearing into its background of trees. The moon had not yet risen so that Long Lane and the bank and hedge above it and the hillside beyond were all in deep shadow.

Alleyn drove the car on to the green near the steps and they got out.

'Hullo,' he said. 'There's somebody still awake up Stile Lane.'

'That's the widow Black's cottage,' said the sergeant. 'There'll be someone looking after her – the brother, no doubt.'

'Looking after her? Why?'

'Did you not hear? She was knocked over by a truck on the way back from the funeral this afternoon. The blind corner up the lane. I've been saying for years it'd happen. The chap was driving dead slow for the turning and she fell clear. He helped her in and reported it to us.'

'Would that be Bruce Gardener's sister?' asked Fox.

'That's right, Mr Fox. We're not likely to disturb them.'

'I don't know so much about that,' Alleyn murmured. 'If it's Bruce up there and he looks out of the window and sees light coming from where he dug the grave and had his own lamp last night, he may come down to investigate. Damn!' He thought for a moment. 'Oh, well,' he said, 'we tell him. Why not? Let's get moving. I'd like you, Sergeant, to act as the boy says he did. Get into the layby in the hedge when the time comes. Not yet. We'll set you up. I'll do the Carter bit. Mr Fox is Bruce. All you have to do is to keep your eyes and ears open and report exactly what you see. Got the lamp? And the shovel? Come on, and quietly does it.'

He opened the lych-gate very cautiously, checking it at the first sign of the squeak. They slid through, one by one and moved quietly up the steps.

'Don't use your torches unless you have to,' Alleyn said and as their eyes adjusted to the dark it thinned and gravestones stood about them. They reached the top. Alleyn led the way round the church: the nave, the north transept, the chancel, until they came to the Passcoigne plot and Sybil Foster's grave. The flowers on the mound smelt heavy in the night air and the plastic covers glinted in the starlight as if phosphorescent.

Fox and McGuiness crouched over the lamp. Presently it flared. The area became explicit in a white glare. The sergeant spent some time regulating the flame. Fox stood up and his gigantic shadow rose against the trees. The lamp hissed. Fox lifted it and put it by the grave. They waited to make sure it was in good order.

'Right,' said Alleyn at last. 'Give us eight minutes to get down, Fox, and then start. Don't look into the light, Sergeant, it'll blind you. Come on.'

The shadow of the church was intensified by the light beyond it and the steps took longer to descend than to climb. When they were back at the car Alleyn murmured, 'Now, I'll show you the layby. It's in the hedge across the lane and a little to our right. About four yards further on there's a gap at the top of the bank with a hurdle gate. You can ease round the post, go through into the field and turn back to the layby. If by any chance somebody comes down the lane and gets nosey we're looking for a missing child thought to be asleep near the hedge. Here we are. Make sure you'll recognize it from the other side. There's that hazel plant sticking up above the level of the hedge.'

They moved along the hedge until they came to the gap.

'Through you go,' Alleyn whispered, 'turn left and then back six paces. You'll have to crawl in, helmet and all. Give one low whistle when you're set and I'll go on into Stile Lane. That's when your obbo begins.'

He watched the shadowy sergeant climb the bank and edge his bulk between the gate-post and the hedge. Then he turned about and looked up at the church. It was transformed. A nimbus of light rose behind it. Tree-tops beyond the Passcoigne plot started up, uncannily defined, like stage scenery, and as he watched, a gargantuan shadow rose, moved enormously over the trees, threw up arms, and the sweeping image of a shovel sank and rose again. Mr Fox had embarked on his pantomime.

The sergeant was taking his time. No whistle. The silence, which is never really silence, of a countryside, breathed out its nocturnal preoccupations: stirrings in the hedgerow, far-distant traffic, the movements of small creatures going about their business in the night.

'Ssst!'

It was the sergeant, back in the gap up the hill. His helmet showed against Mrs Black's lighted window in Stile Lane. Alleyn climbed the bank and leant over the hurdle.

'Artie *is* there,' breathed Sergeant McGuiness. 'In his hidey-hole. Curled up. My Gawd, I nearly crawled in on top of him.'

'Asleep?'

'Sound.'

'It doesn't matter. Come back into the lane and lean into the hollow in the bank below the layby. Your head will be pretty much on a level with his. I simply want to check that he could have seen what he said he saw and heard what he said he heard. Back you come.'

The sergeant had gone. Alleyn slipped into the lane and walked a little way up it. He was now quite close to Mrs Black's cottage. The light behind the window was out. He waited for a moment or two and then retraced his steps, walking, now, in the middle of the road. He wondered if Claude Carter had worn his crêpe-soled shoes last night. He wondered, supposing Daft Artie woke and saw him, if he would repeat his eldritch shriek.

Now he was almost opposite the layby. Not a hint of the sergeant, in blackest shadow under the hedge.

Alleyn paused.

It was as if an ironclad fist struck him on the jaw.

3

He lay in the lane and felt grit against his face and pain and he heard a confusion of sounds. Disembodied voices shouted angrily.

'Mr Fox! Come down here. Mr Fox.'

He had been lifted and rested against a massive thigh. 'I'm all right,' somebody said. He said it. 'Where's Fox? What happened?'

'The bloody kid. He chucked a brick at you. Over my head. Gawd, I thought he'd done you, Mr Alleyn,' said Sergeant McGuiness.

'Where's Fox?'

'Here,' said Fox. His large concerned face blotted out the stars. He was breathing hard. 'Here I am,' he said. 'You'll be all right.'

A furious voice was roaring somewhere out on the hillside beyond the hedge. 'Come back. You damned, bloody young murderer. Come back, till I have the hide off of you.' Footsteps thudded and retreated.

'That's Bruce,' said Alleyn, feeling his jaw. 'Where did he spring from? The cottage?'

'That's right,' somebody said.

Fox was saying, 'Get cracking, Sarge. Sort it out. I'll look after this!'

More retreating foosteps at the run.

'Here, get me up. What hit me?'

'Take it easy, Mr Alleyn. Let me have a look. Caught you on the jaw. Might have broken it.'

'You're telling me. What did?' He struggled to his knees and then, with Fox's help to his feet. 'Damn and blast!' he said. 'Let me get to that bank while my head clears. What hit me?'

'Half a brick. The boy must have woken up. Bruce and the Sarge are chasing him.'

Fox had propped him against the bank and was playing a torch on his face and dabbing it very gently with his handkerchief. 'It's bleeding,' he said.

'Never mind that. Tell me what happened.'

'It seems that when you got as far as here – almost in touching distance of the Sarge – the boy must have woken up, seen you, dark and all though it is, picked up a half-brick from his fireplace and heaved it. It must have passed over the Sarge's head. Then he lit off.'

'But, Bruce?'

'Yes. Bruce. Bruce noticed the light in the graveyard and thought it might be vandals. There's been trouble with them lately. Anyway, he came roaring down the hill and saw the boy in the act. How's it feel now?'

'Damn sore but I don't think it's broken. And the sergeant's chasing Daft Artie?'

'Him and Bruce.'

'No good making a song and dance over it – the boy's not responsible.'

'It's my bet they won't catch him. For a start, they can't see where they're going.'

'I wonder where his home is,' said Alleyn.

'Bruce'll know. It must,' said Fox, still examining Alleyn's jaw, 'have caught you on the flat. There's a raw patch but no cut. We'll have to get you to a doctor.'

'No, we won't,' Alleyn mumbled. 'I'll do all right. Fox, how much could he see from the layby? Enough to recognize me? Go and stand where I was, will you?'

'Are you sure—?'

'Yes. Go on.'

Fox moved away. The light still glowed beyond the church. It was refracted faintly into the centre of the lane. Fox was an identifiable figure. Just.

Alleyn said, 'So we know Artie could have recognized Carter and I suppose, me. Damnation, look at this.'

A window in the parsonage on the far side of the green shone out. Somebody opened it and was revealed as a silhouette. 'Hullo!' said a cultivated voice. 'Is anything the matter?'

The vicar.

'Nothing at all,' Alleyn managed. 'A bit of skylarking in the lane. Some young chaps. We've sorted it out.'

'Is that the police?' asked the vicar plaintively.

'That's us,' Fox shouted. 'Sorry you've been disturbed, sir.'

'Never mind. Is there something going on behind the church? What's that light?'

'We're just making sure there's been no vandalism,' Alleyn improvised. It hurt abominably to raise his voice. 'Everything's in order.'

By this time several more windows along the lane had been opened.

'It's quite all right, sir,' Fox said. 'No trouble. A bunch of young chaps with too much on board.'

'Get that bloody light out,' Alleyn muttered.

Fox, using his own torch, crossed the lane. The lych-gate shrieked. He hurried up the steps and round the church.

'You don't think perhaps I should just pop down?' the vicar asked doubtfully, after a considerable pause.

'Not the slightest need. It's all over,' Alleyn assured him. 'They've bolted.'

Windows began to close. The light behind the church went out.

'Are you sure? Was it those lads from Great Quintern? I didn't hear motorbikes.'

'They hadn't got bikes. Go back to bed, Vicar,' Alleyn urged him. 'You'll catch your death.'

'No matter. Good night, then.'

The window was closed. Alleyn watched Fox's torchlight come bobbing round the church and down the steps. Voices sounded in the field beyond the hedge. Bruce and the sergeant. They came through the hurdle and down the bank.

'I'm here,' Alleyn said. 'Don't walk into me.' The sergeant's torchlight found him.

'Are you all right, sir? 'E's got clean away I'm afraid. It was that bloody dark and there's all them trees.'

Bruce said, 'I'll have the hide off my fine laddie for this. What's possessed the fule? He's never showed violent before. By God, I'll teach him a lesson he won't forget.'

'I suppose it *was* Artie?'

'Nae doubt about it, sir.'

'Where did you come from, Bruce?'

It was as they had thought. Bruce had been keeping company with his shaken sister. She had gone to bed and he was about to return to Quintern Place. He looked out of the window and saw the glare of the lamp in the churchyard.

'It gied me a shock,' he said, and with one of his occasional vivid remarks, 'It was oncanny – as if I mysel' was in two places at once. And then I thought it might be they vandals and up to no good. And I saw the shadow on the trees like mine had been. Digging. Like me. It fair turned my stomach, that.'

'I can imagine.'

'So I came the short cut down the brae to the lane as fast as I could in the dark. I arrived at the hedge and his figure rose up clear against the glow behind the kirk. It was him all right. He stood there for a second and then he hurrled something and let out a bit screech as he did so. I shouted and he bolted along the hedge. The sergeant was in the lane, sir, with you in the light of his torch and flat on your back and him saying by God the bugger's got him and yelling for Mr Fox. So I went roaring after the lad and not a hope in hell of catching him. He's a wild crittur. You'd say he could see in the dark. Who's to tell where he's hiding?'

'In his bed, most likely,' said the sergeant. 'By this time.'

'Aye, you may say so. His mother's cottage is a wee piece further down the lane. Are you greatly injured, Superintendent? What was it he hurrled at you?'

'Half a brick. No, I'm all right.'

Bruce clicked his tongue busily. 'He might have kilt you,' he said.

'Leave it alone, Bruce. Don't pitch into him when you see him. It wouldn't do any good. I mean that.'

'Well,' said Bruce dourly, 'if you say so.'

'I do say so.'

Fox joined them, carrying his doused lamp and the shovel.

Bruce, who wasted no ceremony with Fox whom he seemed to regard as a sort of warrant-officer, asked him in scandalized tones what he thought he'd been doing up yon. 'If you've been tampering with the grave,' he said furiously, 'it's tantamount to sacrilege and there's no doubt in my mind there's a law to deal with it. Now then, what was it? What were you doing with yon shovel?'

'It was dumb show, Bruce,' Alleyn said wearily. 'We were testing the boy's story. Nothing's been disturbed.'

'I've a mind to look for mysel'.'

'Go ahead, by all means if you want to. Have you got a torch?'

'I'll leave it,' Bruce said morosely. 'I dinna like it but I'll leave it.'

'Good night to you then. I think, Br'er Fox,' said Alleyn, 'I'll get in the car.'

His face throbbed enormously and the ground seemed to shift under his feet. Fox piloted him to the car. The sergeant hovered.

When they were underway Fox said he proposed to drive to the outpatients' department at the nearest hospital. Alleyn said he would see Dr Field-Innis in the morning, that he'd had routine tetanus injections and that if he couldn't cope with a chuck under the chin the sooner he put in for retirement the better. He then fainted.

He was out only for a short time, he thought, as they seemed not to have noticed. He said in as natural a manner as he could contrive that he felt sleepy, managed to fold his arms and lower his head, and did, in fact, drift into a sort of doze. He was vaguely aware of Fox giving what is known as 'a shout' over the blower.

Now they were at the station and so, surprisingly, was the district police surgeon.

'There's no concussion,' said the police surgeon, 'and no breakage and your teeth are OK. We'll just clean you up and make you comfortable and send you home to bed, um?'

'Too kind,' said Alleyn.

'You'll be reasonably comfortable tomorrow.'

'Thank you.'

'Don't push it too far, though. Go easy.'

'That,' said Mr Fox in the background, 'will be the day.'

Alleyn grinned, which hurt. So did the cleaning up and dressing.

'There we are!' said the police surgeon jollily. 'It'll be a bit colourful for a day or two and there's some swelling. You

200

won't have a permanent scar.'

'Most reassuring. I'm sorry they knocked you up.'

'What I'm there for, isn't it? Quite an honour in this case. Good morning.'

When he had gone Alleyn said, 'Fox, you're to get on to the Home Secretary.'

'*Me!*' exclaimed the startled Fox. 'Him? Not *me*!'

'Not directly you, but get the Yard and the AC and ask for it to be laid on.'

'What for, though, Mr Alleyn? Lay on what?'

'What do you think? The usual permit.'

'You're *not*—' said Fox, '– you can't be – you're not thinking of digging her up?'

'Aren't I? Can't I? I am, do you know. Not,' said Alleyn, holding his pulsing jaw, 'in quite the sense you mean but – digging her up, Br'er Fox. Yes.'

Chapter Nine

GRAVEYARD (III)

When Alleyn looked in the glass the following morning his face did not appear as awful as it felt. No doubt the full panoply of bruises was yet to develop. He shaved painfully round the dressing, took a bath and decided he was in more or less reasonable form to face the day.

Fox came in to say their Assistant Commissioner was on the telephone. 'If you can speak, that is.'

Alleyn said, 'Of course I can speak,' and found that it was best to do so with the minimum demand upon his lower jaw. He stifled the explosive grunt of pain that the effort cost him.

The telephone was in the passage outside his room.

'Rory?' said the AC. 'Yes. I want a word with you. What's all this about an exhumation?'

'It's not precisely that, sir.'

'What? I can't catch what you say. You sound as if you were talking to your dentist.'

Alleyn thought, I dare say I shall be when there's time for it, but he merely replied that he was sorry and would try to do better.

'I suppose it's the clip on the jaw Fox talked about. Does it hurt?'

'Not much,' Alleyn lied angrily.

'Good. Who did it?'

'The general idea is a naughty boy with a brick.'

'About this exhumation that is not an exhumation. What am I to say to the HS? Confide in me, for Heaven's sake.'

Alleyn confided.

'Sounds devilish far-fetched to me,' grumbled the AC. 'I hope you know what you're about.'

'So do I.'

'You know what I think about hunches.'

'If I may say so, you don't mistrust them any more than I do, sir.'

'All right, all right. We'll go ahead, then. Tomorrow night, you suggest? Sorry you've had a knock. Take care of yourself.'

' "There is none that can compare," ' Alleyn hummed in great discomfort.

> '"With a tow, row bloody row to
>   Our A. Commissionaire."

It's on, Br'er Fox.'

'This'll set the village by the ears. What time?'

'Late tomorrow night. We'll be turning into tombstones our-selves if we keep up these capers.'

'What's our line with the populace?'

'God knows. We hope they won't notice. But what a hope!'

'How about someone accidentally dropped a valuable in the open grave? Such as – er—'

'What?'

'*I* don't know,' said Fox crossly. 'A gold watch?'

'When?' Alleyn asked. 'And whose gold watch?'

'Er. Well. Bruce's? Any time before the interment. I ap-preciate,' Fox confessed, 'that it doesn't sound too hot.'

'Go on.'

'I'm trying to picture it,' said Fox, after a longish pause.

'And how are you getting on?'

'It'd be ludicrous.'

'Perhaps the best way will be to keep quiet and if they do notice tell them nothing. "The police declined to comment." '

'The usual tarpaulin, etcetera, I suppose. I'll lay it on, will I?'

'Do. My face, by the way, had better be the result of a turn-up with a gang outside the village. Where's the sergeant?'

'Down at the "factory". He's going to take a look at Daft Artie.'

Alleyn began to walk about the room, found this jolted his jaw and sat on his bed. 'Br'er Fox,' he said, 'there's that child. Prunella. We can't possibly risk her hearing of it by accident.'

'The whole story?'

'Upon my soul,' Alleyn said after a long pause, 'I'm not at all sure I won't have recourse to your preposterous golden watch, or its equivalent. Look, I'll drop you in the village and get you to call on the vicar and tell him.'

'Some tarradiddle? Or what?' Fox asked.

'The truth but not the whole truth about what we hope to find. *Hope!*' said Alleyn distastefully. 'What a word!'

'I see what you mean. Without wishing to pester—' Fox began. To his surprise and gratification Alleyn gave him a smack on the shoulder.

'All right, fusspot,' he said, 'fat-faced but fit as a flea, that's me. Come on.'

So he drove Fox to the parsonage and continued up Long Lane, passing the gap in the hedge. He looked up at the church and saw three small boys and two women come round from behind the chancel end. There was something self-conscious about the manner of the women's gait and their unconvincing way of pointing out a slanting headstone to each other.

There they go, Alleyn thought. It's all round the village by now. Police up to something round the grave! We'll have a queue for early doors tomorrow night.

He drove past the turning into Stile Lane and on towards the road that led uphill to Mardling Manor on the left and Quintern Place on the right. Keys Lane, where Verity Preston lived, branched off to the left. Alleyn turned in at her gate and found her sitting under her lime trees doing *The Times* crossword.

'I came on an impulse,' he said. 'I want some advice and I think you're the one to give it to me. I don't apologize because after all, in its shabby way it's a compliment. You may not think so, of course.'

'I can't say until I've heard it, can I?' she said. 'Come and sit down.'

When they were settled she said, 'It's no good being heavily tactful and not noticing your face, is it? What's happened?'

'A boy and a brick is my story.'

'Not a local boy, I hope.'

'Your gardener's assistant.'

'Daft Artie!' Verity exclaimed. 'I can't believe it!'

'Why can't you?'

'He doesn't do things like that. He's not violent, only silly.'

'That's what Bruce said. This may have been mere silliness. I may have just happened to be in the path of the trajectory. But I didn't come for advice about Daft Artie. It's about your god-daughter. Is she still staying at Mardling?'

'She went back there after the funeral. Now I come to think of it, she said she was going up to London for a week from tomorrow.'

'Good.'

'Why good?'

'This is not going to be pleasant for you, I know. I think you must have felt – you'd be very unusual if you hadn't – relieved when it was all over, yesterday afternoon. Tidily put away and mercifully done with. There's always that sense of release, isn't there, however deep the grief? Prunella must have felt it, don't you think?'

'I expect she did, poor child. And then there's her youth and her engagement and her natural ebullience. She'll be happy again. If it's about her you want to ask, you're not going to—' Verity exclaimed and stopped short.

'Bother her again? Perhaps. I would like to know what you think. But first of all,' Alleyn broke off. 'This is in confidence. Very strict confidence. I'm sure you'll have no objections at all to keeping it so for forty-eight hours.'

'Very well,' she said uneasily. 'If you say so.'

'It's this. It looks as if we shall be obliged to remove the coffin from Mrs Foster's grave for a very short time. It will be replaced within an hour at the most and no indignity will be done it. I can't tell you any more than that. The question is: should Prunella be told? If she's away in London there may be a fair chance she need never know, but villages being what they are and certain people, the vicar for one, having to be informed, there's always the possibility that it might come out. What do you think?'

Verity looked at him with a sort of incredulous dismay. 'I can't think,' she said. 'It's incomprehensible and grotesque and I wish you hadn't told me.'

'I'm sorry.'

'One keeps forgetting – or I do – that this is a matter of somebody killing somebody whom one had known all one's life. And that's a monstrous thought.'

'Yes, of course it's monstrous. But to us, I'm afraid, it's all in the day's work. But I am concerned about the young Prunella.'

'So of course am I. I am indeed,' said Verity, 'and I do take your point. Do you think perhaps that Gideon Markos should be consulted? Or Nikolas? Or both?'

'Do you?'

'They've – well, they've kind of taken over, you see. Naturally. She's been absorbed into their sort of life and will belong to it.'

'But she's still looking to you, isn't she? I noticed it yesterday at the funeral.'

'Is there anything,' Verity found herself saying, 'that you don't notice?' Alleyn did not answer.

'Look,' Verity said. 'Suppose you – or I, if you like – should tell Nikolas Markos and suggest that they take Prue away?

He's bought a yacht, he informs me. Not the messing-about-in-boats sort but the jet-set, Riviera job. They could waft her away on an extended cruise.'

'Even plutocratic yachts are not necessarily steamed up and ready to sail at the drop of a hat.'

'This one is.'

'Really?'

'He happened to mention it,' said Verity, turning pink. 'He's planning a cruise in four weeks' time. He could put it forward.'

'Are you invited?'

'I can't go,' she said shortly. 'I've got a first night coming up.'

'You know, your suggestion has its points. Even if someone does talk about it, long after it's all over and done with, that's not going to be as bad as knowing it is going to be done *now* and that it's actually happening. Or is it?'

'Not nearly so bad.'

'And in any case,' Alleyn said, more to himself than to her, 'she's going to find out – ultimately. Unless I'm all to blazes.' He stood up. 'I'll leave it to you,' he said. 'The decision. Is that unfair?'

'No. It's good of you to concern yourself. So I talk to Nikolas. Is that it?'

To Verity's surprise he hesitated for a moment.

'Could you, perhaps, suggest he puts forward the cruise because Prunella's had about as much as she can take and would be all the better for a complete change of scene – now?'

'I suppose so. I don't much fancy asking a favour.'

'No? Because he'll be a little too delighted to oblige?'

'Something like that,' said Verity.

2

The next day dawned overcast with the promise of rain. By late afternoon it was coming down inexorably.

'Set in solid,' Fox said, staring out of the station window.

'In one way a hellish bore and in another an advantage.'

'You mean people will be kept indoors?'

'That's right.'

'It'll be heavy going, though,' sighed Fox. 'For our lot.'

'All of that.'

The telephone rang. Alleyn answered it quickly. It was the

Yard. The duty squad with men and equipment was about to leave in a 'nondescript' vehicle and wanted to know if there were any final orders. The sergeant in charge checked over details.

'Just a moment,' Alleyn said. And to Fox, 'What time does the village take its evening meal, would you say?'

'I'll ask McGuiness.' He went into the front office and returned.

'Between five-thirty and six-thirty. And after that they'll be at their tellies.'

'Yes. Hullo,' Alleyn said into the receiver. 'I want you to time it so that you arrive at six o'clock with the least possible amount of fuss. Come to the vicarage. Make it all look like a repair job. No uniform copper. There's a downpour going on here, you'll need to dress for it. I'll be there. You'll go through the church and out by an exit on the far side, which is out of sight from the village. If by any unlikely chance somebody gets curious, you're looking for a leak in the roof. Got it? Good. Put me through to Missing Persons and stay where you are for ten minutes in case there's a change of procedure. Then leave.'

Alleyn waited. He felt the pulse in the bruise on his jaw and knew it beat a little faster. If they give a positive answer, he thought, it's all up. Call off the exercise and back we go to square one.

A voice on the line. 'Hullo? Superintendent Alleyn? You were calling us, sir?'

'Yes. Any reports come in?'

'Nothing, sir. No joy anywhere.'

'Southampton? The stationer's shop?'

'Nothing.'

'Thank God.'

'I beg pardon, Mr Alleyn?'

'Never mind. It's, to coin a phrase, a case of no news being good news. Keep going, though. Until you get orders to the contrary and if any sign or sniff of Carter comes up let me know at once. At once. This is of great importance. Understood?'

'Understood, Mr Alleyn.'

Alleyn hung up and looked at his watch. Four-thirty.

'We give it an hour and then go over,' he said.

The hour passed slowly. Rain streamed down the blinded windowpane. Small occupational noises could be heard in the front office and the intermittent sounds of passing vehicles.

At twenty past five the constable on duty brought in that panacea against anxiety that the Force has unfailingly on tap: strong tea in heavy cups and two recalcitrant biscuits.

Alleyn, with difficulty, swallowed the tea. He carried his cup into the front office where Sergeant McGuiness, with an affectation of nonchalance, said it wouldn't be long now, would it?

'No,' said Alleyn, 'you can gird up your loins such as they are,' and returned to his own room. He and Fox exchanged a nod and put on heavy mackintoshes, sou'westers and gum boots. He looked at his watch. Half past five.

'Give it three minutes,' he said. They waited.

The telephone rang in the front office but not for them. They went through. Sergeant McGuiness was attired in oilskin and sou'wester.

Alleyn said to PC Dance, 'If there's a call for me from Missing Persons, ring Upper Quintern rectory. Have the number under your nose.'

He and Fox and McGuiness went out into the rain and drove to Upper Quintern village. The interior of the car smelt of stale smoke, rubber and petrol. The windscreen wipers jerked to and fro, surface water fanned up from under their wheels and sloshed against the windows. The sky was so blackened with rainclouds that a premature dusk seemed to have fallen on the village. Not a soul was abroad in Long Lane. The red window curtains in the bar of the Passcoigne Arms glowed dimly.

'This is not going to let up,' said Fox.

Alleyn led the way up a steep and slippery path to the vicarage. They were expected and the door was opened before they reached it.

The vicar, white-faced and anxious, welcomed them and took them to his study which was like all parsonic studies with its framed photographs of ordinands and steel engravings of classic monuments, its high fender, its worn chairs and its rows of predictable literature.

'This is a shocking business,' said the vicar. 'I can't tell you how distressing I find it. Is it – I mean, I suppose it must be – absolutely necessary?'

'I'm afraid it is,' said Alleyn.

'Inspector Fox,' said the vicar, looking wistfully at him, 'was very discreet.'

Fox modestly contemplated the far wall of the study.

'He said he thought he should leave it to you to explain.'

'Indeed,' Alleyn rejoined with a long hard stare at his subordinate.

'And I do hope you will. I think I should know. You see, it is consecrated ground.'

'Yes.'

'So – may I, if you please, be told?' asked the vicar with what Alleyn thought rather touching simplicity.

'Of course,' he said. 'I'll tell you why we are doing it and what we think we may find. In honesty I should add that we may find nothing and the operation therefore may prove to have been quite fruitless. But this is the theory.'

The vicar listened.

'I think,' he said, when Alleyn had finished, 'that I've never heard anything more dreadful. And I have heard some very dreadful things. We do, you know.'

'I'm sure.'

'Even in quiet little parishes like this. You'd be surprised, wouldn't he, Sergeant McGuiness?' asked the vicar. He waited for a moment and then said, 'I must ask you to allow me to be present. I would rather not, of course, because I am a squeamish man. But – I don't want to sound pompous – I think it's my duty.'

Alleyn said, 'We'll be glad to have you there. As far as possible we'll try to avoid attracting notice. I've been wondering if by any chance there's a less public way of going to the church than up those steps.'

'There is *our* path. Through the shrubbery and thicket. It will be rather damp but it's short and inconspicuous. I would have to guide you.'

'If you will. I think,' Alleyn said, 'our men have arrived. They're coming here first, I hope you don't mind?'

He went to the window and the others followed. Down below on the 'green' a small delivery van had pulled up. Five men in mackintoshes and wet hats got out. They opened the rear door and took out a large carpenter's kitbag and a corded bundle of considerable size which required two men to carry it.

'In the eye of a beholder,' Alleyn grunted, 'this would look like sheer lunacy.'

'Not to the village,' said the vicar. 'If they notice, they'll only think it's the boiler again.'

'The boiler?'

'Yes. It has become unsafe and is always threatening to explode. Just look at those poor fellows,' said the vicar. 'Should I ask my wife to make tea? Or coffee?'

Alleyn declined this offer. 'Perhaps later,' he said.

The men climbed the path in single file, carrying their gear. Rain bounced off their shoulders and streamed from their hat brims. Alleyn opened the door to them.

'We're in no shape to come into the house, sir,' one of them said. He removed his hat and Bailey was revealed. Thompson stood behind him hung about with well-protected cameras.

'No, no, no. Not a bit of it,' bustled the vicar. 'We've people in and out all day. Haven't we, McGuiness? Come in. Come in.'

They waited, dripping, in the little hall. The vicar kilted up his cassock, found himself a waterproof cape and pulled on a pair of galoshes.

'I'll just get my brolly,' he said and sought it in the porch.

Alleyn asked the men, 'Is that a tent or an enclosure?' A framed tent, they said. It wouldn't take long to erect: there was no wind.

'We go out by the back,' said the vicar. 'Shall I lead the way?'

The passage reeked of wetness and of its own house-smell – something suggestive of economy and floor polish. From behind one door came the sound of children's voices and from the kitchen the whirr of an egg-beater. They arrived at a side door which opened on to the all-pervading sound and sight of rain.

'I'm afraid,' said the vicar, 'it will be rather heavy going. Especially with—' he paused and glanced unhappily at their gear – 'your burden,' he said.

It was indeed heavy going. The shrubbery, a dense untended thicket, came to within a yard of the house and the path plunged directly into it. Water-laden branches slurred across their shoulders and slapped their faces, runnels of water gushed about their feet. They slithered, manoeuvred, fell about and shambled on again. The vicar's umbrella came in for a deal of punishment.

'Not far now,' he said at last and sure enough they were out of the wood and within a few yards of the church door.

The vicar went first. It was already twilight in the church and he switched on lights, one in the nave and one in the south transept which was furnished as a lady-chapel. The men followed him self-consciously down the aisle and Bailey only just fetched up in time to avoid falling over the vicar when he abruptly genuflected before turning right. The margin between tragedy and hysteria is a narrow one and Alleyn suppressed an impulse, as actors say, to 'corpse' – an only too apposite synonym in this context.

The vicar continued into the lady-chapel. 'There's a door here,' he said to Alleyn. 'Rather unusual. It opens directly on the Passcoigne plot. Perhaps—?'

'It will suit admirably,' Alleyn said. 'May we open up our stuff in the church? It will make things a good deal easier.'

'Yes. Very well.'

So the men, helped by Sergeant McGuiness, unfolded their waterproof-covered bundle and soon two shovels, two hurricane lamps, three high-powered torches, a screwdriver and four coils of rope were set out neatly on the lady-chapel floor. A folded mass of heavy plastic and a jointed steel frame were laid across the pews.

Bailey and Thompson chose a separate site in the transept for the assembling of their gear.

Alleyn said, 'Right. We can go. Would you open the door, Vicar?'

It was down a flight of three steps in the corner of the lady-chapel by the south wall. The vicar produced a key that might have hung from the girdle of a Georgian jailer. 'We hardly ever use it,' he said. 'I've oiled the key and brought the lubricant with me.'

'Splendid.'

Presently, with a clicking sound and a formidable screech, the door opened on a downpour so dense that it looked like a multiple sequence of beaded curtains closely hung the one behind the other. The church filled with the insistent drumming of rain and with the smell of wet earth and trees.

Sybil Foster's grave was a dismal sight: the mound of earth, so carefully embellished by Bruce, looked as if it had been washed ashore with its panoply of dead flowers clinging to it – disordered and bespattered with mud.

They got the tent up with some trouble and great inconvenience. It was large enough to allow a wide margin round the grave. On one part of this they spread a groundsheet. This added to an impression of something disreputable that was about to be put on show. The effect was emphasized by the fairground smell of the tent itself. The rain sounded more insistent inside than out.

The men fetched their gear from the church.

Until now, the vicar, at Alleyn's suggestion, had remained in the church. Now, when they were assembled and ready – Fox, Bailey, Thompson, Sergeant McGuiness and the three Yard men, Alleyn went to fetch him.

He was at prayer. He had put off his mackintosh and he knelt there in his well-worn cassock with his hands folded before his lips. So, Alleyn thought, had centuries of parsons, for this reason and that, knelt in St Crispin's, Upper Quintern. He waited.

The vicar crossed himself, opened his eyes, saw Alleyn and got up.

'We're ready, sir,' Alleyn said.

He found the vicar's cape and held it out. 'No thanks,' said the vicar. 'But I'd better take my brolly.'

So with some ado he was brought into the tent where he shut his umbrella and stood quietly in the background, giving no trouble.

They made a pile of sodden flowers in a corner of the tent and then set about the earth mound, heaping it up into a wet repetition of itself. The tent fabric was green and this, in the premature twilight, gave the interior an underwater appearance.

The shovels crunched and slurped. The men, having cleared away the mound, dug deep and presently there was the hard sound of steel on wood. The vicar came nearer. Thompson brought the coils of rope.

The men were expeditious and skilful and what they had to do was soon accomplished. As if in a reverse playback the coffin rose from its bed and was lifted on to the wet earth beside it.

One of the men went to a corner of the tent and fetched the screwdriver.

'You won't need that,' Fox said quickly.

'No, sir?' The man looked at Alleyn.

'No,' Alleyn said. 'What you do now is dig deeper. But very cautiously. One man only. Bailey, will you do it? Clear away the green flooring and then explore with your hands. If the soil is easily moved, then go on – remove it. But with the greatest possible care. Stand as far to the side as you can manage.'

Bailey lowered himself into the grave. Alleyn knelt on the groundsheet looking down and the others in their glistening mackintoshes grouped round him. The vicar stood at the foot of the grave, removed from the rest. They might have been actors in a modern production of the churchyard scene in *Hamlet*.

Bailey's voice, muffled, said, 'It's dark down here, could I have a torch?' They shone their torches into the grave and the beams moved over pine branches. Bailey gathered together armfuls of them and handed them up. 'Did we bring a trowel?' he asked.

The vicar said there was one on the premises, kept for the churchyard guild. Sergeant McGuiness fetched it. While they waited Bailey could be heard scuffling. He dumped handfuls of soil on the lip of the grave. Alleyn examined them. The earth was loamy, friable and quite dry. McGuiness returned with a trowel and the mound at the lip of the grave grew bigger.

'The soil's packed down, like,' Bailey said presently, 'but it's not hard to move. I – I reckon—' his voice wavered, 'I reckon it's been dug over – or filled in – or – hold on.'

'Go steady, now,' Fox said.

'There's something.'

Bailey began to push earth aside with the edge of his hand and brush it away with his palms.

'A bit more light,' he said.

Alleyn shone his own torch in and the light found Bailey's hands, palms down and fingers spread, held in suspended motion over the earth they had disturbed.

'Go on,' Alleyn said. 'Go on.'

The hands came together, parted and swept aside the last of the earth.

Claude Carter's face had been turned into a gargoyle by the pressure of earth and earth lay in streaks across its eyeballs.

3

Before they moved it Thompson photographed the body where it lay. Then with great care and difficulty, it was lifted and stretched out on the groundsheet. Where it had lain they found Claude's rucksack, tightly packed.

'He'd meant to pick up his car,' Fox said, 'and drive to Southampton.'

'I think so.'

Sybil Foster was returned to her grave and covered.

The vicar said, 'I'll go now. May God rest their souls.'

Alleyn saw him into the church. He paused on the steps. 'It's stopped raining,' he said. 'I hadn't noticed. How strange.'

'Are you all right?' Alleyn asked him. 'Will you go back to the vicarage?'

'What? Oh. Oh no. Not just yet. I'm quite all right, thank you. I must pray now for the living, mustn't I?'

'The living?'

'Oh yes,' said the vicar shakily. 'Yes indeed. That's my job. I have to pray for my brother man. The murderer, you know.' He went into the church.

Alleyn returned to the tent.

'It's clearing,' he said. 'I think you'd better stand guard outside.' The Yard men went out.

Bailey and Thompson were at their accustomed tasks. The camera flashed for Claude as assiduously as a pressman's for a celebrity. When they turned him over and his awful face was hidden they disclosed a huge red grin at the nape of the neck.

'Bloody near decapitated,' Thompson whispered and photographed it in close-up.

'Don't exaggerate,' Fox automatically chided. He was searching the rucksack.

'It's not far wrong, Mr Fox,' said Bailey.

'If you've finished,' Alleyn said, 'search him.'

Bailey found a wallet containing twenty pounds, loose change, cigarettes, matches, his pocket-book, a passport and three dirty postcards.

And in the inside breast pocket, a tiny but extremely solid steel box such as a jeweller might use to house a ring. The key was in Claude's wallet.

Alleyn opened the box and disclosed a neatly folded miniature envelope wrapped in a waterproof silk and inside the envelope between two watch-glasses, a stamp: the Czar Alexander with a hole in his head.

'Look here, Fox,' he said.

Fox restrapped the rucksack and came over. He placed his great palms on his knees and regarded the stamp.

'That was a good bit of speculative thinking on your part,' he said. 'And the tin box we found in his room could have left the trace in the rubble, all right. Funny, you know, there it's lain all these years. I suppose Captain Carter stowed it there that evening. Before he was killed.'

'And may well have used some of the cement in the bag that's still rotting quietly away in the corner. And marked the place on the plan in which this poor scoundrel showed such an interest.'

'He wouldn't have tried to sell it in England, surely?'

'We've got to remember it was his by right. Being what he was, he might have settled for a devious approach to a fanatic millionaire collector somewhere abroad whose zeal would get the better of his integrity.'

'Funny,' Fox mused. 'A bit of paper not much bigger than your thumbnail. Not very pretty and flawed at that. And could be worth as much as its own size in a diamond. I don't get it.'

'Collector's passion? Nor I. But it comes high in the list as an incentive to crime.'

'Where'll we put it?'

'Lock the box and give it to me. If I'm knocked on the head again take charge of it yourself. I can't wait till I get it safely stowed at the Yard. In the meantime—'

'We go in for the kill?' said Fox.

'That's it. Unless it comes in of its own accord.'

'Now?'

'When we've cleared up here.' He turned to Bailey and Thompson. They had finished with what was left of Claude Carter and were folding the groundsheet neatly round him and tying him up with rope. They threaded the two shovels inside the rope to make hand-holds.

And everything else being ready they struck the tent, folded it and laid it with its frame across the body. Bailey, Thompson, McGuiness and the Yard men stood on either side. 'Looks a bit less like a corpse,' said Thompson.

'You'll have to go down the steps this time,' Alleyn told them. 'Mr Fox and I will bring the rest of the gear and light the way.'

They took their torches from their pockets. Twilight had closed in now. The after-smell of rain and the pleasant reek of a wood fire hung on the air. Somewhere down in the village a door banged and then the only sound was of water dripping from branches. Sybil's grave looked as if it had never been disturbed.

'Quiet,' said one of the men. 'Isn't it?'

'Shall we move off, then?' Fox said.

He stooped to pick up his load and the other four men groped for their hand-holds under the tent.

'Right?' said Bailey.

But Alleyn had lifted a hand. 'No,' he whispered. 'Not yet. Keep still. Listen.'

Fox was beside him. 'Where?'

'Straight ahead. In the trees.'

He turned his light on the thicket. A cluster of autumnal leaves sprang up and quivered. One after another the torch-beams joined his. This time all the men heard the hidden sound.

They spread out to left and right of Alleyn and moved forward. The light on the thicket was intensified and details of foliage appeared in uncanny precision, as if they carried some significance and must never be forgotten. A twig snapped and the head of a sapling jerked.

'Bloody Daft Artie, by God!' said Sergeant McGuiness.

'Shall we go in?' asked Fox.

'No,' said Alleyn and then, loudly, 'Show yourself. Call it a day and come out.'

The leaves parted but the face that shone whitely between them, blinking in the torchlight, was not Daft Artie's.

'This is it, Bruce,' said Alleyn. 'Come out.'

4

Bruce Gardener sat bolt upright at the table with his arms folded. He still bore the insecure persona of his chosen role: red-gold beard, fresh mouth, fine torso, loud voice, pawky turn of speech, the straightforward Scottish soldier-man with a heart of gold. At first sight the pallor, the bloodshot eyes and the great earthy hands clenched hard on the upper arms were not conspicuous. To Alleyn, sitting opposite him, to Fox, impassive in the background and to the constable with a notebook in the corner, however, these were unmistakable signs.

Alleyn said, 'Shorn of all other matters: motive, opportunity and all the rest of it, what do you say about this one circumstance? Who but you could have dug Sybil Foster's grave four feet deeper than was necessary, killed Carter, buried his body there, covered it, trampled it down and placed the evergreen flooring? On your own statement and that of other witnesses you were there, digging the grave all that afternoon and well into the night. Why were you so long about it?'

Alleyn waited. Gardener stared at the opposite wall. Once or twice his beard twitched and the red mouth moved as if he was about to speak. But nothing came of it.

'Well?' Alleyn said at last and Bruce gave a parody of clearing his throat. 'Clay,' he said loudly.

The constable wrote, '*Ans. Clay*,' and waited.

'So you told me. But there was no sign of clay in that mound of earth. The soil is loamy and easy to shift. So that's no good,' Alleyn said. 'Is it?'

'I'll no' answer any questions till I have my solicitor present.'

'He's on his way. You might, however, like to consider this. On that night after the funeral when we had an acetylene lamp like yours up there by the grave, you, from your sister's window, saw the light and it worried you. You told us so. But you didn't tell us it wasn't Daft Artie who lay in the cubbyhole in the hedge, but you. It wasn't Daft Artie who heaved half a brick at me, it was you. You were so shaken by the thought of us opening the grave that you lost your head, came down the hill, hid in the hedge, chucked the brick and then set up a phoney hunt for an Artie who wasn't there. Right?'

'No comment.'

'You'll have to find some sort of comment, sooner or later, won't you? However, your solicitor will advise you. But suppose Artie was in bed with a cold that evening, how would you feel about that?'

'*Ans. No comment*,' wrote the constable.

'Well,' Alleyn said, 'there's no point in plugging away at it. The case against you hangs on this one point. If you didn't kill and bury Claude Carter, who did? I shall put it to you again when your solicitor comes and he no doubt will advise you to keep quiet. In the meantime I must tell you that not one piece of information about your actions can be raised to contradict the contention that you killed Mrs Foster; that Carter, a man with a record of blackmail, knew it and exercised his knowledge on you and that you, having arranged with him to pay the blackmail if he came to the churchyard that night, had the grave ready, killed him with the shovel you used to dig the grave and buried him there. Two victims in one grave. Is there still no comment?'

In the silence that followed, Alleyn saw, with extreme distaste, tears well up in Bruce's china-blue, slightly squinting eyes and trickle into his beard.

'We were close taegither, her and me,' he said and his voice trembled. 'From the worrrd go we understood each ither. She was more than an employer to me, she was a true friend. Aye. When I think of the plans we made for the beautifying of the property—' His voice broke convincingly.

'Did you plan those superfluous asparagus beds together and were the excavations in the mushroom shed your idea or hers?'

Bruce half rose from his chair. Fox made a slight move and he sank back again.

'Or,' said Alleyn, 'did Captain Carter who, as you informed us, used to confide in you, tell you before he came down to Quintern on the last afternoon of his life that he proposed to bury the Black Alexander stamp somewhere on the premises? And forty years later when you found yourself there did you not think it a good idea to have a look round on your own accord?'

'You can't prove it on me,' he shouted, without a trace of Scots. 'And what about it if you could?'

'Nothing much, I confess. We've got more than enough without that. I merely wondered if you knew when you killed him that Claude Carter had the Black Alexander in his breast pocket. You gave it a second burial.'

Purple-red flooded up into Bruce's face. He clenched his fists and beat them on the table.

'The bastard!' he shouted. 'The bloody bastard. By Christ, he earned what he got!'

The station sergeant tapped on the door. Fox opened it.

'It's his solicitor,' he said.

'Show him in,' said Fox.

5

Verity Preston weeded her long border and wondered where to look for a gardener. She chided herself for taking so personal a view. She remembered that there had been times when she and Bruce had seemed to understand each other over garden matters. It was monstrous to contemplate what they said he had done but she did not think it was untrue.

A shadow fell across the long border. She swivelled round on her knees and there was Alleyn.

'I hope I'm not making a nuisance of myself,' he said, 'but I expect I am. There's something I wanted to ask you.'

He squatted down beside her. 'Have you got beastly couch-grass in your border?' he asked.

'That can hardly be what you wanted to ask but no, I haven't. Only fat-hen, dandelions and wandering-willy.'

He picked up her handfork and began to use it. 'I wanted to know whether the plan of Quintern Place with the spot marked x is still in Markos's care or whether it's been returned.'

'The former, I should imagine. Do you need it?'

'Counsel for the prosecution may.'

'Mrs Jim might know. She's here today, would you like to ask her?'

'In a minute or two, if I may,' he said, shaking the soil off a root of fat-hen and throwing it into the wheelbarrow.

'I suppose,' he said, 'you'll be looking for a replacement.'

'Just what I was thinking. Oh,' Verity exclaimed, 'it's all so flattening and awful. I suppose one will understand it when the trial's over but to me, at present, it's a muddle.'

'Which bits of it?'

'Well, first of all, I suppose what happened at Greengages.'

'After you left?'

'Good Heavens, not before, I do trust.'

'I'll tell you what we believe happened. Some of it we can prove, the rest follows from it. The prosecution will say it's pure conjecture. In a way that doesn't matter. Gardener will be charged with the murder of Claude Carter, not Sybil Foster. However, the one is consequent upon the other. We believe, then, that Gardener and Carter, severally, stayed behind at Greengages, each hoping to get access to Mrs Foster's room, Carter probably to sponge on her, Gardener, if the opportunity presented itself, to do away with her. It all begins from the time when young Markos went to Mrs Foster's room to retrieve his fiancée's bag.'

'I hope,' Verity said indignantly, 'you don't attach—'

'Don't jump the gun like that or we shall never finish. He reported Mrs Foster alive and, it would be improper but I gather, appropriate, to add, kicking.'

'Against the engagement. Yes.'

'At some time before nine o'clock Claude appeared at the reception desk and, representing himself to be an electrician come to mend Mrs Foster's lamp, collected the lilies left at the desk by Bruce and took them upstairs. When he was in the passage something moved him to hide in an alcove opposite her door leaving footprints and a lily-head behind him. We believe he had seen Bruce approaching and that when Bruce left the room after a considerable time, Carter tapped on the door and walked in. He found her dead.

'He dumped the lilies in the bathroom basin. While he was in there, probably with the door ajar, Sister Jackson paid a very brief visit to the room.'

'That large lady who gave evidence? But she didn't say—'

'She did, later on. We'll stick to the main line. Well. Claude took thought. It suited him very well that she was dead. He now collected a much bigger inheritance. He also had, ready made, an instrument for blackmail and Gardener would have the wherewithal to stump up. Luckily for us, he also decided by means of an anonymous letter and a telephone call to have a go at Sister Jackson who had enough sense to report it to us.'

'I suppose you know he went to prison for blackmail?'

'Yes. So much for Greengages. Now for Claude, the Black Alexander and the famous plan.'

Verity listened with her head between her hands, making no further interruptions and with the strangest sense of hearing an account of events that had taken place a very, very long time ago.

'—so Claude's plan matured,' Alleyn was saying. 'He decided to go abroad until things had settled down. Having come to this decision, we think he set about blackmailing Gardener. Gardener appeared to fall for it. No doubt he told Claude he needed time to raise the money and put him off until the day before the funeral. He then said he would have it by that evening and Claude could collect it in the churchyard. And I think,' said Alleyn, 'you can guess the rest.'

'As far as Claude is concerned, yes, I suppose I can. But – Bruce Gardener and Sybil – that's much the worst. That's so – disgusting. All those professions of attachment, all that slop and sorrow act – no, it's beyond everything.'

'You did have your reservations about him, didn't you?'

'They didn't run along homicidal lines,' Verity snapped.

'Not an unusual reaction. You'd be surprised how it crops up after quite appalling cases. Heath, for instance. Some of his acquaintances couldn't believe such a nice chap would behave like that.'

'With Bruce, though, it was simply for cash and comfort?'

'Just that. Twenty-five thousand and a very nice little house which he could let until he retired.'

'Oh, well!' said Verity and gave it up. And then, with great difficulty, she said, 'I would be glad to know – Basil Smythe wasn't in any way involved, was he? I mean – as her doctor he couldn't be held to have been irresponsible or anything?'

'Nothing like that.'

'But – there's something, isn't there?'

'Well, yes. It appears that the Dr Schramm who qualified at Lausanne was never Mr Smythe, and I'm afraid Schramm was *not* a family name of Mr Smythe's mama. But it appears he will inherit his fortune. He evidently suggested – no doubt with great tact – that as the change had not been confirmed by deed poll, Smythe was still his legal name. And Smythe, to Mr Rattisbon's extreme chagrin, it is in the Will.'

'That,' said Verity, 'is I'm afraid all too believable.'

Alleyn waited for a moment and then said, 'You'll see, won't you, why I was so anxious that Prunella should be taken away before we went to work in the churchyard.'

'What? Oh, that. Yes. Yes, of course I do.'

'If she was on the high seas she couldn't be asked as next-of-kin to identify.'

'That would have been – too horrible.'

Alleyn got to his feet. 'Whereas she is now, no doubt, contemplating the flesh-pots of the Côte d'Azure and running herself in as the future daughter-in-law of the Markos millions.'

'Yes,' Verity said, catching her breath in a half-sigh, 'I expect so.'

'You sound as if you regret it.'

'Not really. She's a level-headed child and it's the height of elderly arrogance to condemn the young for having different tastes from one's own. It's not my scene,' said Verity, 'but I think she'll be very happy in it.'

And at the moment, Prunella was very happy indeed. She was stretched out in a chaise-longue looking at the harbour of Antibes, drinking iced lemonade and half-listening to Nikolas and Gideon who were talking about the post from London that had just been brought aboard.

Mr Markos had opened up a newspaper. He gave an instantly stifled exclamation and made a quick movement to refold the paper.

But he was too late. Prunella and Gideon had both looked up as an errant breeze caught at the front page.

BLACK ALEXANDER
FAMOUS STAMP FOUND ON MURDERED MAN

'It's no good, darlings,' Prunella said after a pause, 'trying to hide it all up. I'm bound to hear, you know, sooner or later.'

Gideon kissed her. Mr Markos, after making a deeply sympathetic noise, said, 'Well - perhaps.'

'Go on,' said Prunella. 'You know you're dying to read it.'

So he read it and as he did so the circumspection of the man of affairs and the avid, dotty desire of the collector, were strangely combined in Mr Markos. He folded the paper.

'Darling child,' said Mr Markos. 'You now possess a fortune.'

'I suppose I must.'

He picked up her hands and beat them gently together. 'You will, of course, take advice. It will be a momentous decision. But *if*,' said Mr Markos, kissing first one hand and then the other, '*if* after due deliberation you decide to sell, may your father-in-law have the first refusal? Speaking quite cold-bloodedly, of course,' said Mr Markos.

The well-dressed, expensively gloved and strikingly handsome passenger settled into his seat and fastened his belt.

Heathrow had passed off quietly.

He wondered when it would be advisable to return. Not, he fancied, for some considerable time. As they moved off the label attached to an elegant suitcase in the luggage rack slipped down and dangled over his head.

Dr Basil Schramm
Passenger to New York
Concorde
Flight 123.

Ngaio Marsh

'The finest writer in the English language of the pure, classical, puzzle whodunit. Among the Crime Queens, Ngaio Marsh stands out as an empress.' *Sun*

'Her work is as near flawless as makes no odds: character, plot, wit, good writing and sound technique.' *Sunday Times*

'The brilliant Ngaio Marsh ranks with Agatha Christie and Dorothy Sayers.' *Times Literary Supplement*

FONTANA PAPERBACKS

Fontana Paperbacks: Fiction

Fontana is a leading paperback publisher of both non-fiction, popular and academic, and fiction. Below are some recent fiction titles.

- ☐ THE ROSE STONE Teresa Crane £2.95
- ☐ THE DANCING MEN Duncan Kyle £2.50
- ☐ AN EXCESS OF LOVE Cathy Cash Spellman £3.50
- ☐ THE ANVIL CHORUS Shane Stevens £2.95
- ☐ A SONG TWICE OVER Brenda Jagger £3.50
- ☐ SHELL GAME Douglas Terman £2.95
- ☐ FAMILY TRUTHS Syrell Leahy £2.95
- ☐ ROUGH JUSTICE Jerry Oster £2.50
- ☐ ANOTHER DOOR OPENS Lee Mackenzie £2.25
- ☐ THE MONEY STONES Ian St James £2.95
- ☐ THE BAD AND THE BEAUTIFUL Vera Cowie £2.95
- ☐ RAMAGE'S CHALLENGE Dudley Pope £2.95
- ☐ THE ROAD TO UNDERFALL Mike Jefferies £2.95

You can buy Fontana paperbacks at your local bookshop or newsagent. Or you can order them from Fontana Paperbacks, Cash Sales Department, Box 29, Douglas, Isle of Man. Please send a cheque, postal or money order (not currency) worth the purchase price plus 22p per book for postage (maximum postage required is £3.00 for orders within the UK).

NAME (Block letters) _____

ADDRESS _____

_____

_____